CW00859148

GODS & REAPERS

GODS & GHOSTS BOOK 3

CINDY D. WITHERSPOON

T.H. MORRIS

PROLOGUE
EVA MCRAYNE

AUGUST 5TH

THIS WASN'T the life that I wanted, but it's the life I needed. It's very difficult for me to write those words. On paper, my thoughts take a physical form. They seem as final as a signature on a death certificate. I know that comparison is morbid, but I am surrounded by the tragic stories of others. I have immersed myself in the world of vengeful spirits and hateful gods. It is only right that my soul has been darkened as well.

I won't say that I am happy. I am alone now more often than not. My moments are consumed by Grave Messages or tasks given to me by the Olympian Council. Yet, in my work, I have found a passion that will never leave me. In my tasks as the Sibyl, I have grown into the woman I have always wanted to be. Resilient. Strong. Fearless.

Fearless enough that Joey is convinced I have a death wish. I tend to brush him off, but I can't help but wonder if there is some truth in his words. Perhaps, I embrace the pain caused by the fights against my enemies so that I can feel something. Anything to prove that I am not the icy bitch as the media portrays me.

Yet, I am that icy bitch. I have no tolerance for personal dramas. I do not

1

need a romance that will only leave me stranded in my misery. It was that realization that helped me make the decision to leave all that behind. There was no great love for me. Hell, given the divorce rates these days, that is true for most of the population.

We are leaving to go to the estate in a few hours. I'd purchased a house not far from there some six months ago, but I was never there longer than a day. Why the house? Because I couldn't stay at the estate like I used to. There was too great of a risk in running across Jonah and Lola Barnhardt, the arm candy who was by his side now more often than not.

Jonah. I miss him terribly, but our paths only seem to cross through text messages and Facetime sessions that last for hours. He had been my closest friend for a short amount of time. My virtual confidante when my fears over Cyrus eventually threaten to overwhelm me. I am still convinced that the keeper will find his way out of the prison Apollo threw him in after he tried to drop me off a cliff. But I refuse to write about him. This is about Jonah, not Cyrus. And with Jonah? I love him deeply, though we are only friends. That is all we'll ever be.

Once I accepted that fact to be true, it became easier to listen to his stories about Lola. The last one had been about the day Lola had surprised him at the library. I asked him if the two of them had sex between the bookshelves and his only response was nervous laughter. I took that as a yes.

I listen to these stories as if I am listening to a stranger tell me about his life. I must be detached. Otherwise, I will break the one rule I have set for myself concerning Jonah.

I will never, ever ask him why he didn't want me after he was freed from Ares' influence.

I want Jonah to be happy. I want him to find that one woman he loves more than anything in this life or the next. I will support him every step of the way. After all, that is my true role. To succeed in my work. Support others as long as they see fit to stay in my life. Then wish them a happily ever after that I will never know myself.

The more I think about it, the more reasonable my decision has become. The only person who has the power to hurt me now is myself.

I must finish this entry. I am supposed to be getting ready to go, but I needed to get my thoughts in order first. I wanted to get these emotions and *these fears out on paper before I had to face the one person I hadn't seen for eight months now. I was well aware that time would make Jonah's rejection sting less. But after I take the Oath of Hestia, I would be free of that dull ache.*

Tomorrow at dawn, I will be free of it completely.

ONE

EVA MCRAYNE

I REALLY, really loved the estate. But I really, really didn't want to go today. Terrence was throwing a barbeque and while the rest of the country was getting slammed with a heat wave, Rome was a perfect seventy-five degrees.

Dammit. I looped my curls into a messy bun on top of my head. If it had rained, I could have cancelled. Instead, white puffs of clouds dotted the sky through the windows behind me.

"Evie! Get your butt down here!" Joey called up the stairs. "Pedro is already in the car!"

Pedro. I rolled my eyes as I smoothed out my pale green t-shirt. Joey's first official boyfriend had become a staple over the past few months. He was nice enough. A real charmer. He and Joey were adorable together. Sickeningly so.

I grabbed my sunglasses and ran to the garage to see Pedro already sitting in the driver's seat of his Aston Martin. The dude was loaded. Thank Olympus for that. He took care of Joey now even more than I did.

"Get in, chica!" Pedro flashed his bright white teeth at me. "Terrence promised mesquite just for me."

"Is that right?" I slid into the back of the roadster. "Then you better press on the gas. Between Spader and Liz, you ain't got a prayer, Pedro."

"You don't know that. When I was growing up, we used to fight jaguars for food. Two ethereal beings are nothing."

I glanced out the side window as Joey climbed in with his Nikon. He kissed Pedro and I made a face behind my hand.

"Are you boring Evie with your stories of Columbia again, babe?" Joey locked hands with our driver. "You should switch them up. Give her some good ones from Florida."

I rolled my eyes once more. Pedro was a Columbian immigrant who had risen to the Ivy Leagues once his parents escaped for Miami. Yay. Good for him.

"Evie, you have got to get in a better mood," Joey twisted around to look at me as Pedro lowered the top of the convertible. "You know, you're not representing the sun god very well right now."

"Leave her alone, Joey," Pedro came to my defense. A move that was completely unnecessary. "Our Eva is tired from her flight this morning. That is all."

"Uh huh."

"Oh, be quiet." I pouted at Joey as Pedro headed down the back-roads to the estate. "It's not my fault I got stuck with the cops all night. You could've stayed with me."

"You find the corpse, you deal with the aftermath, Evie. That's our arrangement."

"I want that in writing."

"It's in our contracts." Joey laughed until I popped him on the shoulder. "Ow!"

"Anyway, I'll be fine once we get there. You know me, Joey. All gloom and doom until the spotlight hits."

"You know, on *Rainbow Brite*, you'd be that little gray man that hates kittens and flowers."

"Well, you'd be-"

"Children, children, we're here," Pedro whistled to get our attention. "And look! The driveway is already full."

Of course, it was. I waited for Pedro to park before I climbed out over the side. I tugged my shorts down, slid my sunglasses into place, and smiled when Nella Manville ran around the side yard to throw her arms around Pedro.

"Pedro! You're home!"

"*Sì*, Nelliana!" He boomed. "I found a few stowaways on the cruise ship. Thought they could join us."

Did I mention that Pedro was one of the Grannison-Morris Elevenths? He traveled often but happened to be in town the last time Joey came to Rome to visit Terrence. I'd stayed in L.A. It was better that way. Easier.

"Evie!" Nella finally noticed me standing next to the car when Joey and Pedro stopped yammering at her. "Jeez, it's been forever since you've been home!"

"Not that long-"

"Eight months, if you want to know," Royale Spader came around the side yard with a grin on his face and a blonde girl with pink highlights on his arm. "Come on. Party's back here. Not in the driveway."

"Oh, is that-" The girl started and Spader patted her hand.

"That's just Evie. Evie, Heidi. Heidi, Evie."

"I love your show." She started chattering at me. "You're so brave and-"

I didn't hear the rest. I had spotted the one person I'd spent the past eight months trying to get out of my head. Jonah Rowe dressed in shorts and a blue polo was still a sight that made my heart want to stop.

So, too, did the curvy brunette that hung around his neck. She pressed a kiss against his cheek and laughed at the face he made. Suddenly, I was all too aware of why I had avoided the estate like a plague. I'd still talked to Jonah, but through FaceTime. Video calls. I'd been busy.

And so had he. With her.

"Guys!" Pedro whistled. "Party's just got here!"

I switched on the celebrity persona like the pro that I was. I could get through this. I would get through this.

"Joey! Pedro!'

The two of them were swarmed and I took a step back in the

crowd. For the first time since I'd been coming to the estate, I felt out of place. Lost.

"Evie?" Jonah approached me with the brunette in tow. "Holy-how did Joey get you here in time? I thought you were in Detroit."

"I took the red eye flight," I smiled at him as the brunette threw her arms around his waist. "This must be Lola."

"It's so nice to meet you, Eva," She grinned at me. "You have to sit with us. Tell us all about Detroit."

I didn't want to talk about Detroit. Hell, I didn't want to talk to her at all.

"You know Detroit is nothing but burned-out buildings and busted factories. But I can make up some stories if you want."

"Evie found a body last night," Joey threw his arm around my shoulders. "Gang hit. She spent the night talking to the cops."

"Thank you for the spoiler alert," I grumbled while Joey kissed me on the cheek. "Go play somewhere else."

"Just trying to ease the tension," Joey said innocently, "I smell Terrence's barbecue. Have got to go!"

"What tension?" I glared at him. "There's no tension."

Joey dashed off, and I was happy to be rid of him. Nothing negative, but he was just so damn sappy that I needed space away from his giddiness.

Funny how I'd wanted him to leave. I was now free of Joey, but face to face with Jonah's girlfriend. Fabulous.

"I have to admit that that would've been cool to report on," Lola sounded almost wistful. "Down here, the most exciting news is when someone's cow breaks from the pasture and holds up traffic on the road."

"Jonah mentioned you were a reporter." I glanced over at Jonah, who was looking down on her with an expression I didn't like. It was too much like Pedro after he and Joey had kept me up all night banging around in his bedroom. I put my focus back on her. "What network are you with again?"

"I'm local at the moment, but I have my eye on other avenues." She grinned. "I kept trying to get J. to move out to L.A. with me. He won't do it."

Why would he? Jonah hates big cities. He only came to L.A. to be with me.

No. I knew that wasn't true. He came to *help* me. Not *be* with me. There was a huge difference.

"You're awfully quiet, J.," Lola leaned her head back to look up at him. "You good?"

"Yeah, fine. Just letting you two chitchat."

Jesus, this was awkward. I decided to take the most graceful exit I could think of.

"I'm going to go mingle. I'll catch up with you two later. It's nice to meet you."

I slipped around them and wondered if I should hide out inside until Apollo could send one of the keepers to come get me. I knew this was a bad idea. Why I let Joey convince me otherwise was beyond me.

I never made it to the house. I got caught up in a bear hug by Terrence, who lifted me off my feet.

"Goldilocks!"

"Papa Bear!" I teased him. "Put me down!"

"Evie, how have you been?" Terrence pulled me over to the grill. "How's the road?"

"Fantastic. How's the estate?"

"Fantastic!" Terrence pushed a plate my way. "Got some goodies with your name on them."

Of course, he did. Terrence was forever trying to get me to eat a full plate of food. I didn't have the heart to tell him it was never going to happen.

I grabbed the hot dog and took a bite to be polite. Perfection as usual.

"Jonah seems to be doing great with Lola," I commented. "What do you think of her as his girlfriend? Step up from Vera, ain't she?"

"Girlfriend?" Terrence frowned. "Eva, J. and Lo ain't like that. They're not in love. They're just friends with benefits."

Uh huh. I pulled back the tab on my soda. I didn't believe that for a second. I'd seen the way he looked at her. That was not a 'friendly' expression.

"They go on dates. They have sex. They are all over each other.

And she's here at the estate," I ticked each point off on my fingers. "Sounds like a girlfriend to me."

"That's because you're too innocent, Evie."

I went to take another bite of the hotdog and put it right back on the plate. I couldn't force myself to do it. I pushed it towards Terrence. "You finish this."

"You literally took one bite."

"That's enough."

"For a bird!" Terrence grumbled under his breath. He picked up the hotdog and took a bite. "You know, if you actually ate something, you wouldn't be so grumpy all the time."

"How do you know I'm grumpy? You haven't seen me in forever."

"True." He finished the food he made for me. I kept the soda though. "What about you? Have you found a Pedro yet?"

"No. I don't like men who get better manicures than I do."

"Evie! I mean someone to hang out with."

"You know better than that, Terrence." I leaned against the grill just in time to spot Lola once again on Jonah's lap. I made a face when he kissed her. "How is that not a relationship?"

"It's not. But it's not like you care, right? J. said the two of you talked it out after the Emmys."

"Yeah, we did. I'm just trying to understand the whole 'friends with benefits' thing."

"I can teach you," Spader slid up beside me. He threw his arm around my shoulders. "We'd have fun."

"We. As in me and you or you and Heidi?"

"Who? Oh, yeah. Not her. Just you."

"Spader," I turned towards him. "I don't think you would know what to do with yourself if I ever took you up on one of your pick-up lines."

"Oh, I'd know what to do."

"Uh huh. Then do it."

Spader jerked upright. "Um, what?"

"Show me what you got to seduce me with." I crossed my arms over my chest. "Take your best shot."

Spader's mouth dropped open. He closed it then ran his hand through his spiked hair before he looked the other way. Spader cupped his hand around his ear.

"What's that, Heidi?" He hollered across the yard. "Geez, Evie, I gotta go. See ya!"

Spader took off like a shot and Terrence cracked up. He laughed so hard, I thought he was going to hurt himself.

"That look on his face," He gasped. "I can't...Evie, you're so mean!"

"Nope, just used Spader to make my point. That's the reaction I always get if a guy tries to approach me. Most of the time, they keep their distance."

"Because you are an intimidating woman who's not afraid to let her light shine," Terrence pointed his spatula at me while I hopped up on the adjoining picnic table. "Seriously, Evie. I imagine you think most men are dicks. Some are, but others don't fit because they're blinded by you. When the one comes along that isn't intimidated by the shine, that's the one you jump on."

I shrugged. "I've yet to meet him."

Terrence rolled his eyes at me. "He's your best friend, Evie."

"The one'" I used air quotes to emphasize my point. "Is not Jonah. 'The one' for me doesn't exist. Terrence, Jonah made it perfectly clear that he doesn't see me as any more than a friend. I'm respecting that."

"I'm just saying. You should jump on it."

"How the hell am I going to jump on Jonah if there is another woman hanging off his lap?" I examined my manicure. "Besides, I'm over it."

"Over Jonah?"

"I can't get over someone I never had. I mean the whole love and romance crap. I'm done."

"What does that mean?" Terrence narrowed his eyes at me. "Evie, you can't stop yourself from falling in love. It's already happened."

"Yes, I can, and no, it hasn't."

"Explain this. Because the only thing that comes to mind when you say that is a nunnery."

"That's what I'm going to do. In the Olympian sense. I'm taking Hestia's oath tomorrow."

Terrence frowned and pulled out his phone. I couldn't help but laugh that my friend was googling Hestia's Oath. He must have found it, because he stared at the phone before he focused on me. "Eva, why would you do this? This is damn unnatural!"

"No, it's not. Magick is the most natural thing there is."

"But..." He read it and his eyes widened. "You'll lose your ability to fall in love."

"Not a problem."

"You have to remain a virgin?" Terrence stared at me. "Remain? You don't fit the criteria then."

"Yes, I do."

"Never?"

"Never."

Terrence squinted his eyes as he scrutinized my face.

"But you're twenty-six."

"Exactly. If I haven't found anyone even remotely interested by my age, then what's the point of even searching?"

"You're serious about this. You are actually going to neuter your ability to love?"

"Where's the drawback here, Terrence? I lose the ability to fall in love, I won't care how alone I am. I lose desire? Don't have it, so whatever." I shrugged. "It's a win-win for me."

"Evie, this is a mistake," Terrence shook his head. "I believe that with every fiber of my being. Like...down in my gut."

I swallowed the last of my soda. "Well, if it *is* wrong, which I doubt, then there will be some miracle to stop me. Right?"

"You know what could avoid your need for a miracle? If you just changed your mind."

"I don't think that's going to happen, Terrence. But I appreciate the sentiment." I gestured to the people around us. Everyone paired off with someone else. "All that? That's not made for me."

"How do you know?"

"Because the scant few moments I have had like that were stolen ones. So it's time to stop pretending and accept my fate as the spinster. I'll go adopt a few cats next week to seal the deal."

Terrence fixed another hot dog. He didn't laugh at my attempt at humor. "So your mind is made up, then? How long have you thought this out?"

"Just over eight months. Hestia makes you wait before she will perform the ritual. Gives you time to decide if that's what you really want."

"Is it?"

"Is it what?"

"Is this what you really want, Evie?" Terrence bit into the hotdog and swallowed. "Because I don't think so."

I took a breath as my memories took me back not to the night in my garage, but to Santa Fe. My one perfect day where - for a little while at least - I was happy. But I wasn't going to lie to myself about it. We had been pretending. Pretending to be other people. Pretending to ourselves. That thought stung. I heard Lola laughing, so I looked over to see her dangling from Jonah's lap.

"Yeah, Terrence," I turned my attention back to him. "Yeah, it is. Because if I don't feel anything? I won't be hurt by anything."

Terrence sighed. "I foresee it not coming to pass, Evie."

"Oh?" I raised an eyebrow. "So now you're a psychic?"

Terrence lowered the lid of the grill. "Eva, I'm not as smart as Reena, or as receptive as Jonathan, or as mentally creative as Jonah. But I know that the man Jonah is when he's with you is the man he's meant to be. You two fit together. Anybody who's been around the two of you together for more than five minutes can see it. And if you become some emotional eunuch, you won't just be wrecking your life, but Jonah's, too."

He patted my shoulder then headed back to mingle in the crowd I had been avoiding. I just stayed there, surprised at his words.

What the hell did he mean by that? How would I be wrecking Jonah's life?

I shook my head. It didn't matter. Terrence's words may have struck a cord with me, but I knew better. I knew the conversations I had with Jonah. I knew where he stood, alright. And it wasn't with me.

I hopped down from the table as Spader waved me over to where he was sitting. My little spectacle with him forgiven.

"Sit down, Evie. Stop being a stranger."

"Hanging out with Terrence makes me a stranger?"

"Damn right it does," Spader smirked at me, "Because everyone knows *you* of all people ain't getting second helpings of anything."

"Shut up!" I laughed and pushed him on the shoulder. "It's not like you're complaining. You never turn down my plate when I offer it to you."

"Hell, no, I don't. It's too good to waste. Look at Pedro and Joey. They are already three plates deep."

"Hmm," I rested my chin on my hand. "Those two aren't worried about calories in the slightest. They always burn it off after dark."

Spader laughed. "They probably won't be waiting till nightfall. You know how it goes when you're in the honeymoon phase."

"No, actually," I turned my head towards him. "I don't."

Spader gave me a knowing look. "Oh, right. You're still innocent."

I frowned at him. "You knew that? There's no way."

"Oh, yes, there is, Evie," Spader grinned. "All the signs are there."

"Like what?" I held up my hand before he could respond. "You know what? Forget it. I don't want to know."

"You sure? Could help you."

"No, thanks. I plan on keeping it for a while."

"Forever is not 'awhile'," Terrence piped up and picked up a French fry when he joined us. "Evie's going to become an Olympian nun."

"Terrence!"

"What? You didn't tell me to keep it a secret."

"Ugh, can we just stop talking about this?"

"Oh really?" Spader's eyebrows raised. "You're taking the Oath of Hestia?"

I looked at him. What the hell? Was the guy a mind reader? "How could you possibly know about that?"

Spader snickered. "Eva, is it *that* surprising that I know more than you give me credit for?"

He let that hang there. I wasn't about to add on to it. He eventually smiled.

"Don't worry," He raised a hand. "I won't tell you that it's a mistake, or you'll change your mind, or anything Terrence said. You do you, babe. You're a grown woman."

"Wait a second." That was so far removed from Spader that I was shocked. "You're actually supporting my decision?"

"Of course," Spader said. "If you've made up your mind, what could I say to change it?"

"Well, thank you, Spader. That's very nice of you."

Spader fiddled with his phone for a second and mine buzzed. I lifted it out to see a picture of a naked man from the waist down. I frowned at it when I realized it was from Spader.

"But as a grown woman, you should know what you're missing."

"Is that thing real?"

"Oh, yeah. It's real."

"Huh. I didn't realize they came in miniature sizes." I deleted the picture. "And now? You're blocked."

Spader gaped at me. "You can't block me. I'm trying to help you."

"Dick pic is automatic grounds for blockage." I shrugged. "No exceptions."

Spader laughed. A reaction that I didn't expect in the least.

"What the hell is so damn funny?"

"That wasn't even me," He replied. "But you still made a snap decision on a wrong notion."

I felt my eyes narrow. First Terrence, now Spader. What I should have done was ask where he got another guy's dick pic, but I was too annoyed to press the issue.

"Spader, you sending that picture to prove a point is...disturbing," I began, "but I don't have time for this. I've made up my mind. I know what my life will be like if I don't fix this now."

"Spader!" I saw Heidi in a bikini rush over to the table. The damn thing could barely be classified as clothing. "We're headed to the lake!"

"One minute, baby!" Spader called, then he turned to face me again. " I hear you Eva. I won't judge your choices. All I will say is this. Four years ago, when you went to that expo in New York, you knew that Katharine had tricked you into saying the Sibyl's oath. Two years ago, you knew you'd do the Covington episode and never see Rome or Jonah again. One year ago, you knew Cyrus was the be-all-end-all, and his word was law. And now, you know what your life will be like after you make a five-minute decision that will alter the rest of your immortal days. Imagine what you'll know tomorrow."

I narrowed my eyes at Spader as he ran off with the Heidi girl. I knew he meant well. Terrence, too. But they didn't know what it was like to be so damn alone all the time. They had each other. They had their significant others. Their playthings.

"Eva, come on!"

Joey bounded over to me and lifted me off the picnic bench. He was saved from the glare I threw at him thanks to my sunglasses.

"Why can't I just stay here?" I grumbled. "I grew up next to the water. I live in Malibu. What the hell do I need to go to a lake for?"

"God but damn, you are hateful today," Joey threw his arm around my shoulders. "You went to see Chronos last week. Did you absorb his personality or something?"

"No," I pushed him a little. "I'm just not in the mood to be lectured at."

"Lectured?"

"Yeah. Terrence and Spader. I told them about the Hestia thing."

Joey went quiet and tightened his grip around my shoulders. He knew all about it. He was also in full support of my decision.

"They don't understand, Evie. They won't understand. Why'd you even tell them?"

"It just came out.

"You're still meeting with Hestia tomorrow? Before your flight?"

"Of course. I have to show up, Joey, or I lose my one shot at getting this done."

"Eva."

I looked around to see Jonathan. The protector guide extended a beautiful silver chain that had a golden charm.

"I haven't seen you for eight months, dear girl," He gave me a warm smile. "That meant your birthday came and went, so you didn't get your present."

I held the chain with one hand and the pendant in the palm of the other. It was as gorgeous as the bracelet he had given me a week after we first met. As gorgeous as the dagger Jonah gave me, which now sat locked away in a safe in my home office.

"Jonathan, I love it," I told him. "Thank you. But what does the inscription mean?"

"It's Latin, my dear," Jonathan answered. "It means 'Know Thyself.'"

I wasn't used to getting gifts. Promotional merchandise that companies sent me in hopes for free advertising didn't count. So, I was touched. I passed the necklace back to Jonathan.

"Put it on me?"

The old protector guide smiled. "Of course."

He slipped the chain around my neck and I held it against the base of my throat while he clasped it in place.

"Go on to the lake, Joseph. I wish to steal Eva away for a moment." Jonathan took my hand and placed it on the crook of his elbow. "Walk with me."

"Sure."

We headed away from the party and strolled around the shore.

"Shall I tell you the story of the necklace, Eva?"

"Please."

"It belonged to my late wife," He smiled at my look of surprise. "Before you say you can't accept it, you already have."

I didn't know what to say to that.

"I want you to consider those words, Evie. Remember the vision I showed you? It may still come to pass if you act too rashly."

"So this is about Jonah." I studied the ground as we walked. "Jonathan, the stipulation you gave me was to be physically alive when the battles were over. There was nothing about love in that equation."

I knew that's where this was coming from. So he had heard about my oath then.

"Love has everything to do with it, dear child."

"Jonathan, I adore you. I adore Jonah, too. But he's fine." I stopped and the spirit did as well. "Isn't it obvious? Take today for example. Jonah has barely said five words to me. Whatever. The point is? He's happy. That's all that matters."

Jonathan gave me a knowing chuckle that made it clear that he knew something I didn't. "Jonah hasn't spoken much to you because your armor is up. What you saw wasn't happiness, Eva. It's infatuation. Jonah's had an eye on you the whole time you've been here. But you've determinedly had your back to him. That is *not* judgement, I assure you. Merely an observation."

"Have I?" I frowned. "I didn't realize I was acting that way."

Jonathan nodded. "Body language, my dear. You're speaking very clearly that you want no part of him. Now, is that true? Yes or no, I will not judge you, you have my word."

I considered my next words very carefully. I didn't dare give too much away.

"Of course, that's not true. Jonah is still one of my best friends. I'm simply respecting the boundaries he set himself. I am keeping my distance."

"Lola's presence has nothing to do with that?"

"It does. I'm trying to respect her, too. I know what Terrence said, but the two of them have been all over each other. I am not going to go over and interrupt them."

Jonathan smiled. "Let me let you in on something, my Eva. The reason why Jonah and Lola are so affectionate today is because Lola is leaving town."

"I'm sorry?"

Jonathan nodded. "She's going to London for a job at a news desk there. No small feat for an American newscaster. This cookout is a farewell."

I sighed then rubbed my forehead. "Then I shouldn't be here at all."

"Pardon?"

"The focus should be on Lola. You should be with the rest of them, Jonathan. Not trying to convince me to hold out hope a little longer."

"Eva, that's not what I meant."

"I know. You are far too kind to say it out loud. So I will say it for you. This is a celebration. A farewell for a woman I didn't even know." I hugged him. "I'm going to go."

"Eva, are you certain?"

"Yes." I stepped back. "I don't want to be the downer on her last day."

Jonathan nodded. "Very well. Come home again soon, child. We miss you."

The Sullivan House was a four mile walk from the estate. When I bought the place, I never imagined I would walk to it. But I wasn't going to pull Joey away.

The walk was good for me. It gave me time to think of what Terrence had told me. What Spader had told me. But more importantly? I considered Jonathan's words. He said Jonah was infatuated with the newscaster. And when that infatuation ended? I knew that meant he would move onto someone else. There was always someone else for him. Someone who wasn't me.

I had to get over my feelings for Jonah. I knew that. It didn't matter what Terrence said about wrecking Jonah's life. It didn't matter what Jonathan said in an attempt to keep me standing in the wings. Their words were sweet, but meaningless. Jonah was the only one who could make decisions about his life. And I was tired of hoping. Tired of waiting for something that was never going to happen. Tired of the rejection I received whenever I tried to get close to someone.

I entered the Sullivan House then tossed my keys on the table. I dropped down on the couch and considered my upcoming appearance. It was a *Ted Talk*. And I had just the right topic for it.

A rap on the glass made me jump up. I headed back to the kitchen and heard a muffled voice through the glass.

"Eva? You in there?"

"Jonah? What the hell are you doing here?"

I went to the back door to look at him through the glass. I convinced myself that it was better that way. Jonah looked me in the eye, and I had to turn away.

"I saw you leave," he answered. "Just wanted to make sure you were ok."

"You noticed?" I said in a tone colder than I intended.

"Of course, I noticed,' Jonah stuffed his hands in his pockets. "You might not want me around anymore, and I get it, but I still want to know if you're okay."

"Now wait one damn minute." I jerked the door open. "I never said I didn't want you around me."

"You never come home, you only want to FaceTime, and you snubbed me at the barbeque. What else am I supposed to think?"

"I never come home because I'm busy with work, Jonah," I stood aside and pinched the bridge of my nose as I gave in. "Come in."

Jonah crossed the threshold before he turned back to me.

"I'm sorry if I seemed like a bitch at the party. I wasn't trying to be. I was just respecting the boundaries you set. Respect you and Lola. That's all."

The truth was, I missed Jonah desperately. It took everything I had not to throw myself in his arms. He didn't want that. He'd told me himself he didn't want that.

"Anyway, I was being a downer, so I left. Better that way."

"Eva, why did you think you were a downer?" Jonah asked. "Everyone wanted to see you, even Lola. She wanted to meet you before she went to the U.K. because I talk about you so much. I just thought you had no interest in being around *me*.

"You know me better than that." I whispered. "And for the record? I thought you didn't want to be around *me*. From what I'd heard before the party, you and Lola were pretty solid. I didn't want to interrupt you two. Please understand that."

"Eva, Lola and I are friends who just happen to have a physical relationship," Jonah said. "We wanted to have time together before she moved to London. But you weren't interrupting anything. I was looking forward to talking to you. I missed the hell out of you. But that 'don't talk to me' across your forehead might as well have been a neon sign."

"Jonathan brought that to my attention. I didn't realize how I was coming across." I considered my next words. "I've missed the hell out of you, too, Jonah."

"Come here."

Jonah pulled me into his embrace, and I closed my eyes to keep my tears back. He would always seem like home to me. I had a feeling that would never change.

I held him back until I caught the whiff of a woman's perfume on his clothes. That was enough to make me loosen up.

"When does Lola go to London?" I cleared my throat to hide the emotion from it. "I know you'll want every second with her before she leaves."

"Two days from now," Jonah said. "I've got time. And because I know you, Superstar? It's not Lola's perfume. She doesn't wear perfume. You smell Nella's perfume. We were laughing ourselves silly playing flag football."

Uh huh.

"I don't know what you're talking about."

Jonah gave me a look and I laughed. I couldn't help it. He really did know me better than anyone ever would.

Stop it, I scolded myself. *It's only as a friend.*

His next words confirmed it.

"So, friends?" Jonah smiled. "I think we both let rumors get the best of us."

"Always friends," I willed the ache in my chest to stop. It would be completely gone in a few more hours. "Blue and gold, right?"

"Blue and gold eternal," Jonah said with a grin. "Will you come back? I've kind of been hoping to see your revenge body."

I frowned. "My what?"

"Well, clearly you've been doing *something*." Jonah regarded me. "I thought Hell hath frozen over and someone had you working out."

"Hell is perfectly safe at the moment. I'm not working out. I've been trying to take up running."

That was good. Better than telling him that I'd been trying to outrun my memories.

"Trying?"

"Yeah. Trying. I hate running with a passion." Now, I regarded him. "You really want me to come back?"

"I do. Bring a bathing suit. You can get in the lake."

"Give me a minute."

I slipped upstairs and grabbed a bikini from my dresser. I put it on beneath my outfit then grabbed an extra t-shirt to throw over it. I came back downstairs and tugged at my bun to tighten it.

"I walked back," I said as I approached him. "But we can take the Rover if you want."

"We can walk, no problem," Jonah said. "The party is going to continue until three a.m. at least. We haven't had much fun lately, so they're not about to let the party end too soon."

I grabbed my keys as we exited the house. I kept my hands under the extra shirt. Helped me keep them to myself.

"New jewelry?" Jonah pointed to my necklace. "It's nice."

"It is. Jonathan gave it to me."

"Oh, yeah." Jonah nodded. "That must be the birthday present he's been keeping warm for you. It's pretty damn awesome."

"Jonathan said it belonged to his wife back in the day."

"Really? Can I see it?"

We stopped and Jonah lifted the pendant off my throat. I felt my breath catch when his fingers grazed against my skin. I hated myself for that reaction.

"It's Latin."

"It means something like "Know thyself".

Jonah lowered the pendant back into place. "Good philosophy to have."

"I'm pretty sure it's a cryptic message. You know how Jonathan is."

"You'll figure it out someday." Jonah gave me a small smile and we resumed our walk. "So, what's on tap tomorrow? Joey said you have an appearance. He wouldn't say what it was for."

"Oh. I'm doing another damn *Ted Talk*," I shrugged. "Haven't the slightest clue what I want to say. I'll write out something tonight and memorize it on the plane tomorrow."

"Another *Ted Talk*? And you didn't tell me?" Jonah stuffed his hands in his pockets. "I could come to see it in person."

"No, you can't." I dodged a chunk of asphalt from the road. "One, I hate doing *Ted Talks*. So I'm going to do my part and bounce. There's no use in you making a trip all the way to New York to see it. And two, you'll be busy tomorrow, I'm sure."

"Lola is just a friend, Evie."

"And you are always there for your friends." I parroted back words that I had heard him say a million times. "So be there for your friend. If she's going to London, I get why you want to spend so much time together. I'm fine."

Spend as much time as you want with her. Making out with her. Hanging all over her. Then, once she is good and settled across the ocean, you can use the Astralimes to keep it all up.

I hated myself for my thoughts. I really, really did. I hated myself for the jealousy I held for the woman. It was stupid. I had no reason to be jealous. I had no claim on Jonah. He'd given me no indication that we'd be anything more than what we were.

I had to put this behind me. Every moment I could cling to was a fraudulent one. I had to remember that more than anything else.

"Who all is going with you?" Jonah glanced my way. "Joey and Pedro?"

"No. They are taking Pedro's boat out. Something to do with romance on the high seas." I made a face and Jonah laughed. "It's ridiculous and sappy, but hey. Whatever makes them happy."

"Did you just make a rhyme?"

"Ew. Not on purpose. I'm no poet."

"Rhyming 'sappy' and 'happy' doesn't make you a poet, Superstar." Jonah laughed again and I hoped he'd dropped the whole *Ted Talk* thing. Instead, he went right back on topic. "Who'll be there to support you?"

"I don't need support, Jonah." I shrugged. It was only the truth. I'd done so many appearances on my own, it didn't faze me anymore. "This won't be the first time I walk into a theatre alone. It won't be my last. I'm just going to talk then leave. No more. No less. It's no big deal."

"You seriously don't want anyone there with you?" Jonah frowned. "You usually relish at the chance to have your people in the audience. When did that change, Superstar?"

"Um, Jonah? Things didn't change. I tend to be alone unless I'm on location. I thought you knew that." I shifted the shirt I carried. Maybe he didn't. Jonah never traveled with me. He didn't ask questions about my interviews or promotional gigs. I shoved back my memories of both Cyrus and Joey telling me that was a red flag. I didn't need the reminders when it was all too obvious now. "Anyway, I'm used to being alone."

"That's sad."

"Not really. The only person I have to answer to is myself. I don't have to ask for permission, I can come and go as I please. And if I need praise that badly after I've done something? Then I'm in the wrong line of work."

It was only the truth. I'd made my peace with it. As Jonah always said, it was what it was.

Jonah smiled just a bit. "It's nice to see you, Eva. It's nice to be talking to you again."

I knew that tone. The one that said he didn't agree with me, but he wasn't going to force the issue. There was something else in his tone, too. Something that sounded like regret.

Of course, there was. He'd left a perfectly good celebration to get...what had Joey called me? The grey man on *Rainbow Brite*?

"I told you I was a downer." I stopped. "You sure you want me around tonight, Jonah? I don't blame you one bit if you don't."

"Why do you think you're a downer?" Jonah tilted his head towards me. "Eva, no one is saying that but you, I promise. And given your new status as a loner, company that's not like the vultures in L.A. would do you good."

"You think so?"

Jonah clasped me by the elbow and initiated the Astralimes. We appeared right next to the lake where everyone was having the time of their lives.

"You didn't have to use the Astralimes."

"Worth it." He grinned. "Had to get you back here before you took off in the other direction."

"You're back!" Lola strolled up in a bikini that told me exactly why she and Jonah had made their little arrangement. She wrapped her arm around his waist then grinned at me. "Where'd you go?"

"Had to get a swimsuit," I lied. I'd gotten better at that over the past few months. "Jonah was nice enough to give me a lift back."

"You change," She shoved Jonah playfully. "You have way too much clothes on."

Why did I let Jonah talk me into coming back? Was I really that much of a masochist?

Jonah started to take off his shirt and I was saved when Joey ran up to grab my arm.

"You're actually going to get in the water?"

"I never said that. I figured I could work on my tan or something."

"With a shirt on?"

"Joey? You're doing that thing again."

"What thing?"

"Getting on my nerves."

"You two are funny," Lola giggled so I had to turn back around. "No wonder the crowds love you."

"We're a riot." I responded drily. "Joey is the real star. I'm just the face."

"You gonna strip down, too?"

Jonah wrapped his arm around Lola's shoulders. I forced myself to keep my eyes on his face. This didn't matter. The sharp pain in my heart whenever I saw the two of them together didn't matter. I could do this. I *would* this. I blinked when I realized Jonah was still talking.

"I'm sorry? I missed that last part."

"I asked if you were going to wait a little longer before you got in the water."

"How much longer until it's dark?"

"Evie!" Jonah looked up at the sky then down at me. "I swear, you're hopeless."

"Fine." I muttered. I passed Joey my shirt and pulled the green one over my head. I'd gone with a standard white two piece with every intention of hiding it under the shirt. I stripped out of the shorts, too when Spader whistled.

"That's not something a nun would wear!"

I flipped him off and Joey passed me the extra shirt.

"You can't wear that in the water!" Lola caught my arm as I started to put it on. "Come on!"

"Really, its-"

I ended up dropping the shirt on the shoreline as she dragged me into the water. Whatever. I'd just hide under the waves then.

I swam out far enough that I was covered. I broke the surface seconds before Terrence swam up beneath me, lifted me up, and threw me back over his shoulders.

I hit the water with a splash and came up laughing.

"Go drown someone else!" I laughed as Terrence splashed me. "Dammit, Terrence!"

"Uh huh. Made you laugh." He grinned. "Let's play a game."

"Like what?"

"How about a chicken fight?" Spader swam up next to us. "You can ride me, Evie."

"Ride you?"

"On my shoulders," He grinned. "Course, that's not your only option."

"I've already embarrassed you once today, Spader." I wiped water out of my eyes. "I'm about to do it again."

"Oh, just get on."

"I don't know how to play this game."

"Easy. The girls climb up and you try to knock each other off."

Jonah got Nella on his shoulders while Terrence got Lola on his and Reena got Douglas on hers.

"Hey!" Douglas protested with a laugh. "I'm not a girl!"

"I subvert girl tropes, dude," Reena said. "You know that."

"Up." Spader tapped his shoulder. "Get on top of me."

I grumbled under my breath as I straddled the back of Spader's head.

"If no one has ever told you this, Spades, you're a creeper."

"Just callin' it like I see it...ow!"

I smacked the top of his head. "Shut up and let's just see if we can lose this as quickly as possible."

"Oh, trying to lose so you can vanish, huh?"

"Yes!" I snapped at him. "Or just dunk me now. That'd be better."

Spader backed away from the game as it got started.

"Spader, what the hell are you doing?"

"Giving you a platform to shine on."

"I don't need a damn platform. You wanted to play this stupid game. Let's play it."

He didn't move. Whenever I tried to throw myself backwards in the water, he would lean forward so I couldn't. I growled softly to myself before I leaned over his head.

"You are killing me, Spader. Either play the game or put me down."

"Oh, calm down. It's not like Jonah hasn't seen you naked before. I heard about the garage thing."

"First off, I wasn't naked, and it was dark as hell. So, no. He hasn't seen me anywhere close to naked. Put me down."

"He sees you naked nightly in his dreams," Spader grinned. "Don't think he doesn't. You know what? Let's get him. You teasing him and lighting the fire to his dreams could be your last great act as an emotional creature."

"Spader, no!"

"Hey Jonah! Nella!" Spader called over my words. "Eva said y'all ain't got shit on us!"

"I hate you so much."

I had seconds to react as Nella grabbed at me so that we locked arms. I tried to loosen up. I tried to throw myself off balance. But Spader held onto me

"Dammit, Evie! Fall!" Nella laughed.

"I'm trying! Spader won't let me!"

Nella raised her eyebrow, then deliberately pitched herself backward. Jonah looked at her in surprise once she bobbed her head back up.

"What the hell, Nella?" Jonah asked.

"Hey," Nella shrugged, "Goldie's stronger than she looks!"

"Nella!"

"What?" She grinned up at me. "You are."

"Lola!" I called over to Jonah's 'friend'. "Come knock me off. Please!"

"Sorry!" Lola laughed. "I'm over here trying to drop Doug!"

"See, Goldie!" Spader laughed. "You ain't getting away!"

"Fine. You wanna play dirty? I can, too."

"What are you-"

"Spader sent me a picture of his-"

I hit the water so hard, I inhaled a ton of it. I came up sputtering as I tried to cough and laugh at the same time.

"Uh huh. Knew that was yours."

Spader shook his head. "Party foul, Eva. You're just mad because I reminded you that you wanted it."

"What are ya'll talking about?" Jonah swam over, but he kept his distance from me. No surprise there. "Spader sent you a picture of his what?"

"Barbie doll collection." I grinned sweetly at Spader, who glared at me. "He keeps it in his closet. He's convinced that I want it, but I don't want to play with his toys."

"You're too damn harsh, Evie."

"So, who's winning?" I pushed away from Spader and waded next to Jonah. "Lola or Doug?"

"I am, of course," Lola called. "Doug wants to be a gentleman, so he's holding back!"

"Go for it, Doug!"

Jonah laughed when Lola stuck her tongue out at him. She squealed when she landed in the water.

I watched as Jonah swam over to her. I saw him lift her up and she pressed herself against him.

"Oh, that's nice," Lola purred. "I think we need to go inside for a bit."

What in the hell was she talking about?

"Dammit, Evie," Spader swam up next to me as Lola pulled

Jonah into yet another make out session. "You were supposed to tease him! Now, Lola's getting the benefits."

"What benefits?"

Spader and Terrence both cut their eyes over at me. I got it.

"Oh, for god's' sake! Drop it, you two. That," I gestured towards Lola and Jonah. "Is not for me. I don't know how to make that any more obvious. Hell, I don't know how *Jonah* can make it more obvious!"

"Come on, Evie. Let's go for a swim." Nella shook water from her eyes. "It can't make you feel great having to watch that."

"It doesn't matter. That's the point I keep trying to make." I rubbed my hand over my eyes. "Jonah can do whatever he wants. It doesn't bother me in the slightest."

"Right," Nella drew out the word. "You comin'?"

I dove under the water and went as deep as I could before I actually began to swim. The shadows covered everything. Even the long strands of plant life that stroked at my skin when I swam over them.

I was fine. Better than fine. For once, I was taking control of something in my life. I hadn't told Jonah yet, but I knew I would soon. I knew he'd probably be relieved. He wouldn't worry about hurting my feelings when he told me he had found someone else. Again.

Nella and I lapped the lake twice before we finally left the water. It wasn't until I stepped on the shore that I realized my legs were shaking.

"Evie, catch!"

I caught the t-shirt Joey threw at me as Pedro wrapped my shoulders up in a towel. "Thanks, but can I get out of the water first?"

"Sure, sure," Pedro spoke reassuringly. "We are only trying to ensure your comfort, chica."

Right. Joey had told him about my issues before. I wasn't surprised by the gesture. I should have seen it as sweet, but when I noticed the others cutting their eyes over at me as I dried off, all I could think about was why I was like this in the first place.

I dropped the shirt over my head and sat in on the dock to watch the volleyball game that had started while I was in the water.

"Hey," Joey sat next to me and mimicked my seating position with his knees drawn up to his chest. "You hanging in there?"

"I'm good," I turned to look at him. "Why?"

"I know how hard it is to see Jonah and Lola together. I'm just checking on you."

"There's no reason to check on me."

"Sure, there is," Joey studied me. "I know it hurts like hell, but now, maybe you can move on. The oath tomorrow will help."

"Jonah is not the reason I am taking that oath tomorrow."

"Well, regardless of your reasons, I'm proud of you. You're taking steps to make yourself feel better." Joey slung his arm around my neck. "Always remember, you got me. You don't need a ton of folk, anyway."

I didn't respond to that. He wouldn't have heard me anyway. He and Pedro fell into a conversation about their little romantic getaway.

"Evie, can we talk to you for a second?" Terrence cut his eyes over at Joey. "Alone?"

"We?"

"Yeah. Me and Spader."

"Why don't you go harass Jonah like you're harassing me?"

"Can't," Spader came up behind Terrence. "He and Lola went into the house to get drinks. We all know what they are really doing."

"That's not an image I want in my head."

"Come on."

Terrence lifted me up. I excused myself from Joey and the conversation I was no longer a part of to follow them. When we reached the tree line, they stopped.

"What?"

"What's with Joey and Pedro swooping in like they did?" Terrence rocked back on his heels. "I'm curious."

"I don't know what you're talking about."

"Sure, you do." Spader pulled out a joint and lit it. "That shit doesn't remind you of anyone?"

"They brought me a towel and it's supposed to remind me of someone?"

"No. They wrapped you up tighter than a pig in a blanket trying to hide you." Terrence took the joint. "You have nothing to be ashamed of. You gotta stop letting other people screw with your head to make you believe otherwise."

"You've lost me, Terrence."

"Evie," Terrence came in closer like he was about to tell me a secret code. "You're out here being beautiful, splashing around, and having fun. Then Joey and Pete come over, get you out of the water, make sure you're back to hiding, then go on about their day? Don't that seem a tad familiar to you? Keeping you in check and isolating you?"

I met Terrence's eyes and then pinched the bridge of my nose.

"Now, I get it. You're referring to Cyrus. But this is different."

"How is it different?"

"Because Joey doesn't leave me black and blue?" I gestured to the joint. "Give me that."

"The same principles apply, Evie."

"Or maybe, they are just trying to be nice. Maybe it's their way of showing me they care."

I nearly choked on the smoke when Spader responded.

"No offense, Evie, but you wouldn't recognize someone taking care of you if it bit you on the ass."

"Explain that."

"I shouldn't have to."

"Obviously, you do, since I'm the glorified idiot. What are you saying, Spader?"

Spader looked more serious than I'd ever seen him.

"Eva, this isn't fun, crude Spader talking, this is real. Cyrus beat you when you disagreed with him. Told you that his way was the only way, non-negotiable. Now, Joey and Petey over there decide to swaddle you up in a towel, and distance you away from people you already haven't seen for almost a year. That's not caring, Eva. There is another motive behind it. If it is malicious or shady, I don't know. But they weren't showing that they care. That was what Jonathan did. What we did and do for you. Have we ever told you to hide who you are? Have we ever told you who you could and couldn't talk to? You've been here for weeks in the past and not once did we pull you to the side and say, 'Just stay here. You've got us.'"

I stared at Spader as my stomach started to sink. Joey wouldn't do that to me. Would he?

Of course, he would. I turned back towards the lake. Everyone abandoned me eventually. They got what they could and then vanished.

"Eva?"

I blinked back the tears in my eyes then turned towards them with the plastic smile I had perfected over the years.

"You are both very sweet and I love you dearly for it."

"Cut the act, Eva." Spader snapped. "This is serious."

"You think I don't know that?" I responded with the same amount of heat that Spader had thrown at me. "You think I don't remember what I went through? Do you honestly believe that I'm not aware of the fact that Joey is using me for the show and my money? Pedro for the same reasons? I do, alright? I get it. But what the hell does it matter? They are going to drop me eventually. Everybody fucking drops me. At least, just for one minute, let me pretend that someone gives an actual damn about me."

I turned towards the house and remembered that I couldn't go there. I turned towards the lake and wondered if I could run home from the other shoreline. I wanted to run. I needed to run.

There was nowhere to go. Terrence caught my arm and pulled me into a hug. I stiffened against him.

"Don't." I let my voice return back to normal. "Don't do that pity crap with me, Terrence. I can't stand it."

"Eva, can you take that armor down for one *goddamn* second?" Terrence said sternly. "This is *not* pity. It's love. Affection. Everyone doesn't abandon you. *We* are here for you."

"No."

"No, what?"

"No, I can't take the armor down. I can't. I'll never stop crying if I do."

"I don't think it's a good idea for you to go back to the Sullivan House tonight." Terrence loosened his grip so that I could breathe. "Stay with us. You need to get away from Joey for a little while."

"I can't stay. I have to meet with Hestia at dawn and then catch a flight to New York. I still have to write my monologue, too."

"We'll get you set up in a room. You can leave in the morning." Terrence gave me a soft smile. "I'll even make you pancakes."

"I don't know why you even bother. I only eat one bite."

"That caring thing just bit you on the ass, Evie," Spader threw his arm around my neck. "Told you so."

"Shut up."

I let Spader pull me against his side, and he kissed me on the side of the head. Any other time, I would have shoved him away. But I knew I'd just prove his point.

"If I'm staying here, I need a clean set of clothes. I also need my work bag and my luggage. Let me borrow your car to go get it."

"Are you going to bring it back?"

"If it doesn't break down on the four-mile drive? Then, yes. I am also going to take a shower. I am covered in lake gunk."

"Ok. Let's go get the keys."

I followed Spader to the mudroom where the keyrings were kept. I took the keys from him as Jonah and Lola passed by the door without realizing we were there.

They were flushed. Laughing. I heard Lola say something about doing it again.

"Evie," Spader caught my arm. "Don't let this get to you. I don't think Jonah understands what he's doing."

"Jonah is a grown man. He can do whatever he wants. I don't factor into that equation."

"He loves you, Eva."

"If Jonah loves me the way everyone else says he does, then Jonah would be with me. There would be no apologies. No friends with benefits. No make out sessions in front of me or running off to have sex while I'm around." I palmed the keys Spader passed me. "So everyone else is wrong. He doesn't love me anymore than he

33

loves Reena or Nella. The sooner ya'll stop trying to convince me otherwise, the better."

"How do you not see-"

"I'm done talking about this." I found his car key on the ring and the rest jingled as they fell into place. "I'll be back in a few hours. Tell Jonah so he doesn't have to leave Lola again."

"Yeah, ok."

I went to the garage and started up Spader's old Buick. I was nearly home when the tears I had held back all day started. I pulled into the driveway and stayed in the car as I cried not for Jonah, but for all the lies I had wanted to believe so badly.

———

I made it back to the estate three hours later. Joey and Pedro were nowhere to be found, but I spotted a bonfire on the shore. So, I left my bags in Spader's car and walked towards it. The flames were beautiful. Mesmerizing.

"Evie, you gotta stop leaving us behind!" Joey grinned up from his spot next to Pedro. "Spader said something about staying at the estate tonight?"

"Yeah," I ignored the looks Terrence and Spader were giving me. "I need a change of scenery, is all."

"You're spending the night?" Lola grinned as well. "Oh, that's awesome. I'm staying tonight, too. Maybe we can talk over dinner or something."

Not sure how we're going to talk if you constantly have your mouth on Jonah, but ok.

I kept that thought to myself. Instead, I dropped down next to Joey.

"Sure. I'd like that."

"We actually had a movie date planned for the trio of us," Joey said. "So maybe Eva doesn't need to-"

"You had nothing planned." Reena was all smiles, but there was something in her voice that was a little firm. "You and Pedro were going to hang out here then go home before you shipped out tomorrow on your little love boat. So why are you lying?"

I focused on Joey. My best friend ducked his face behind a red cup to drink before answering.

"We wanted to surprise Evie," He laughed. "I guess there's no point now."

"Yeah, ok," Reena shrugged. "So, what are we going to do tonight?"

"Well, we have this great campfire. Terrence brought the stuff to make s'mores," Lola sat up from where she had been laying her head on Jonah's shoulder. "Let's tell ghost stories!"

Great. Yeah, that was an idea.

I didn't say that out loud. Instead, I tucked a strand of hair behind my ear as she continued.

"Jonah used to write the best ones. Tell us one, J."

Jonah patted my leg. I glanced down at his hand and wondered why the hell he'd done that. I saw Lola reach behind Jonah's neck to play with his hair, so I pulled my leg out of his reach. He was just being nice. Nothing more, nothing less.

"Before I knew I was an Eleventh, I was in Charleston taking the tour for Fort Johnson," Jonah began. "While the tour guide was talking, I actually, plain as day, I saw a group of spirits fighting tooth and nail from the Civil War. I was scared as hell. I even heard the cannons. Could you imagine seeing explosions and nothing blowing up? People around me are not even batting an eye?"

"What happened?" Lola leaned forward. "Did they say anything?"

"Not a word. They just fought each other. Vanished after a few minutes."

"You saw a residual haunting."

"What is it called, Eva?" Lola focused on me now. "I've never heard of those."

You would have if you've ever seen my show.

I didn't say that out loud either. Instead, I cleared my throat and tried again.

"A residual haunting. It's when the energy created by a specific

35

event gets caught in a time loop. Like, an old video tape stuck on repeat."

"I bet you have a million stories." Lola breathed out. "Your turn."

Jesus, really? I glanced over at Jonah to make sure he was finished. He gestured for me to go ahead, so I took a moment. I stared into the flames as I began to speak.

"All ghost stories are love stories. The widow who walks the shore, waiting for her husband to return from sea. The saintly grandmother who remains in her home after her passing to ensure her babies are protected. Even those spirits who try to harm the living have love in their stories. Because they loved the place they are trying to protect."

I paused for a second before I continued.

"I read an account once that really stuck with me. A woman lost her beloved husband when he was fighting in Iraq. She was a believer in the spirit world. She became convinced that he would reach out to her from beyond his grave. Nothing ever happened. The paranormal events never occurred. So she turned to her own memories. She couldn't stop thinking about the man she had lost. Her mind would wander back to their happiest days. Then, she began to think of what could have been. The what ifs of a future that was never to be."

I paused again. This time, long enough to get the rest of my words together.

"You see, it wasn't the paranormal that haunted the widow. There was no ghost in the true sense for her to fear. She wasn't haunted by a spirit. She was haunted by her own mind. Her memories became her obsession. Her dreams of what could have been took over her every moment until she became like a spirit herself. She stopped eating, stopped going to work. She damned herself into a hell of her own making."

"Makes sense." Lola nodded. "I'm agnostic, wasn't raised in the church, so we were taught that there was no Hell, just the hells we create with our focus and thoughts. If thoughts are strong enough to create dark places, why can't they create hauntings?"

"That was so depressing, chica," Pedro looped his arm through mine and rested his head on my shoulder. "Tell us a funny one. Like the time Joey walked in and that spiritess threw an old bowl at his head."

"I'll let Joey tell that one."

"I didn't think it was sad. I thought it was beautiful." Lola returned her head to Jonah's shoulder. "I'm no romantic, but even I felt something hearing that."

I heard her, but I wasn't really listening. In my mind, I was already writing the words I was going to say before a packed theatre in New York.

Joey goosed me on the side and broke my train of thought. Didn't matter. I already had it down.

"What?"

"Didn't you?"

"Did I what?"

"Demand to go back into a hotel room after a ghost threw you out." He grinned at me before he turned back to the others. "Hand to God, I have it on tape. Evie was thrown through a door by a spirit in Montana. When I asked her if she was going back in, she did her little sword trick and said "Of course, I am. My new Louis Vuitton is in there."

That got a laugh. I shrugged. "It was vintage. I wasn't letting the spirit have it."

"Why did you have a Louis Vuitton bag with you ?" Nella asked.

"What can I say?" I replied, trying for humor, though I wasn't really feeling it. "I'm a fancy ghost hunter."

"Very fancy," Jonah leaned forward with a smile. "First time we ever saw you, you were wearing what? Two-hundred-dollar jeans?"

"Five hundred." I scoffed at the very thought of Calvin Klein's costing two hundred dollars. "And I was trying to intimidate ya'll into keeping your distance. It was a...a thing."

"Didn't work in the slightest, Evie," Spader leaned back on his arms. "Look at you now. Adopted into the fold."

"That's sweet, Spader."

"What time are you heading upstairs, Evie?" Pedro got off me and I shook my shoulder out. "We will stay until you are settled in. Then, I am afraid, Joey and I will make our exit."

"Ya'll can go now-"

"No, no. It won't do for us to just leave you. We brought you to the party. We'll see you to the end of it."

TWO

JONAH ROWE

JONAH COULDN'T THINK of a better night. The bonfire, the laughter, Lola snuggled up next to him after another day of fabulous sex. He was going to miss that when she took off for London, but there was no reason why he couldn't visit her occasionally.

It was Pedro that caught his attention. The Columbian was asking Eva what time she was going to bed so they could hang around until she crashed? What the hell did it matter to them?

"Eva has been hanging with us since before you returned from your wintering in Hawaii, Pete," Jonah told him. "I promise we'll make sure the world doesn't end while you're gone. If you don't have time to hang anymore, then get. No ill feelings."

"Of course, we could," Pedro nodded. "But that would be exceedingly rude of us."

"No, go," Eva patted Pedro's hand. "Ya'll have fun on your little adventure."

"No doubt about that, Evie," Joey leaned forward as if to stand. He didn't though. "You sure we can't bring you anything back?"

"Very," She turned away from Jonah, so he couldn't see her face. "There is absolutely nothing on that boat you could bring back for me. It's a sex trip, Joey. I'm not stupid."

"I mean, you could always make balloons-"

"Will you just go?" Eva laughed. "Be safe. I'll see you in a couple of days."

Pedro and Joey gave Eva a weird look. Even Lola noticed it and jabbed Jonah in the side with her elbow. What the hell was up with these guys?

Joey was the first to stand.

"Okay then," He said rather breezily. "We'll send a postcard!"

"We know what you'll be doing already, Joey," Jonah muttered. "So, hard pass."

Joey narrowed his eyes slightly, but then they left. Jonah thought the two of them had been acting weird all day. But the thing that stuck out the most was when Terrence mentioned to him how they saw fit to cover up Eva like she'd been indecent when she got out of the lake. Eva had already had one bastard trying to rule over her. Two more was overkill.

"Glad they're gone." Spader grinned as he pulled out a huge pouch. "Now Lo can get baked with us good-fashioned one final time."

"Light it up, Spader!" Lola clapped her hands. "Gimme!"

"Tell me about London, Lola," Eva rested back against a log and stretched her legs out. She'd come back in yoga pants, so the firelight glowed yellow against the black of them. "What type of reporting are you doing? Please don't say entertainment. I think I'll scream if I have to think about work right now."

Liar. Jonah eyed her. She'd been thinking about that *Ted Talk* monologue when she told them that ghost story. Hell, he'd be surprised if she didn't use it. There were some great lines in there.

"Oh! I'm a crime reporter. I'll be stationed in White Chapel." Lola took a hit then passed it to Jonah. "I can't wait."

"White Chapel? That's Jack the Ripper territory," Eva took a joint from Reena and a lighter. "Wait, sorry. That slipped. Please, continue."

"No, it's good!" Lola pulled off her joint. "I already knew that. Eva, I'm not a gradual person at all. *At all.* When I make shifts in my life, they tend to be big. So a friend of mine from our old Creative

Writing class said there was an opening in London--he's living there now--and he knew I was ready to move past the sticks. So, I looked into it and son of a bitch, I got it. It was a little tedious getting the visa stuff squared away. Never had to before."

"If you've never been, London is great. It's got a little bit of everything there. History, a modern metropolitan city. It's really something to see."

"I take it you've filmed the show there?" Lola leaned back into Jonah, so he began to play with her hair. She wiggled against him and he knew exactly what that meant.

"Yeah, it's a paranormal favorite," Eva knocked some ash onto the ground beside her. "Plus, promotional tours. Photoshoots. Things like that."

"Eva also helped me out concerning London," Jonah said after a pull from his joint. "I'd always been an Anglophile, and Eva set up a trip. We went together. "

"No kidding?" Lola grinned. "Eva, Jonah always brags on you. What other spots did you film in the U.K.?"

"Eh, I'm alright," Eva gave him a small smile. "It was a fun trip though."

She took the water Terrence passed her then twisted it in her hands.

"Um, everywhere, really. The only part of the world I haven't filmed something in is the Middle East, but with the war going on, we can't get permission."

"You've been trying to get a permit to film in a warzone?"

Jonah took his hit. This was new. He hadn't seen any locations like that on his research lists.

"Yeah. It's the perfect spot, don't you think? We could spotlight the human rights abuses to help get the attention of the U.N. Maybe put some families at ease about their loved ones."

"I know wartime correspondents have to go through some pretty rigorous training." Lola spoke, her eyes wide. "But it's still danger-ous. They get kidnapped all the time."

"Not all that worried about it being dangerous," Eva pointed out.

"Everywhere is dangerous. But not everywhere needs the help these people do."

"You can't get permission though? Why?"

"Because of the military. They don't want me to play on their battlefield. Whatever. It'll happen. But tell me more about yourself, Lola," Eva changed the subject. "What do you do on your off time? What's your 'meeting Jonah' story?"

"You really want to know about me?"

"Sure. You're a part of the group. Why would I not want to get to know you?"

Under any other circumstances, Jonah would have been leery. But seeing as how Lola wasn't his girlfriend, such qualms didn't exist. For her part, Lola took another pull from her joint and started speaking.

"I met Jonah in our Creative Class," she began. "I had the biggest crush on him, but he didn't notice me at all."

"I *did* notice you," Jonah laughed. "I just had a *lot* of shit going on at the time."

"I get that now," Lola laughed as well. "But we started doing study groups and started talking, so we realized we were on the same page. Wanted fun, aren't trying to get married...just hanging out."

Jonah looked over at Eva. So far so good. He just hoped she wouldn't view Lola like she did Vera.

"And you're a local here?" Eva continued the conversation. Another good sign. "You have no accent."

Lola smiled again, but it was just a bit solemn. "I've wanted to do news ever since I saw Barbara Walters for the first time. But I came to find out that people *really* frowned on Southern accents. Especially heavy ones. So, between watching talk shows and taking a couple elocution classes, I learned to suppress my country accent. Did you have to do that when Theia started grooming you?"

"Oh, yes," Eva stubbed out her joint and folded her hands over her stomach. "My accent was the first thing to go. But it slipped out during the first episode and the viewing panel loved it. Said it made me more realistic, so Theia let me keep using it."

"More realistic?"

"Yeah. People like to think you're a blank slate. A doll that they can mend and mold however they see fit. If the audience likes it, it stays as part of the character they have created for you. If they don't, it gets scratched."

"See?" Jonah sat back. "That's why I'm always myself nowadays. Playing a character is just too damn tedious. Besides, I couldn't suppress my accent if I tried."

That got a laugh and Eva shook her head.

"No, there's no way you could. And you shouldn't."

"I agree," Lola kissed Jonah quick on the mouth. "It's sexy as hell, J. Keep it."

"Lo," Jonah smirked at her. "I've never heard that my voice was sexy. Country and stupid, but never sexy."

"It is." Eva said it quietly, but it was firm. "Don't you ever change one damn thing, Blueberry."

That was surprising. Jonah shifted a little beneath Lola. He wasn't sure what to make of Eva's comment.

"See? Eva knows what's up." Lola pop kissed him again. "So stop arguing."

"On that note, I think I'm going to go back inside," Eva got to her feet and dusted off her pants. "I have to be up before dawn."

"What? Why?" Jonah looked up at her. "When are you leaving for New York?"

"Tomorrow afternoon. I have a meeting at first light. Lola, it was nice to meet you. Best wishes in London. Guys, good night."

Eva threw a wave as she headed back towards the house. Jonah couldn't watch her go. Lola had his full attention as she leaned on him.

"So, skinny dipping?" She laughed. "It's the perfect night for it!"

Jonah laughed. "No place I'd rather be, sexy."

"Come on, baby."

"You guys comin'?"

"Nah, J.," Spader stood up with a stretch. "I think I'm heading inside."

"Me, too," Terrence grabbed the bucket to fill with water. "Been a long day, brother."

"Enjoy the lake, you two." Reena yawned. "I'm going to paint."

Terrence doused out the fire and the trio headed inside. Lola watched them go before she stood to remove her shirt.

"Ready?"

"I'm always ready, Lo."

They headed out to the lake once again. Another night of reckless abandon and frivolity guaranteed. It was always fun with Lola. There was never any question.

Yet, a part of Jonah would have happily traded it for a Marvel movie marathon with Eva.

Jonah shook his head before he dove into the water. He couldn't think that way. Not tonight. Not anymore.

———

Jonah woke up out of a solid sleep at 3:45 a.m. He groaned to himself and Lola shifted in her sleep. They'd passed out less than an hour ago. What the actual hell was he doing awake?

Jonah tried to go back to sleep. Fifteen minutes of fighting it and he got up. He strolled to the window that overlooked the backyard just in time to see Eva tying her shoe on the steps of the gazebo. She got up, stretched, then headed towards the lake.

What was she doing? It took Jonah a second, but he remembered what she had said about taking up running. So, she had been serious then.

Jonah watched Eva start her run at the edge of the lake. She was likely going to run the route from there to the spot at Lake Run, the mini park area where the lake ran into Washee River. So.... twelve miles total, there and back. He grinned when he had an idea. Eva would have a nice little surprise when she got back.

———

Jonah didn't go back to sleep but returned to his room. Lola was used to getting up before dawn, so when he woke her, she had given him one final goodbye in the sheets then headed off. Now, he was reading online wrestling articles until he saw Eva's figure running back in the security lights that gleamed bright against the early morning. Jonah grinned as he watched her run up to the gazebo, pause to catch her breath, and then freeze when she saw what he'd done.

A bottle of water, a thermos of coffee, and toast rolled up in a napkin and foil sat waiting for her, along with a note.

Gotta replace all those nutrients you just sweat out, Superstar! Hope this helps.

Eva approached the note as if it were a snake. She picked it up, and Jonah noticed she didn't move for a bit. When she sat down on the stairs, she opened the water and he couldn't wait any longer. Jonah went through the house and bounded to the back door. Once he reached it, he forced himself to walk.

"Mornin'."

Eva looked up, obviously surprised to see him. When he reached her, he gestured to the stairs.

"May I?"

"Sure," She gave him a small smile as she scooted over. "Thank you for this. It was very sweet."

"Of course," Jonah said. "I thought you'd be pleasantly surprised to see some food when you were through."

Eva took a half slice of toast and pushed the rest toward Jonah. "Has Lola left?"

Jonah nodded. "Yeah. But she was still here when I got up and put this together for you."

Eva took a bite of the toast then bumped his shoulder with hers.

"You were right. I was pleasantly surprised."

She smiled and Jonah's heart flipped. He shifted against the stairs. He told himself his reaction was because Eva didn't smile that often. Not a real smile, at least. It was quite the thing to behold.

Yeah, that sounded good in his head. Jonah took the opportunity to change the subject.

"So what kind of shit is going down that you have to meet someone at dawn?"

"Nothing bad," Eva shrugged. "It's just the only time she has available."

"She?"

"Hestia. She's exceedingly busy."

"Hestia? Goddess of the hearth and home?"

"The very same," Eva had begun crumpling up her toast. "Talk about staying in your lane. Her mortal cover is the owner of a log house company."

"Nifty. What's she helping you with?"

"Nothing much, really." Eva began to toss the crumbs out across the grass around them. "She's willing to help me become more effective in my interactions with people, and also, mentor me on how to deal with worthless emotions."

"That's always a good skill to pick up." Jonah rested his elbows on his knees. "I think it'll help you get over some things."

Even in the early morning darkness, Jonah saw something change in Eva's expression. There was a sadness there he couldn't place.

"I think so," She gave him a small smile when she finally responded. "She has a great success rate."

"Hestia was always the sweetest goddess, or was depicted as such in the stories," Jonah said. "She always seemed up and up. My only thing was the chastity. The stories said the same about Athena and Artemis, but that was false. Hestia, though? She truly is a virgin goddess. Can you imagine never having sex?"

Eva drank from her coffee thermos again, which made Jonah's eyes narrow slightly. Drinking water or eating food during a conversation was a stalling technique. One that bought a person time to think of something to say. Eva had pulled that thermos twice already after questions. Was she hiding something?

"I won't even try to know the mind of Hestia," Eva said, at last. "Maybe being focused on her duties was enough for her."

"That didn't answer my question."

Eva sat the thermos down and leaned back to focus on the backyard.

"Yeah, Jonah. I can imagine never having sex. You can't miss what you've never had."

"That doesn't mean it's bad, just means a person doesn't know what they're missing," Jonah said. "It's pretty damn fun, not to mention good cardio. I'll tell you a funny story. Remember when I told you about my friend, Nelson?"

"Your accountant friend?"

"Yeah, him." Jonah nodded. "Well, he was a car wreck some time ago; nothing very serious. Just soreness and shit. I asked him if he was doing physical therapy. You know what he said? 'Fuck that noise. I get all the physical therapy I need having sex with Tamara. I nearly spit out my punch when I heard that."

Eva tilted her head as if she was trying to get the joke. Jonah knew she was clueless, but he didn't think she was *that* clueless. In the end, she shrugged.

"Either way, I understand where Hestia is coming from. What's the point of being tied to your physical urges?"

"You'll understand one day, Evie."

"I don't think so, but thanks for the vote of confidence." She gave him that plastic smile she always used for talk shows. Jonah thought she seemed desperate to change the subject. He was right when she spoke again. "What's the plan today? Lola has two more days, right?"

"Yeah, but we said our goodbyes," Jonah answered. "She's gonna wrap up her last days with her parents and sister. My plan was some Gotch Bible and maybe some gaming. It was nice to be less stressed, and I want to keep that up, you know?"

"You should keep it up. You deserve to chill out. Have zero drama."

Eva stood up and he did, too. He reached out to tuck a strand of her sweaty hair behind her ear.

"You heading out, Evie?"

"Yeah. I have to get cleaned up. Thanks again for breakfast."

"Two bites of toast is not breakfast."

Eva smiled a little at that. "You gonna stay up? I'll come say goodbye then. I don't want to do that just yet."

Jonah still wondered...no, he *knew*...Eva was hiding something. But he wasn't about to be the one to bring the mood down after some light-hearted conversation. He forced himself to file it away. Were it important, Eva would share it with him.

"Yeah, I'll be up," He replied. "But the next time you see me, I may be a sweaty mess."

"That's not so bad. You may be a sweaty mess, but your workouts always make you so happy." She turned towards the house. "That alone makes the mess less noticeable."

Jonah laughed at that. "That's good to know. Well, keep me posted on when you leave, Superstar. I'll be in the gym."

He clutched Eva's hand, kissed her on the cheek, then headed off.

He had to leave her quick or else he'd kiss her once again. Probably make a fool of himself and piss her off. He'd already been in the doghouse with Eva yesterday. He didn't want to be there again.

THREE

JONAH ROWE

"You're up early."

Jonah had heard Terrence banging around in the kitchen, so he thought he'd stop by there first. His brother had the entire counter covered with bowls.

"Geez, Terrence," Jonah teased. "Is it a holiday I didn't know about? You're set to make a feast."

"Nah, man. Making Evie pancakes before she heads out." Terrence ducked into the fridge. "Hoping it'll help change her mind."

"Change her mind about leaving? I don't think she can cancel, Terrence."

"Nothing is set in stone yet."

"Ok. I think we're talking about two different things. What's going on?"

"I'm talking about this meeting with Hestia," Terrence sat the eggs on the counter. "What are you talking about?"

"I'm confused. The Hestia meeting is a good thing. Why would you want Eva to cancel it?"

Terrence stared at Jonah with wide eyes. Jonah narrowed his. He was missing something. Something big.

"What do you know that I don't, Terrence?"

"Dude, it's not my place. If she didn't tell you, I'm not going to."

Jonah straightened up. He *knew* Eva had been hiding something. "Terrence, you know Eva is a fortress right now. We were just talking outside and she danced around some of my questions so well I thought she'd resumed ballet. What's going on, man?"

Terrence cracked a few eggs and took a whisk to them. Before Jonah could tell Terrence to just spit it out, he started talking.

"Eva's going to take the Oath of Hestia this morning. It's a damn shame, man."

"The Oath of Hestia?" Jonah racked his brain, but he couldn't come up with anything. "She can't worship another god other than Apollo. So what's the big deal?"

Terrence sighed. "This is why she should be saying this instead of me."

"Terrence, talk. You're my source at the moment. If I need to know something, you've got to tell me."

"The oath of Hestia is the equivalent of the Olympian nuns, J. It nullifies any emotions you have related to love, sex, desire. All of it."

Jonah simply stood there as Terrence's words washed over him. "You've got to be kidding."

"Am I laughing, J.?"

"C'mon man," Jonah looked away, flabbergasted. "She wants to be a damn Vestal Virgin? Why would Eva want to do *that*?"

Terrence sighed. It was clear that he didn't want to have this conversation.

"She's burnt out, man. Everything has been a fuck up to her, and she decided she wasn't gonna put herself through that anymore. So she is not only making the choice to live chaste, she's also killing the impulse."

"You can't kill desire. You know what Jonathan says-"

"Yeah, I know. But this oath thing seems to do the trick."

"I don't understand." Jonah still stared at Terrence. "Why the hell would she do this?"

"I'm not going to speak for her, J. I'm not. All I'm going to say is that she's convinced that she'll always be alone and that by taking the oath, she'll stop being hurt when the people she loves lets her down."

"That's bullshit!" Jonah couldn't believe it. Why would Eva make such a totalitarian decision and not even tell him? If she cut off her emotions, she'd be wrecking *his* life, too! "Eva can't do this! She'll ruin *my* life, too! I'm going to talk to her. She's making a huge mistake."

Jonah turned before Terrence could say anything else and bounded up the stairs two at a time. He reached her room so fast; he hadn't even broken a sweat. Eva's door was ajar. Jonah didn't have the time for modesty or subtlety. He just burst right in.

"Eva, what the hell is all this about?"

He froze. Eva was gone.

Her bed was made up, the drawer empty, the closet closed. She'd just left. It must have been recent since her lavender scent was still in the air.

But that didn't matter. Eva had blazed without saying goodbye. She just made a decision and ran with it, Jonah be damned.

Just like Vera.

"Jonah? What in the world are you doing?"

He turned to see Eva in the doorway. She was dressed to leave, but she was there. Her confusion was evident.

"I thought you left."

"No, I just put my luggage downstairs so that the airport driver could pick everything up. I heard you run in here and thought I'd see what's going on'."

Eva stepped into the room with a look of concern on her face. Jonah didn't know if he should hug her or shake her.

"Jonah, sit down. You're pale." She took his arm. "What's wrong?"

Jonah didn't doubt he was pale. As cold as he felt, he doubted that pale would be much of a stretch.

"Eva...you're going to become a Vestal Virgin? Why? What's happened that made you think that's the only way?"

Now, Eva was the one who paled. Her lips parted, but she shook her head. She pulled him over to the bed and Jonah sat on the edge of it. She sat down beside him.

"It's not just one thing, Jonah." She began to fiddle with the pendant around her neck. The one Jonathan had given her. "It's a combination of everything that has happened in my life. I'm tired of hoping that someone will love me, then being crushed when they don't. I'm tired of being disappointed every damn time. I want to free myself from that hurt."

Jonah tried very hard not to minimize Eva's feelings because they were valid. But at the same time, he needed to get his point across, too.

"Eva, that can't be undone," He told her. "You make that decision and that's it. It's emotional suicide. A permanent solution to a temporary problem. Because of Cyrus, you're going to kill your love and romantic impulses for the remainder of all time?"

"It's not just Cyrus. It's not just love in the romantic sense. Jonah, remember when you told me that sometimes, taking a risk sucks?"

He nodded.

"Every risk I have ever taken with someone has ended badly for me. Every single one. When I was a kid, I used to hope that I could be good enough for Janet to love me. She died hating me. Cyrus? Same thing. I didn't want a romantic love with him, but I wanted him to love me as a person. It took him nearly throwing me off a cliff to make me see that I'll never be good enough for anyone. I'm useful to a point, and when people are done with me? I get discarded. I have to take that pain away when that happens, Jonah. I do."

"Eva-"

"I can't lie to myself anymore. I can' t keep saying 'Maybe this year' or 'Maybe if I was like this or that'. I just can't."

Jonah looked at Eva hopelessly. "You really think this is the only way to have a happy life. Eva, forever is a *long* time. I mean, you're going to outlive us all. When Terrence, Reena, and I are distant memories, dust in the wind...you'll still be here. Surely you don't want to be alone for all eternity?"

"Don't say that about passing."

"It's true-"

"I don't care," Eva turned to him with tears in her eyes. "Please, just don't."

"All I'm saying is that you don't realize how long forever is." He clinched the side of the bed with both fists. "You don't. And if you do this, Evie..."

He almost said it. He was so close to telling her the truth. About how she would destroy his future along with hers. Maybe he should tell her. Maybe that would get through.

"This isn't about sex, Jonah. It's not about romance or even basic affection. It's the exact opposite of that. Put yourself in my position. Imagine that you didn't have Nana, but Janet. Imagine if Terrence turned against you. Reena beat you every chance she got. And everyone you tried to make happy decided you weren't enough. What decision would you make?"

Jonah regarded Eva. "I'd move heaven and earth finding *new* people, then."

"I tried that." She whispered. "It didn't work."

"Eva, please. There has to be another way. You'll figure this out, but you can't just kill your desire."

"I don't have desire, Jonah."

"Yes, you do. You just don't know it. When we were in the garage-"

He stopped talking when she started to stand. He caught her wrist and she turned to face him.

"Look, if you're pissed at me over what happened, I don't blame you."

"I'm not pissed at you, Jonah. Stop thinking that I am."

Jonah didn't let Eva go. He couldn't make himself let her go.

"Has anyone been encouraging this?" He ventured. "Joey, perhaps? Has he been hyping this up like it's some amazing step?"

"Joey has been supportive of the idea. I understand why."

"Tell me then."

"He's the one who found me the last time, remember?"

Jonah had to think of what 'the last time' had been. It took a minute for him to realize exactly what she was talking about. The night she had taken a blade to her wrists after one of Cyrus' meltdowns.

"Maybe the need to do shit like that will go away, too."

Jonah wanted to protest. He wanted to hide her away. But shit like that would make him as bad as Cyrus. He had to be the good guy. Always.

"I don't want you to do it, Eva."

Eva looked Jonah in the eye. "But you won't try to stop me?"

Jonah had fought evil spirits, rogue Elevenths, vampires, monsters, and demon dogs. But the next thing he did was by far the hardest he'd ever done.

"No, I won't try to stop you. You've made your mind up. I don't have the right."

Eva's shoulders dropped and she closed her eyes. Jonah had one last ace up his sleeve. One last thing for her to consider.

"I want you to do what is right for you." He continued. "But I want you to consider something. If you lose the ability to love, then you lose the ability to love, period. You won't love us anymore. You won't love anything. Those people you work so hard to save on *Grave*? They'll be just another episode. The passion you feel towards your projects? It'll be gone, too."

Eva opened her eyes and the pain Jonah saw in them was damn near enough to drown in.

"I can't keep living like this, Jonah."

"Can you afford not to?"

Eva looked up at the ceiling and Jonah waited. He waited and he hoped. She pulled her arm free when her phone rang from her back pocket. Eva took it out and gestured to him with it.

"It's Hestia." She lifted the phone up to her ear and turned her back on him. "Good morning, Lady Hestia. I'm ready when you are."

Jonah closed his eyes and bowed his head. He felt sick as he listened to Eva's side of the phone call, but what could he do? If this was the path she had chosen for herself, who was he to stop her?

"Excuse me? I don't believe I heard you right."

Jonah stared at the rug. Eva went silent. He looked up and her eyes were closed.

"Hestia, that can't be right. I'm not important enough for all that." Eva went silent again. "And there is nothing that can be done?"

Once again, silence before Eva responded to whatever Hestia told her.

"Very well. Thank you for considering my request."

Eva hung up the phone and Jonah held his breath. She stayed frozen in place before she spoke.

"Hestia has cancelled the ritual."

"What?"

"She cancelled the ritual. I can't take her oath."

"I don't understand."

Eva didn't turn to face him when he stood. It wasn't until he closed the gap between them that he realized she was shaking.

"Eva?"

"Can I be alone for a few moments?"

"Why?"

"Because I am trying my damnedest not to cry in front of you right now."

Jonah closed the distance between them and wrapped her up against him. He was relieved, but he didn't dare show it.

"It's for the best, Superstar. You'll see. Someday-"

"Stop saying that." Her voice was thick with emotion. "There is no 'someday' for me."

"You don't know that." He whispered as she bowed her head forward. "Evie, you don't."

Eva tried to step away from him, but he held on tighter. Jonah felt as if something precious had nearly slipped through his fingers, but he had managed to hold onto it.

"We'll get through this, Superstar. One day at a time. You'll see."

She didn't respond, but she shook in his arms. Jonah knew there was no point for words. Not right now. Eva needed time to get herself together. She needed him to be a presence.

The two of them stood there long enough for the sun to start filtering through the blinds. It was then that Eva tapped his arm and he let her go.

"I, um," She cleared her throat and tried again. "I still have to leave by eight. My flight leaves from Raleigh at nine."

"It's not even six a.m." Jonah kept his hand on her arm as if he had to convince himself that she was still there. "You got time to lay back down. What time did you wake up?"

"3:45. I wanted to get my run in before I left."

Jonah stiffened. The action didn't go unnoticed by Eva.

"What?" She questioned. "I thought you were a morning person."

"I am," Jonah said hastily. "It's awesome you found a way to be up that early without your beloved coffee."

"You really think I didn't have coffee before I left?"

"Well, Terrence was downstairs making you pancakes. I bet he's pissed because he thinks you left without having them. Why don't you go make his day, Superstar."

Eva headed out the door and Jonah followed her. He ran his hand through his hair as they entered the kitchen. Terrence was putting the batches of pancakes in freezer bags, but he stopped when he spotted them. His entire face lit up and he bounded around the kitchen island to sweep Eva off her feet.

"You didn't go!" He laughed. "Thank God, Evie. You have no idea. Sit down. Eat."

"Only if you cut one in half and put the other half on Jonah's plate." She patted him on the back. "Hestia decided I wasn't good enough to join up."

"She's right. You're too good to live a loveless life," Terrence said in a voice so boisterous that Jonah laughed. "Let's talk about food. Jonah, I know you prefer your fruit topping, so I got you. But what will the topping be for your little bit, Evie? Syrup and butter, or fruit?"

"Just butter."

She sat at the counter and Jonah slid in beside her. He tried to stop himself from cutting glances at her. Eva was pale. Her hands kept shaking every time she reached for something. He watched as she dropped her fork twice. Then the cap to the bottle water Terrence passed her. Eva was upset. Very upset. But Jonah knew that Hestia had saved Eva from making the worst mistake of her life.

Even if Eva herself didn't believe that at the moment.

He also knew he had to stop staring at her. So when Terrence gave him his plate, he focused on the food. Jonah was cutting a triangle with his fork when Eva tapped his hand.

"Yes?"

"Thanks for talking to me this morning." She picked up her fork. "I guess I should've told you, but I always lost my nerve."

"Eva, you needn't apologize." Jonah was in much better spirits now, but he also realized that Eva still wasn't okay. So, he had to be considerate of that, no matter the sunnier demeanor within him now. "I wish you had talked to me, but it's over and done with. Water under a bridge."

Eva said nothing as she focused on cutting up the pancake on her plate. It was obvious where her mind was, and Jonah became damned determined to get her thoughts on something else.

"So, Eva, please tell me," Jonah fastened on an event he had heard about the night before. "Why exactly did Joey and Pedro see fit to wrap you up at the lake yesterday? What was the deal with that? It was almost like they didn't approve of you or something."

Eva didn't answer right away. She cut a sliver off her pancake then popped it in her mouth.

"They know how I am. I think they were just trying to make sure I was comfortable." Eva narrowed her eyes at Terrence. "What all did you tell Jonah?"

"Concerning what?"

"Joey."

"Not a damn thing. Ok, I told him about the lake thing. And the oath." Terrence answered. "But you know we're all smarter than the average bear, Eva. More receptive, too."

"He's right Superstar," Jonah carried on. "You didn't see it, but Joey and Pedro kept cutting their eyes at you when you were in the water, like they didn't green light that particular bikini or something. It was just weird."

"Knowing those two, they probably thought I looked tacky in it," Eva dropped her fork as she looked between them. "Oh, come on.

You know how Joey can be sometimes. It's like I told Terrence and Spader yesterday, it's just the way they show that they care."

"They show that they care by shading and undercutting someone who's rebuilding their self-esteem?" Jonah scoffed. Was Eva truly molded into thinking all criticism was a blessing? "Well, I'll start 'caring' about Joey by telling him that he's not very smart and has a kangaroo pouch."

"Right," Terrence caught on, "And I'll start 'caring' about Pedro by telling him that were it not for the money he's amassed, he would have no friends outside of Jonathan, and probably Trip."

"You don't like him?" Eva asked. She sounded genuinely surprised. "But I thought you all loved him."

"No." Terrence took another bite of pancakes. "I've known Pedro since we were both thirteen. We got to the estate at the same time. He was a pompous ass *before* he was rich. But I didn't rock the boat. Our energies won't mesh with everyone's, after all."

Eva raised an eyebrow at Terrence. She started to respond when her phone rang. She pulled it out of her back pocket and put it on speaker.

"Hey, Grizzly."

Jonah and Terrence looked at each other. That was convenient timing.

"Evie, are you done with Hestia yet?"

"I didn't go." Eva popped another piece of pancake in her mouth. "It's a long story, Joey."

"You didn't go?"

"No and I don't want to talk about it. Why are you calling? I thought you and Pedro wouldn't come up for air any time soon."

"Listen, I need you to take some equipment to New York for me. Forgot all about it. I had it sent to the airport already. Should be waiting for you."

"Yeah, no problem."

"You are still going to New York, right?"

"I'll be there unless the plane crashes."

"Thanks, baby girl," Joey sighed. "Sorry about the Hestia thing. Maybe she'll reschedule with you."

"She won't."

"See you in a few days, alright?"

"See you."

Eva disconnected the call. "Joey and his kangaroo pouch are perfectly normal. No aggression, no takedowns."

"Apart from him being butt hurt you didn't go see Hestia," Jonah observed. Eva might be jaded to the actions of her best friend and roommate, but *he* wasn't, and never would be. "What was in that arrangement for him?"

"Not a thing."

Eva pushed her plate away and got up to go to the fridge. Jonah watched her grab some more waters then bring them back to the counter.

"Here's what I'm curious about." Terrence sat up as he took the bottle Eva offered him. "Pedro's loaded. We all know that. So why is he shacking up with Joey and by extension, you?"

"I figure it's because the two of them are damn near inseparable."

"Uh-huh, that or you have more than him by heads and shoulders, and he likes the cushy spot."

"Ok, look. There's nothing to worry about." Eva sipped on her water. "Can we talk about something else?"

"Not yet," Jonah wiped his hands on a napkin as he twisted around to face her. "I didn't realize that Pedro was now roommate number two."

"He stays with Joey." Eva shrugged a little as she pushed her plate away. "Seemed kinda bitchy to kick him out when the two of them are so happy."

"And he helps out?" Jonah raised his hand when Eva started to protest. "I just wanna make sure they ain't taking advantage, Superstar."

"You know Joey doesn't make the money I do. Pedro, either." She propped her chin on her hand. "I understand that. Besides, having them around makes the house less empty. That's going to be even more important now."

Jonah nodded, not willing to push Eva any lower than she already was. "I just don't want you to be getting screwed."

Eva's phone rang again, and Jonah halfway expected Joey to be calling her back. Instead, she frowned as she put it on speaker.

"McRayne."

"Miss McRayne, I am a representative of the Raleigh-Durham travel fleet. I have arrived at the Grannison-Morris estate to drive you to the airport."

"You're very early. My flight doesn't leave until nine."

"My apologies, ma'am. We received a call from Theia Productions. Your flight time was changed to seven-thirty."

"Give me five minutes."

Eva hung up. "That's my cue. I better get going."

Jonah sat back and looked her over. "Never a dull moment, huh?"

"Not with me around."

She hugged Terrence goodbye as Jonah stood. Eva stepped up to him and wrapped her arms around his waist. Jonah didn't want her to leave. Not when she hadn't been home for a full twenty-four hours.

"Knock 'em dead, Superstar."

"It's a *Ted Talk*. That audience is already dead."

Eva released Jonah, threw them both a final wave, and was gone.

"That shit was set up, man."

Jonah turned around as Terrence grabbed the plates. "You think?"

"Damn straight I do. Joey finds out she's still with us and suddenly, she is being whisked away to the airport three hours before her flight?"

Jonah nodded. "I'm thinking the same thing. I've been thinking things have been weird with Joey for months now."

"Really?" Terrence asked with a frown.

"Yeah." Jonah sat back down. "I had suspicions after Joey repeatedly said that Eva was moving on, transitioning to new things...this, that, and the other. I've no doubts that Eva's been busy, but it seemed like Joey was being extra. When I told Eva I understood she didn't want me around anymore, she looked so shocked and hurt that I realized there is a disconnect. Joey is...I don't know, man. Something is up."

"It can't have anything to do with Olympus or Cyrus. He's been gone for ages now."

"No," Jonah agreed. "But maybe Cyrus was the shield or the gatekeeper. Or hell, maybe Joey picked up a thing or two from him. Whatever it is, I don't like it."

"What do we know about Joey?" Terrence asked. "Really?"

"Why do you say that?"

"I don't know, man. All I know is what we saw yesterday."

Jonah sat down and racked his brains. "He grew up in the backwater with a wildly religious family. Almost extremism. He likes guns and technology."

"And apparently, being controlling," Terrence added.

"Maybe that's where he gets the controlling factor from." Jonah pressed his fingers together and pointed them at Terrence. "The religious background. You know how Bible people are."

"True." Terrence shook his head. "I don't know why Evie bought that house to begin with when she could just stay with us."

"What's that got to do with Joey?"

"Nothin' other than he'd have a hell of a time isolating her if they stayed here when they were in town."

"They seemed like they were trying to keep her insulated," Jonah wondered aloud. "Just makes me suspect they're up to something. There's an extra motive here."

"Well, I ain't interrupting their little cruise to find out." Terrence took a sip of his water. "We could go talk to Trip. They're buddies."

"Hell no," Jonah spat. "Let's just get Reena to look Pedro up. The *only* reason she hadn't is because she knew Jonathan wanted to give him a chance. "

"That, and he was the golden boy before Yale." Terrence shrugged at Jonah's expression. "He was. Everybody doted on Pedro thanks to his sob stories about Columbia."

"What sob stories?" Jonah asked. "Remember, I didn't grow up with ya'll."

"Pedro's folks were farmers in Columbia. Close to the jungles or some shit. They immigrated to the States when the cartels moved in. Florida, I think."

"Cartels." Jonah's eyes narrowed. "Please don't tell me his family was involved."

"Not the *whole* family," Terrence said hastily. "Just his mom and her brothers. Pedro got out. Made something of himself and went to the Ivy League."

Jonah was unmoved. "You do realize the Ivy League is overrated in a lot of respects?"

"*College* is overrated in a lot of respects," Terrence grunted. "But that's why Pedro was so golden. He persevered, the whole 'pull up by your own bootstraps thing'. You get the picture."

"I don't like this, Terrence."

"I didn't think you would. That's why we didn't pull you away from Lola yesterday. Figured you deserved a few hours of bliss before we dropped our concerns on you."

"It's not like that," Jonah told Terrence. "Family is not a concern. I wasn't all that fond of Pedro, either. Remember how I told you we got off on the wrong foot when I simply asked what he did for a living when I saw the Ferrari, and he accused me of being a racist and assuming he stole it?"

"Yeah, of course," Terrence cackled. "You were *not* happy after that."

"Of course, I wasn't," Jonah grumbled. "*You* know I'm not a fucking racist. *He* was the one that jumped to the conclusion that I thought he stole it."

"The point is now, right?"

"Yeah."

"And the three of them are separated because of their schedules, right?"

"Yeah, so?"

"So it's seven a.m. and I got zero sleep." Terrence stood upright. "So unless you want to talk about the party yesterday, I'm going back to bed."

"What else is there to talk about?"

Terrence thought about it and shrugged. "Nothing I guess.

Unless you're up to talking about how damn hot Lo was yesterday. I was green, brother."

Jonah snorted. "Lola was always hot. I just didn't notice it sooner."

"You gotta tell me, man," Terrence coaxed, "What will you miss most?"

"You're *really* asking me that question?"

"Yeah," Terrence said. "I have no shame. None."

Jonah considered not answering, but in the end, he grinned. "Those curves, man."

Terrence laughed. "I knew it! Voluptuous is where it's at, man. No one wants some bony, uber-athletic woman."

"Oh, athletic women are perfect," Jonah said, though his mind was on only one. "Women are more than just bodies."

Terrence wasn't stupid. He knew exactly where Jonah's mind went. He just smiled.

"I gotcha man," He said. "I gotcha."

FOUR

EVA MCRAYNE

I SHOULD HAVE SPENT the flight from Raleigh to LaGuardia polishing up my speech. That would have been the responsible thing to do. Instead, I stared out the window and tried to stay awake. I should have known getting up so early was going to wreck my plans for the rest of the day. I guess it didn't matter since Hestia destroyed my plans for the day anyway.

I tried not to think about my phone call with her. I tried not to think about what this latest rejection meant for me. I would still be alone, but now, I was forced to suffer all the feelings that went with that loneliness for eternity.

"I have just received word from the Oracles, Representative," Hestia had told me in that no-nonsense tone she had perfected. "If you take my oath, then two separate worlds will forever fall into chaos. I refuse to allow you into my service."

Refused. That's how she said it. When I tried to protest, Hestia remained as resolute in denying me peace as I had been in taking her oath.

"The Fates have agreed with the Oracles. I am sorry. There is nothing else that can be done."

So now, I was right back to square one. I wiped the tear away from the corner of my eye as I remembered the conversation. How my heart had sank to the very bottom of my stomach when Hestia snatched my chance at actual peace away.

I'd tried not to think about the things Jonah had said before my phone call from the goddess. I had tried not to look at the panic in his eyes. A panic I didn't understand. But it was what he said that confused me more than anything.

I don't want you to do it.

Why in the hell had he said that? Of all people, Jonah would have benefited the most from my decision. I wouldn't be the constant reminder of his possession. I wouldn't be the heartbroken idiot still clinging to him because I couldn't let him go.

I swallowed my tears before they could overwhelm me. There had to be another way. Some mystical person who was good enough to see my pain for what it was and ease me of it.

Until I found that person, I'd just have to figure out another way to protect myself when the inevitable happened. When everyone was gone, and I'd still be as I have always been. Maybe I should get closer to the immortals. Apollo had been trying to get me to do that - make friends outside of my Eleventh Percent bubble. Then, when I had told him I was going to take Hestia's oath, Apollo had flipped a proverbial switch. At first, he'd asked me about Jonah. Then, Apollo argued that Jonah was my soulmate and he only needed time to see it. I shut those arguments down with the truth.

I told Apollo everything. I told him about our day in Santa Fe. I told him about the events in the garage and the conversation where Jonah had apologized. Finally, I told him about Lola. About the dates and the stories Jonah had told me about their time together. In the end, my father simply squeezed my shoulder. He'd promised to create a list of eligible Olympian bachelors for me by the weeks' end. I told him that if he even considered doing such a thing, I'd go straight to the Titan headquarters in Italy and pick a fight so brutal, they'd have no choice but to take me down.

I was absolutely serious. I wasn't going to let my *father* become my gilded pimp. Besides, I didn't trust new people enough to get close to them. I had a whole history full of reasons why.

"Miss McRayne," The stewardess came over from her perch in the steward's cabin. "Be getting ready to land."

"Yeah," I sipped on my water then capped it. "I'm ready."

I watched the ground come up to meet me when the wheels touched down. The day was hot. Sticky. New York was awful during the summer. Even as far out as LaGuardia. No wonder everyone tried to escape it once the snow thawed.

I waited until I saw the equipment cases being unloaded before I looped my bag around my shoulder and headed out. I thanked the crew as I always did then descended down the stairs. A man in a black suit was waiting by a black Audi SUV.

Had the theatre sent him? I racked my brain as I tried to remember the protocol. It had been awhile since I'd done a damn *Ted Talk*.

"Hi, did the theatre send you?"

The man opened the rear door and another, larger man got out. He was wearing sunglasses, but I could see the wicked scar that ran down his cheek. The man reached back into the Audi and pulled at an arm. Joey stumbled out of the backseat and I nearly screamed.

My friend had been beaten to hell. His right eye had swollen shut. His nose and mouth had been busted. The man shoved him to the first man I had seen and then pulled Pedro out as well. Joey's boyfriend was in worse shape than Joey.

"What the actual hell is going-"

I started when a third man approached me. I was seconds away from willing my weapon when I felt a barrel press against the back of my skull.

"One move and I got orders to pull this trigger."

I felt my breath catch, but I did as he asked. I watched the first man raise his handgun to the back of Joey's head. That need to scream threatened to overwhelm me again.

"Move. Show me that you're not a liar, Lawson."

"Vic, man-"

Joey started, but he couldn't finish. I was looking for an opening. If I could get the gun away from the man behind me, then I could take out the one holding Joey and Pedro at bay.

Joey fell towards the equipment cases, then fell on his ass as he wrapped an arm around his ribs.

"It's all there," Joey coughed. "Every damn grain."

What was he talking about? I narrowed my eyes. Why would he be talking about grain?

"Joey!"

I hissed when the man behind me smacked the butt of the gun against the top of my spine.

"You said don't move, asshole. You never said don't speak."

That earned me another smack across the back of the head. He dug his fingers into my shoulder until I was forced down on my knees. From this angle, I could see Joey and Pedro better. I could also see the white bricks that were being lifted out of the equipment cases.

I felt myself go absolutely numb as I realized what I was watching. The bricks were cocaine. Had to be. The leader gestured for his men to take the cases to their SUV. Once they were loaded up, I was lifted to my feet by the collar of my shirt.

"This isn't what we agreed on, Lawson."

"You only gave me four hours." Joey grunted and the man kicked him twice in the ribs. "Dammit!"

"Put the bitch in the car."

What?

The man behind me shoved me forward and I pretended to stumble. I fell to my knees, but when he started to lift me back up, I kicked out, smacking his gun out of his hand. The bastard grunted before he grabbed at me, but I was faster. I scrambled up and dove for the gun when two shots were fired.

I wrapped my hands around the butt of it and twisted around just in time for the man I was fighting with to slam into me. I cracked my head against the asphalt when I heard gunshots going off around me.

"I oughta blow your god damn head off."

I was jerked up again, but this time, it was by the leader of this little party. He pressed the muzzle of his gun beneath my chin as he held me tight against him.

"Drop the gun, Lawson." He barked. "Now!"

Don't drop that gun, Joey. Please don't drop that gun.

Somehow, Joey had gotten to his feet. He was hurt. Dragging one leg behind him. And I could see the tears streaming down his face as he aimed the gun at us.

Us. I was still a human shield at the moment.

"You killed him!" Joey yelled. "You killed him!"

The gun beneath my chin began to glow a bright red as sirens filled the air. The man who had me started dragging me to the car. Joey did something I never would have suspected.

He opened fire.

I yelled as a bullet punctured through my arm. I jerked myself to the side when the leader pulled his trigger. The bullet that was meant to go into my brain had gone into his instead.

I fell flat on my back as the other men began to scatter. They were jumping back into the SUV, to leave the rest of us behind. Joey came over to where I was pinned beneath the body. I saw him raise the gun again. I turned my head as Joey unloaded the clip into the man's body.

"You killed my Pedro," He whispered. "You killed him."

I couldn't breathe from the weight of the drug dealer, but Joey had forgotten I was there. He turned away from me then dropped down next to Pedro. The last image I saw before I passed out was of Joey smacking against the asphalt as more gunshots exploded above me.

FIVE

JONAH ROWE

JONAH SPENT the rest of the morning alternating between helping out around the estate and working out. He'd needed something to keep his mind off the events that had happened before dawn. Eva nearly taking the oath to nullify her emotions. Joey's invasive phone call then the flight that had taken her away two hours before she was supposed to go.

Then, there was the other thing. The initial event. The one thing that Jonah had never expected in a million years. The one he needed to forget entirely.

"Dude, you are hella distracted this morning." Spader threw a weighted ball at him and he caught it with both hands. "You still riding high from yesterday?"

"Wouldn't you be?"

"Yeah, but I'd have taken full advantage of Lo's last two days in the States."

"I bet you would," Terrence dropped a free weight back on the stand. "You sure as hell chickened out yesterday."

"That was different. Evie threw me off my game."

"What?" Jonah grabbed his towel to run it over his hair. "What game?"

"She called me out when I was screwing around with her. Told me to go ahead and shoot my shot."

"And?"

"I got this part," Terrence grinned. "Spader turned whiter than usual before he ran away."

"You ran?"

"Damn straight I did." Spader huffed as he sat on the bench behind him. "She wasn't supposed to tell me to go for it. Threw me off."

Jonah laughed out loud. "You're a damn coward. I wish Heidi had seen that shit."

"Fine. I'm a coward." Spader snorted. "Eva looked at me with those fire eyes and all I could think of was Apollo ripping my head off."

"He does have that reputation." Jonah grabbed the pull up bar over his head. "But I don't think that's the real reason."

"Don't go trying to psychoanalyze me, J. We were just playing around." Spader began to work on arm curls. "Besides, I'm not the only coward in here."

"And what exactly have I done that matches taking it like a bitch when you get put on the spot?" Jonah wanted to know. "Please, tell me."

"You really want to know, J.?"

"Yeah, actually." Jonah popped his neck muscles before he adjusted his grip on the bar. "I do."

"Lola."

Jonah raised his eyebrows at Spader. "You're gonna have to explain that one."

"You ran, J. You had your shot in L.A. and you ran away from it just like I did. Hid behind Lola for nearly a year." Spader shrugged. "You're gonna keep runnin' and hidin' until it's too late."

Jonah nearly sneered, but hey, this was Spader. "When you have a girlfriend for longer than three dates, then we'll talk. Until then, well...I hope you at least gave Heidi a ride home."

"No judgement." Spader adjusted the strap of his glove then met his gaze. "If I had a woman like Lola hanging all over me, I'd have done the same thing. But don't get pissed at me for calling it like it is, man. Ain't none of us blind."

"There is no anger here, Spader," Jonah replied. And it was true. Annoyance, but not anger. "I'm not blind either. Heidi is the *only* woman you've brought around that we've seen past a month. I'm just curious whether it's them or not. There is an old saying....'When you've got an issue, it's *you*."

"We ain't talking about me. You're deflecting."

"I am not."

"Yeah, man, you are. I got my issues, but it's because I know I haven't found the right one yet. When I do, I sure as hell won't be screwing someone else right in front of them."

"It wasn't like that, Spader."

"Sure, it was. I heard Jonathan tell Evie that she had the bitch mask on around you and that was true. But you weren't innocent in that, either. I mean, come on, man. Put yourself in her position. Would you have approached Eva if she had been all over somebody else?"

Jonah slowly turned his eyes up to Spader. "I show affection to the woman I'm with, Spader. It was no disrespect to Eva at all. As a matter of fact, I think that whole thing was orchestrated by Joey and Pedro."

"There you are, deflecting again-"

"Guys!"

Reena rushed in from the hallway. She looked stunned. Almost shell-shocked. Jonah released the bar, alarmed at Reena's face. The awkward, tense conversation beforehand evaporated instantly.

"What's the matter, Re?"

Reena looked so dumbstruck that the expression made her look like a stranger. "Pedro was murdered. Joey is in surgery with two gunshots, and Eva is being held for questioning."

"What the hell?"

Reena shoved her phone into Jonah's hands. "Just look."

She hit 'play' and a newscaster began to speak. Behind the man was a picture of Eva and Joey from the Emmys. Both grinning up at the crowds from the red carpet.

"Breaking news this hour," The man fiddled with some papers on his desk. "A shoot out at LaGuardia Airport this afternoon has led to two deaths and two people being injured. Joseph Lawson, known for his role as the cameraman on *Grave Messages*, was found with two gunshot wounds. His companion, Pedro Garcia, died at the scene."

The man checked his papers. He was giddy but was trying damn hard to hide it.

"NYPD has taken Eva McRayne into custody at this hour for questioning. We reached out to Theia Productions, but have received no comment from them. Stay tuned as this story develops."

The video stopped. It just fucking stopped.

"Eva shot Joey? And Pedro?" Terrence broke the shocked silence around them. "Dude, no. That can't be real."

"Eva didn't shoot Joey, Terrence," Reena said. "There's no way in Hell that happened. Eva doesn't even like guns."

"Can you *really* have blamed her for offing Pedro if she did?" Spader was just as shocked as them, but still attempting glibness.

"Not the time, dude," Jonah said as he pulled out his own phone. "Not the time at all."

Jonah pressed the contact on his call list. If anyone could get them answers, it'd be Patience. The Networker was a gold mine of information.

Two rings later, he answered. "Jonah, good to hear from you."

"Good to talk to you," Jonah passed Reena her phone back. He couldn't stand to look at the image on the screen. "I need your help, Patience. A friend of ours has been detained by NYPD. We need you to get her out."

"What's the charge?"

"Murder, I think. Her name is Eva McRayne."

The line went silent for a moment. "The Olympian?"

"Yes."

"As much as I want to assist you, Jonah, McRayne doesn't fall into our jurisdiction." Patience must have been walking. Jonah could hear gravel crunch beneath his feet. "Is this in regard to the events at LaGuardia this morning?"

"You saw the news, huh?"

"Not quite. We have an agent on scene. Marlon Debois."

"I thought this was out of your jurisdiction."

"No, Miss McRayne is out of my jurisdiction. The murder of an Eleventh Percenter is not."

"So, you guys are looking into Eva, too?"

"No. We are much more interested in the Spirit Reaper's corpse that Miss McRayne was pulled out from under."

"Huh?" Jonah croaked. "Spirit Reaper?"

That got everyone's attention, but Jonah kept his focus on the call.

"Yes, Spirit Reaper," Patience answered. "Went by the name of Victor Albertson. While his sister continued in the family business of southern barbecue, he used ethereal powers to rise in the ranks of the drug game."

"Drug game," Jonah repeated. "You had the corpse of an Eleventh dealer, but there are no drugs on the scene, right?"

"Not one bit," Patience answered, his voice troubled. "That's what's most disturbing."

"Ok, look. Eva is a suspect in Pedro's murder, right?"

"Yes."

"Then you guys detain her. We can talk to her. Find out what really happened." Jonah caught Reena's eye and she nodded. "Eva's not a shooter, Patience. She hates guns. Out of the two of them, Joey is the gun fanatic."

"We will have to wait, Jonah. I am sure her legal team is trying to go for bail. She has no criminal record, but homicide is a capital offense."

"What happens if they let her out?"

"Then she will fall into our hands. We will have to detain her until the investigation is complete."

"Then why can't you make that happen?" Jonah demanded. "Eva's wardrobe costs more than the entire NYPD. She'll post bail."

"Right now, it is up to her legal team," Patience stopped talking for a minute. "Hang on. That's Marlon."

Jonah looked up in frustration. Nobody spoke during the pause. There was nothing they could say, really, to make this better.

"Jonah," Patience came back in less than three minutes. "Eva is being released. Marlon is waiting at the detention center to detain her."

"Wait, what?" Jonah gripped his phone so tightly it could've snapped. "I told you she'd post bail!"

"No bail," Patience said. "Eva won't be charged because there is no evidence she was involved in the crime. It turns out that she was also shot. She's saying it was Lawson, but lucky for her, it was a through and through."

"Joey shot Eva?"

"I don't know that for certain."

"Where is Marlon taking her?" Jonah clinched his hand into a fist then released it. "Can she come here?"

"No, I'm sorry. We still have to question her ourselves, Jonah. She'll be kept at our detention center in D.C."

"D.C." Jonah straightened. "We have a friend who works in that branch named Katarina Ocean. Tell Eva we'll be there in a few minutes."

"No, Jonah, you won't," Patience said. "Standard Spectral Law protocol mandates that Astralimes travel is prohibited at ethereal crime scenes or detention centers. Any attempts will land you in an ethereal steel holding cell at the Median."

"Dude," Jonah was frustrated and worried all at once. "What are we supposed to do?"

"Jonah," Patience sounded anything but. "You have a driver's license, don't you?"

With that, he hung up. Jonah wasn't pissed. Patience was in work mode and had no time for small talk.

"I'm going to D.C.," He said. "I'm going to go get Eva."

"Jonah," Terrence sighed. "You know the ethereal world is a *little* fucked up right now? You need to clear it with Jonathan first.

"Why?" Jonah demanded. "He's not my damn father."

"No," Spader shot back. "Jonathan actually cares about you."

"I don't have time for this. I have to get on the road."

"Jonah, Eva isn't going anywhere." Reena clasped his arm to keep him focused. Or to keep him from jumping in the damn car. "If she is in custody with the Networkers, then we know she's safe. I get that you want to go, but you have time to talk to Jonathan."

"We'll go, too." Terrence folded his arms across his chest. "There's a lot that ain't right about this. You go talk to Jonathan. I'll pack food."

"*You* guys have to stay," Jonah insisted. "On account of said fucked up situations. You're gonna need as many hands on deck as possible should anything go down. Besides, Terrence, Jonathan is sending you on recon on some Spirit Reapers. That was the other reason you threw the barbecue, remember? Because you'd have to be all business for a while."

Terrence's expression darkened. "Yeah, I know. But this is different, man."

"Stay here. I'll go talk to Jonathan."

Jonah left the group and headed to the protector guide's study. He knocked once before he entered.

"Jonathan, I gotta go. Eva is in some shit with the Networkers. I'm going to get her."

Jonathan sat back in his chair. "Pardon?"

"I don't have time to explain it. Call Patience, he's involved. I have to head out."

"Jonah, it is far too dangerous for you to leave Rome at this time. Allow me to contact Patience. I will speak with the Curaie as well. Perhaps they can give us information on Eva's predicament."

"Jonathan, she got tangled up in some mess with Joey and Pedro," Jonah spat. "There was a damn drug kingpin involved. Eva got shot, and she's saying Joey did it. He was shot as well, too. But Pedro? Gone. The drug lord spirit reaper, too."

At the words spirit reaper, Jonathan stood. Jonah knew that would get his attention. He saw Eva in the same light a grandfather would see a favorite grandchild. He sure as hell wouldn't want her in the same state as a damn reaper.

"Go. But be careful, Jonah."

"Always, Jonathan."

With that, Jonah left the study and went to his room. He

changed clothes, grabbed a travel bag, and headed downstairs to see the others waiting.

"You should take Evie's Rover." Spader passed him a set of keys. "It'll make it to D.C. Your car might not."

"I need to leave now. I can't go by the house-"

"It's in the drive, J." Terrence clapped him on the shoulder. "You were busy? So were we."

Jonah thought about it. Made sense. He took the keys and left without another word.

———

The fact that Jonah was on the road at a time like this was a testament to how much he cared about Eva. A woman he considered one of his best friends.

No, he didn't need the road trip to tell him how much he cared about Eva. Jonah couldn't stop thinking about the horrible conversation he'd had with Spader earlier that day when Spader had accused him of hiding. He hadn't been hiding, dammit. He'd been enjoying his life with a woman who had the same goals as he did. No strings. No attachments. They both knew it would end eventually with no hard feelings or hurt pride.

The exact opposite of what had happened with Eva in L.A. Jonah grimaced at the memory. He knew she had been hurt when she found out about Lola, but he didn't need to explain his actions away to her. They were friends. If he'd given Eva any indication otherwise - outside of the possession, that is - then it had to stop.

Jonah tightened his grip on the steering wheel. *All* of it had to stop. No more embraces, no more brushing up against each other. No more grabbing her hand or holding her on the couch when they watched movies. She'd gotten the wrong idea. Maybe he was to blame. Maybe Eva was so inexperienced with relationships that she misread his affection and it was her fault for not understanding his motives in the first place.

It didn't matter. He wasn't going to do that to her. Not anymore. Jonah had made peace with himself over the events in L.A. He'd pushed them to the back of his mind and refused to think about them. No matter how many times they tried to come to the surface every time he smelled lavender.

File it away, Jonah. That ain't the issue right now.

But it was, at least, a little. Eva had been moments away from taking an oath that would have destroyed him. He knew why, too. Jonah knew that if she had gone through with it, then there would be no hope for the future. It was a stupid thought. If he was determined to remain friends with Eva, then the future didn't matter.

Then again, maybe it did. It was the future that gave Jonah the most pause. He couldn't have a relationship with Eva knowing that someday, he would physically die and leave her behind. That wasn't fair to either of them. If he was a coward, it was for that reason alone. He considered Eva's response when he'd said that very thing during their conversation about Hestia's damn oath. She'd gotten emotional. No surprise there. Eva tended to walk away if he talked about his own mortality.

So, no. Eva wasn't 'the one', as Spader had implied. You can't be soulmates with someone and it not be able to last forever. And who the hell wanted 'forever' anyway? Jonah was much more interested in having agreements like the one he'd had with Lola. He wasn't ready for a damn full-time relationship. He wasn't ready for all the shit that went along with it. The emotions, the strings. It was as bad as a marriage, which was something he'd never be interested in.

He was so lost in thought that he almost didn't notice the lady with tire trouble on the side of the road, frantically flagging him down.

Jonah pulled over but didn't leave his car just yet. He'd seen one too many horror movies and had been through one too many horror experiences *personally* to walk blindly into this situation. He closed his eyes, took a deep breath, and willed the actors in his mind to perform. Spectral Sight was activated.

There were spirits and spiritesses here and there, which was a good sign. But that was just the first part.

He focused on the lady. Moment of truth.

There were spirits around her. Four of them. Both sets of grand-parents, maybe?

Jonah sighed in relief. That was a good sign.

He stepped out of his car and got a better look at the woman. She looked to be in her early thirties, tall, and no stranger to working outside if her well-worn jeans and sun-faded shirt were any indication. Her dark brown hair was in shambles, but that was likely due to her toiling with the tire. Nothing about the scene was suspicious.

Which made Jonah that much more suspicious.

He pocketed his hands and clutched the handles of his batons as he approached the woman.

"Oh, thank you, darlin'!" The lady threw her hair out of her face and closed the remaining distance between them. "Can you help me with this flat tire? My daddy lent me his truck just for a day, and I popped the damn thing! Musta been a nail in the road or somethin'!"

Jonah realized something now that he had a closer look at the woman. Her features were largely plain and unremarkable, but there was still a certain beauty about her. It was an immutable, natural thing about her. But he remained iffy.

His expression did not go unnoticed by the woman, who shook her head.

"Are you okay, darlin'?" she asked. "You look like somethin' bad is 'bout to happen."

Jonah could have sworn to himself. He'd gotten so suspicious of every stranger in the past few months that he saw threats every-where. There was nothing wrong with this woman. The only threat she carried was potentially bursting into tears if her father's tire didn't get fixed. "I'm sorry, ma'am. I-I have a lot on my mind."

He replaced the flat tire with the spare. The woman was so relieved that she raised her hands in a silent cheer.

"Thank you so much!" she exclaimed. "You got me out of a bad way! Name's Mary Anna. Mary Anna Greene."

She extended a hand. Jonah's hands weren't that clean due to the tire, but neither were Mary Anna's, so he shook it without reservation.

"Jonah Rowe."

He had to admit that this woman broke his tension somewhat. His mind had been so occupied with concerned thoughts about Eva and Cyrus that he'd probably have wrecked his car because his mind hadn't been on the road. Mary Anna may very well have saved his physical life.

"My daddy would love you, Jonah!" she said. "He'd appreciate the fact that some men ain't forgotten how to treat a lady."

Her drawl was even heavier than Terrence's, but it sounded better from her. It pulled him in somewhat, but he remembered that he had more pressing matters. It wasn't a time for light-hearted fare.

"My nana beat that into my head," he told her in a deflective sort of way. "But I'm glad that I was able to help you, Mary Anna. Got to blaze now."

"Wait two minutes!" Mary Anna ran back to her father's truck. "I gotta give you something!"

"Oh no worries, Mary Anna," said Jonah. "No charge—"

"Naw, darlin'!" Mary Anna was insistent. "Can't let you leave without something!"

She pulled a long-stemmed red rose out of the truck and extended it. Jonah looked at it and then raised his gaze to her. She shrugged.

"I got a thing of roses in here for my mama," she explained. "It's her birthday. I know it ain't the manliest present, but it's all I had on hand, and it's the gesture that counts, right? Give it to some pretty lady in your life."

Jonah was well aware that the flash in his eyes didn't go unnoticed. Mary Anna regarded him.

"You alright, darlin'? Was it the lady thing? Are you embarrassed?"

Jonah steeled himself. Like he was going to discuss himself with a stranger. "I'll make sure the rose winds up somewhere great," he promised. He took the rose rather absently and accidentally palmed two of the thorns. "*Ah,* dammit." The punctures were negligent, but annoying just the same.

"Aw," Mary Anna frowned. "I didn't mean for you to do that."

"It's fine, I promise." Jonah pulled out a napkin and wiped his hand. It wasn't the biggest deal. "I really have to go now, Mary Anna. But thank you. This has been … serene."

Jonah didn't know what else to say. Serenity may very well not be an option where he was going.

Mary Anna smiled. "'Course, darlin'." She patted his wrist to avoid the hand with the cuts. "Take care and God bless!"

Jonah sped off. That was an interesting experience, to say the least. Of course, his mind still swirled about with whatever fresh shit he might face when he reached Eva but interspersed with those worries were pleasant thoughts about the sweet, considerate, quietly attractive farm woman, Mary Anna Greene.

———

Mary Anna watched Jonah's car for a distance, and then lowered her eyes to the blood-spotted napkin in her grasp. Simple sleight of hand was all it took to make it hers. Jonah hadn't noticed a thing. She brought the napkin to her nose and took in the scent as though it were a rare fragrance.

"Mmm." Her eyes closed in bliss. "His very blood is perfect."

She looked at the bouquet of roses in the seat of the pickup and looked over the cherry-red roses with a smile. "And *you'll* serve your purpose as well," she murmured.

Finally, she snapped the fingers of her left hand, and the spirits around her became visible to the naked eye.

"He bought it," she said to them. "Now leave here, lest I vanquish you."

SIX

JONAH ROWE

JONAH GOT to the D.C. headquarters of the Networkers after dark. Eva's Rover was a great ride, but damn if it wasn't slow on the interstates. He took the stairs two at a time before he damn near ran through the glass doors. The receptionist at the counter didn't seem to be phased as he slid to a stop in front of her.

"Evenin'," Jonah caught his breath before he tried again. "Evenin', ma'am. I need to see a woman detained here."

"I'm sorry." The woman didn't look away from her screen as she typed. "Visitors are prohibited this late. You will have to come back tomorrow between the hours of nine and two."

"I didn't drive like a bat out of hell from North Carolina to be told about visiting hours." Jonah snapped. "Bring Katarina Ocean out here. She'll let me in."

"I'm sorry, sir, Ms. Ocean is not available."

Jonah was seconds away from yelling at the woman. He gripped the edge of the counter as he leaned against it.

"You are going to unlock that damn door behind you-"

"Mr. Rowe."

Jonah turned to see a slender black man approach him. Dude

was his height with a bald head that gleamed under the fluorescent lights. From his accent, Jonah wagered he was Cajun.

"Who are you?"

"Agent Marlon DeBois. Patience told me to expect you," The man gestured for him to follow him. "Come with me."

"Where is Eva?" Jonah heard the door click when Marlon ran his card through a slot. "Is she alright?"

"McRayne is in shock. That is the difficulty we are facing at the moment."

"Shock?"

"Indeed. She was taken from the hospital straight to the precinct." Marlon explained. "She went into shock prior to that."

Jonah ran his tongue over his teeth in annoyance. "Patience said she had been shot."

"She had. Left bicep. McRayne is exceedingly fortunate. Should have gone through her chest."

"So what happened?" Jonah questioned as the two men walked the barren corridors. "What do you know?"

"Nothing. The security footage of the airport didn't extend to the private airfield. Two subjects are deceased, so they can't tell us anything. Lawson is unconscious, which leaves only McRayne to tell the tale. She ain't talkin'."

Marlon ran his little card through another slot. The door clicked open.

"I'd move her to the interrogation rooms, but it won't do any good. I cannot allow you entrance to her cell."

Cell? As Jonah followed the Networker, he realized just how serious this was. They passed by solid white doors with little bars over square windows. Ethereal steel. Jonah would recognize the metal anywhere.

"Eva's innocent, sir," Jonah tried. "She wouldn't have shot Pedro. She would have stabbed him."

"That's not very encouraging, Jonah."

Goddammit.

"Let me try this again," Jonah tucked his hands in his pockets. "I can get Eva to talk, but I need to be in the room with her. I get ya'll have your regulations, but if you want the truth, you gotta let me in."

Marlon stopped and eyed Jonah. "I've already explained her current state. You think you can break a woman out of shock?"

"Eva and I are..." Jonah searched for the right words. "We're close friends. If she's gonna talk, it'll be with me."

Marlon twisted at the waist as if he were looking for someone behind him. Finally, he returned his focus onto Jonah.

"I'll allow it. You have five minutes. If she don't talk, I'm pulling you out."

Five minutes? That was it? Whatever. Jonah had to take what he could get at this point.

"Deal."

"I will be recording the conversation," Marlon continued walking. "And every inch of the cell is being monitored. Do not, under any circumstances, try anything other than talking."

"I didn't bring a cake with a nail file in it, if that's what you're getting at," Jonah muttered. "Whatever, man. Just let me go talk to her."

The two of them walked for another five minutes. Jonah was surprised the place was so big, but then again, it was a jail. A busy one if the number of occupied cells he passed were any indication.

At long last, the Networker stopped in front of a solid white door.

"This where she's at?"

Jonah peered through the bars of the small window. Eva was sitting on the cot with her knees pulled up to her chest and her head resting against her folded arms. An ache filled Jonah at the sight of her. She seemed so damn small in that cell. The bright orange jumpsuit she had on made her seem even paler than usual.

"Five minutes." Marlon slid the card through the lock. "If she ain't talking by then, I'm pulling you out."

"Thanks for the reminder." Jonah took a step back then entered the cell. He waited until he heard the door echo shut before he walked over to the cot. "Hey, Superstar."

Eva didn't move. Jonah sat on the edge of the cot and touched her elbow. Maybe she was asleep.

"Superstar? Sit up."

It took a second for Eva to do as he said. Well, she sort of did what he asked. She turned her head and looked at him, but Jonah didn't know if she actually *saw* him. Her golden eyes seemed too glassy. Too bright.

"Jonah?" She whispered. "What are you doing here?"

"I came to see what the hell is going on with you." He leaned forward so that his elbows rested against his knees. His hands clasped together in front of him. "You wanna tell me what happened?"

Eva started to return her head back to her knees, but Jonah knew better than to let her do that. He placed a hand on the back of her head to stop her and felt a knot against the back of her skull.

Was there a fight? The only thing Patience had told him was about a shootout.

"Let me check you over. You could have wounds you don't even know about."

Jonah expected her trademark 'I'm fine', but Eva didn't protest in the slightest. She unfolded herself when he nudged her chin up to check her neck. There was a ring burned into the smooth skin there. Jonah took note of it, then moved to her arms. Aside from the bandage that was stained brown, she seemed fine.

Thank god for that. Now, if he could just get her to talk.

"Pedro is gone, Eva." Jonah released her arm and resisted the urge to pull her against him. "What did he do to make you shoot him?"

Eva's face remained impassive. She stared at a corner of the room close to the cot. Jonah barely heard her when she whispered.

"I didn't shoot him."

"You didn't? The cops, the Networkers, they all seem to think otherwise."

Eva scrunched up her nose and Jonah knew that meant she was holding back tears. That was good. A woman in shock did not show emotion like that.

"What about Joey? He took two to the chest. Might not make it. What'd he do to deserve that?"

This time, Eva put her head in her hands and began to sob. Jonah stared at her, unnerved and a little frightened. He had never once seen Eva breakdown like this. He didn't think she had it in her. Eva was too damn strong to resort to full blown tears. In trying to snap her out of it, had he gone too far?

"Eva, I'm sorry. I was just tryin'-"

"The men in black shot them," She turned her head away from him as she tried to calm down. She took another minute, but Jonah didn't move an inch. If he spoke, he knew she'd shut down again. "It...they used me, Jonah."

"Explain that."

"The equipment cases." She whispered. "Those men were after the equipment cases. They met me when the plane landed. They had Joey and Pedro and-"

Her face twisted again. She struggled as she tried to maintain herself. This time, Eva was successful.

"The cases were full of cocaine. I had no idea. The men were calling Joey a liar. I was going to fight, but one of them had a gun to my head. I didn't start struggling' until it was too late."

Jonah went numb. He couldn't feel anything as he stared at her. Not even his own fingernails as they cut into his palm.

"Then what? When did Pedro get shot, Eva?"

"I don't know. There were six men there. Their leader grabbed me. Used me as a shield. Pedro was gone by then. Had to be. That's when Joey opened fire and I got hit."

Jonah closed his eyes as the numbness was replaced by a rage he had to stamp out. It wouldn't do Eva a damn bit of good if he went off at the moment.

He had two minutes, tops. Less, if Marlon had started the clock when he unlocked the door.

"Be straight with me, Eva. I ain't playing around with this. Did you know about the cocaine?"

"No," She whispered as she met his eyes. She then closed hers. "No, I didn't know about the drugs. Joey and Pedro used me as a cover, Jonah. I'm a damn fool for thinking they *wouldn't* use me, but they did. I had no idea what was going on when I stepped off that plane. I still don't."

Jonah reached out to wrap an arm around her neck. He pulled her head down to his shoulder. He believed her. He knew Eva well enough to know when she was lying. At that moment, the cell door opened and Marlon stepped inside.

"Jonah, come with me."

He didn't want to. He didn't want to let Eva go. Not when she needed him so damn bad. Jonah glared at the man but he sat Eva back up.

"I'll be back."

Jonah found himself following the Networker out into the hallway. The cell door sounded hollow when it connected with the lock.

"I told you, she's innocent. She had no idea that drugs were being transported on that plane. Let her out."

"It's not that simple, Jonah." Marlon rocked back on his heels. "If Lawson and Garcia were involved in the drug trade-"

"They were. Eva just said it."

"Then Eva is now a target." Marlon continued. "She needs to hide out for awhile until we have a chance to capture the men who attacked them on that airfield."

"Why would Eva be a target?" Jonah asked. "You heard what I just heard in there."

"Boy, do you not know how this works?" Marlon frowned at him. "Patience brags on you, but you aren't matching his description at the moment. Just saying."

Jonah gritted his teeth. He hated being spoken to like he was stupid with a passion, but Marlon was ethereal law enforcement. The Tenth police might have been stuck on stupid ninety percent of the time, but Jonah still had some deference for Spectral Law.

"Marlon, I mean no disrespect here," He said in a measured tone, "But you don't know me. Don't assume you do, and I would prefer it if it didn't talk to me like I'm stupid. Just...don't. Now, the reason *why* I asked the question why Eva would be a target is because one, Patience said that that Albertson guy was the leader who is now gone, so the head is cut off the snake, and two, no product was found at the scene, which means they must have their stash. So why would they come after Eva at *this* point?"

"Because Eva is the only witness who can identify them. She is probably - whether she realizes it or not - sitting on top of the rest of the cocaine that Lawson and Garcia stole from the cartel. It is infinitely safer if she remains here."

"You think Joey and Pedro were stealing from a cartel?"

"That is the only reason an event of this magnitude would occur. Jonah, when a drug lord falls, his second-in-command takes on his previous role. It is how the business thrives. So the head of the snake theory sounds nice, but it's not realistic. I can just about guarantee they have files on all three of them just in case shit goes bad. Well, it did."

"Marlon?"

Jonah recognized that voice, and turned to see Katarina Ocean.

"Jonah!" She hugged him. "Fancy seeing you here!"

"Not here because I wanted to be," Jonah muttered. "I tried to speak to you, but the damn bearded lady at the front wouldn't let me."

"Don't talk about Veronica like that," Marlon said sternly.

"Guys, please," Katarina said. "We have an issue. A massive shipment of cocaine has just been moved offshore via a freighter. From New York."

Marlon froze. Jonah looked at him.

"What's that mean?"

Marlon pulled something from his pocket. Jonah recognized it is a Tally that Spectral Law practitioners used to contact each other. "These bastards are trying to run."

Jonah glanced back at the white door before he made his decision.

"You gonna go do a raid or somethin'?"

"That's the plan." Marlon spoke into the tally. "42, location?"

A woman's voice came back through. "Hudson Plastics. Dock 214B."

"Give me twenty minutes. Briefing." Marlon pocketed the tally. "I have to go. Eva will remain with us for the foreseeable future."

"She can't leave even if this raid goes right?"

"No. It isn't safe. You disagree, you can go over my head."

Marlon moved past him and Jonah called out to him before he could get very far.

"Marlon."

The Networker stopped and Jonah closed the distance.

"Let me help."

Marlon's eyes immediately darkened, but Jonah spoke up once more. This man's attempts to micromanage were annoying him hugely, but he was trying to keep himself in check.

"Before you shoot it down, Katarina will vouch for me," He told The Networker. "Patience will, too. And I know that the S.P.G. has done tons of assignments with consultants, namely Felix Duscere. So if you shoot it down, it is for one of two reasons; one, you've decided you don't like me and want to lock me out, or two, you were in on this operation with Albertson."

"Jonah!" Katarina chided.

Jonah shrugged. Yeah, it was an asshole thing to say, but Marlon was being an asshole. Jonah was simply taking the cue from him.

Marlon stuffed his hands in pockets and tilted his head at Jonah. He narrowed his eyes.

"What'd you say?"

"You heard." Jonah stared him down. "Get on the phone. Talk to whoever you gotta talk to. Or I'm going to show up anyway."

"This is an S.P.G. investigation you're trying to fuck with," Marlon approached him. "You wanna end up in one of those cells? No. So your best bet is to go to New York and talk to your girl's buddy to get us answers to the fuckers he was working with."

"Okay," Jonah nodded. "I now see that ethereal law has its assholes the same way Tenth laws do. One phone call, and I'll have the tabloids here, reporting on how you're apprehending a celebrity just because you can."

Marlon's eyes flashed. Katarina shook her head slowly. Jonah was unfazed by both.

"You're an asshole, Marlon. I'm just matching you."

"You can't expose this location," Marlon narrowed his eyes at him. "Do you not realize where you are? The next step for most of these assholes is the Plane with No Name. You call the goddamn media, and it'll go straight to the Curaie."

"All you gotta do is share your toys, Networker. Let me go with you."

"Why do you want to go so bad?"

"First of all, it's 'badly'," Jonah corrected him. He was being an asshole and was aware of it. But Marlon created this situation. Jonah himself just adapted accordingly. "And not that it's any of your business, but Eva is important to me. I know for a fact that she had no knowledge of any of this. My suspicion is Joey, since *he* is one who is the addict. I want her cleared, and maybe, I can help expedite that. I'm not bound by red tape."

"Uh huh."

"Dude, I ain't asking. I'm doing you a courtesy by requesting-"

"Katarina, get Rowe a vest. You fuck up and take a bullet, that's on you, understand?"

"Or maybe I save *you* from one," Jonah murmured.

"Jonah, please," Katarina implored as a vest appeared in her hands. "Be reasonable. Marlon has been working for almost a hundred hours straight, subsisting on coffee and nutritional supplements."

"What?" Jonah looked at the guy again. He must have been a zombie by now. "Why didn't you explain that?? Why didn't you send me to another Networker if you're running on fumes?"

"If Patience tells me to escort you to Mars, I'd damn do it." Marlon cut his eyes over to Katarina. "Thanks, Ocean."

"I know you're not really a hard ass," She shrugged. "Thought Jonah should know that too."

"Whatever. Get him his gear then show him to the muster room."

"On it." Katarina saluted. "This way, Jonah."

Jonah headed after Katarina. It was hard as hell to do knowing that Eva was stuck in that damn cage. He thought back to his conversation with her. How her eyes looked.

"Kat, there was something up with Eva. Her eyes were strange. Glassy."

"Oh, that's just the truth serum." She slipped her card in a lock. "Standard interrogation procedure. It'll wear off soon."

"Truth serum?" Jonah exclaimed. "Katarina, I was told that Eva was dead silent until I showed up. I thought truth serum forced you to talk. Had she said anything to anyone, due to that serum?"

"No." She frowned. "She didn't speak at all until you showed up. It's strange."

"That *is* strange," Jonah said. "Why would it work in the first place, though? Why is it standard procedure? I was told that stuff like poisons and mind-altering things don't work well on Elevenths."

"No, Jonah." Katarina looked him in his face. "Poisons and mind-altering things don't work on *you*. You are a blue aura. You balance it right out. The rest of us, not so much."

"Ok. Why did they use it on Eva then? She's a tenth."

"No, she's not. She's a demi-god." Katarina stopped next to a cracked door. "That's one step below actual god, J. It's not the same."

"But-"

"Jackson," Katarina pushed open a door with her shoulder. The man she spoke too was sitting in an office chair, bag of chips in one hand as he watched a wall of screens. "You are watching McRayne, right?"

"Suppose so."

"Ok. Has she said anything when no one is there?"

"No. Barbie hasn't said a word. Stares of into the corner at times, but she hasn't said anything."

Katarina nodded. "It'll pass, Jonah. When you return from New York, I'm sure she'll be back to right again."

"Still unnerving as hell to think you'd just drug someone."

Katarina shut the door and continued. They were coming close to an enclosed area with a gate around it when she spoke again.

"What could Eva have said that's got you so worried?"

"What?"

"When you found out about the truth serum. You asked if she

had said anything to anyone. I'm simply curious what you mean by that since you knew she hadn't said anything about the shooting."

Jonah sighed. "I don't know, Katarina. Anything, I guess. Eva has had a difficult life. She could have unloaded her whole life in there and been entirely alone with no support. It was likely that, I suppose."

"I've read her file. I know what you mean."

"Ya'll have a file on Eva?"

"Of course, we do. We keep files on everyone who becomes embroiled in our world."

Jonah wasn't even angry. It made sense. "I know you have one on me. Please tell me it's been updated from the volatile basket case ya'll had me determined as earlier."

"Um, you're the Blue Aura. If Jonathan would allow it, we'd track everything from your food to your sleep schedule."

"Oh, god," Jonah complained. "You're joking."

Katarina was silent. Jonah stared down at her.

"You're not joking."

Katarina sighed. "Jonah, I consider you a friend now. A dear friend. But it is wise policy to watch our friends. Look at Eva's former associate, Cyrus Alexius."

"I'm nothing like him!"

"The principle is still the same. You know the old saying. Keep your enemies close, but your friends closer."

Jonah thought about it when Katarina stopped in front of a series of shelves. She began passing him clothes. Black pants, black shirt, bulletproof vest.

"You really think Lawson was behind all this?" She asked quietly. "Or do you think he was following Pedro's lead?"

Jonah chose his words carefully. He was biased, but that wouldn't help. "Joey is a heroin addict in recovery. Pedro has family members who apparently got big in the cartels. Just based on those alone, Pedro was tailing Joey along. Either he was an enabler, or he liked having a lap dog."

"Did you know them well? Maybe you know something that could help."

"Help with what?"

"I don't know, J. Help with the raid? Help get Eva out of here?" Katarina studied him. "Think on it. You have ten minutes before the meeting in the muster room."

"What the hell is a muster room?"

"Cop speak for meeting hall." She chuckled. "Hurry up. They'll leave without you."

Jonah waited until Katarina stationed herself by the door, but as he removed his shirt, he heard voices filter to the back of the room. He turned just in time to see Marlon storm over to him.

"You already approved this," Jonah reminded Marlon. "So too late-"

"Eva is being released." Marlon muttered. "Apparently, Apollo threw such a fit that the Curaie agreed to release her into your care."

Jonah felt a rush of relief so great, he dropped his arms. "What about the investigation? The raid?"

"It's still happening'." Marlon pocketed his tally. "But you ain't going. Get the girl and go."

"Where is she now?"

"Still in her cell. Get your shirt back on. I'll take you back."

Jonah dropped the black shirt and pulled his polo back on. Katarina smiled, hugged him goodbye, and went the opposite direction.

Why hadn't he thought to contact Apollo? He should have done that on the drive.

Marlon was quiet until they reached the hall Eva was on. His voice made Jonah jump when he heard it. "Apollo has also refused our assistance in guarding McRayne. He said he was going to send one of his own men."

"Did he say who?"

"A Ulysses somebody."

Ulysses. The man-bun keeper who had helped Eva the night Cyrus had tried to throw her off a cliff. Jonah didn't remember much about the keeper other than his warm nature.

"Ok. Let me get her home, man."

"Eva is not allowed on Estate grounds due to the current investigation. Neither can she go back to the residence she purchased in Rome until we know for certain it is clear. Do you understand?"

Dammit. Eva couldn't go to the estate? The Sullivan House was off limits, too? Jonah considered L.A., but that was too far for backup. He pulled out his phone and made the call.

"Jonathan, Eva's being released into my custody. But she is not allowed at the estate and the Sullivan House is too dangerous. Any ideas?"

"Indeed. We shall put her at the Milverton Hotel downtown. Joseph, too."

"Joey? Why Joey?"

"The bullets that struck Joseph were ethereal. I was able to arrange his medical care be put in our hands."

"Kinda wished you'd let the tenth doctors deal with him. It'd hurt longer."

"Jonah," Jonathan had a warning tone in his voice. "We must save all we can."

"I'll call when we reach town."

Jonah disconnected the phone call just as Marlon unlocked Eva's cell door. The Networker stood to the side so he could enter. Eva was still curled up into herself, and once again, she didn't move when Jonah approached her.

"Superstar, it's time to go."

She lifted her head off her arms and stared at him. Her eyes were still glassy, but rimmed with red. Had she been crying again? What the hell had made her so emotional?

Jonah knew the answer to that question. He didn't have time to deal with Joey's betrayal right now.

"We're going home?"

"Um, no. We're going to a hotel in Rome. It'll be safer for you."

"Will you be there?"

"Yeah. I'll be staying at the hotel with you."

"Then it's home if you're there."

Jonah felt his face warm up. He didn't have time for that, either. Instead, he lifted her to her feet then wrapped his arm around her waist when she stumbled.

"I got you, Superstar."

Jonah led her after Marlon as noise filled the halls around them. Loud bangs and muted shouts. "What the hell?"

"Other prisoners." Marlon responded as he continued. "They don't like it when someone is cut free that ain't them."

Jonah kept going until they reached the parking lot. He helped Eva into the Rover and ignored the way his stomach fluttered every time his fingertips brushed against her skin. It took him right back to the night in her garage. The kiss in the kitchen.

Yeah, he remembered everything. Every little detail. He didn't think he would ever be able to forget them.

Jonah got in and pulled them into traffic before he heard Eva's quiet voice.

"You came to get me? Why?"

Jonah allowed the question to marinate for a second. Maybe one day, Eva would understand that he would do anything for her.

"First of all, you're my best friend, Superstar," He said. "I may not be a superhero, but I make time for my friends. And second of all, I believe you. I know you better than to think you're a drug trafficker on the side."

"Best friend? I thought that was Terrence."

"Nah, different set of rules for Terrence. Don't tell him I said that. Might hurt his feelings."

Eva returned her gaze out the window, and Jonah wondered if the truth serum was still flowing through her. She was too quiet. Too withdrawn.

"Superstar, I know you're not ok. Nobody would be ok in this situation. But I gotta ask you. Why'd you break down back there?"

"Break down?"

"Yeah. The cryin' thing. I've never seen you cry before. Threw me, is all."

"I cry all the time, Jonah. I just never let you see it."

"Why?"

"Because it's no good for you to see me like that or anyone for that matter. I'm the pillar. The soldier. I'm not allowed to break down."

Jonah didn't know what to say to that. He understood Eva's words more than he liked to admit. He wasn't about to get into it with her. Not right now. Later, when he was driving at ninety-two miles and she wasn't drugged out of her mind.

There were so many questions he could ask her right now and the truth serum would force a straight answer out of her. Questions like why she had really stayed away from Rome for so long. Was she gone all the time because of work? Was it because she didn't want to risk running into him and Lola? Why had she taken his apology on the cliffs that night so damn hard in the first place?

It wasn't right. Jonah may have been able to get the answers he wanted, but at what cost? He trusted Eva to tell him the truth. She had always been honest with him. The truth serum was just a cheap gimmick used by strangers to get answers she didn't have. Jonah didn't need drugs with her.

"The drug lord at the airport was a spirit reaper," He broke the silence in the car to keep himself from slipping up and asking her those very questions. "Joey and Pedro were messing with the wrong crowd when they hooked up with them."

Eva kept looking out of the window and watched most of Virginia fly past them before she spoke again. "What exactly is a spirit reaper, Jonah? I know you explained them to me in Romania but refresh my memory."

"In a nutshell, a Spirit Reaper is an Eleventh Percenter who has chosen to use their ethereality for the dark side," Jonah answered. "That's why the color of their aura has a darker shade. They usurp innocent spirits and spiritesses, which increases their power. Some are more hardcore than others—" Jonah shuddered involuntarily and hoped that Eva missed it, "—but I didn't realize they had drug lords in their ranks. I sure as hell didn't expect Joey to ever get tangled up in one."

Eva ignored his prompt to get her to talk. Instead, she whispered so low, he barely heard her over the noise of the tires on the road.

"I've seen him."

"At the Sullivan House?"

"Yes. And the condo. Joey never introduced us. I never cared to be introduced to him, either."

Jonah tightened his grip on the steering wheel then let up before he broke it. Albertson had been inside her home? Joey had actually let a fucking spirit reaper around *his* Eva?

No. Not *his* Eva. He couldn't think like that.

"I've seen him in spirit, too. Since the airport."

That was enough to pull Jonah out of his thoughts and back to the conversation.

"You couldn't have seen him."

"I have. I see him now. He is in the backseat, leering at me. You can't see him, Jonah?"

Jonah, still unnerved at her expression, glanced into the rearview mirror. He halfway expected to see a spirit, but the backseat was empty. "You see him now?"

"You don't?"

"I wouldn't have been able to. Eleventh Percenters can't see the spirits of other Eleventh Percenters. Something to do with height-ened spiritual attunement. Ask Reena for a more detailed explanation."

"Then how can I see him?"

"That's a good question," Jonah said. "See, when a Tenth passes into Spirit, they can choose to stay on Earth plane or cross to the Other Side. But when an *Eleventh* passes, we go to the Other Side. Period."

"That's what always happens, Jonah?"

Jonah swallowed and didn't answer. "You shouldn't be able to see the spirit of that evil Eleventh, Eva. Maybe it had something to do with your being the Sibyl or something."

Eva still looked afraid. She didn't even look like she believed Jonah's hypothesis. That was fine. Jonah didn't believe it much either. It just sounded nice.

"He called Joey a liar," Eva muttered to herself. "Why would he call Joey a liar? Why would he murder Pedro?"

"Let's talk about something else." Jonah grabbed her hand from her lap to hold it against the middle console. The more Eva talked about what had happened, the more Jonah wanted to take her mind off it. "How did filming go in Detroit.?"

"Fine. Caught some pretty convincing evidence for a cold case that the police won't even fathom as real since it came from the spirit of the victim."

They talked about her locations for a long while, but somewhere close to the Virginia-North Carolina line, Eva went silent. She still held onto his hand for dear life, but her thoughts were a million miles away.

No. Her thoughts were at the Milverton Inn and Suites. Her game face was back on when they pulled into a parking space there shortly after midnight.

Jonah read over a text message he received from Reena. "Eva, Reena is in the lobby. Joey is in the Apex suite, not the Governor's. Jonathan must have set it up."

"Okay," Eva said slowly, "What's with the expression?"

"The Apex suite was where Turk Landry stayed while they taped the Rome season of *ScarYous Tales of the Paranormal.*"

"Listen, Superstar. Akshara is here. Reena's gonna help us out, too. Terrence couldn't get away. We'll get Joey fixed up and figure all this craziness out."

"I don't think there's much to figure out, Jonah." Eva sounded sad when she said it. "Joey and Pedro used me. What else is there to say?"

Eva withdrew her hand from his. Jonah started to grab it back but thought better of it. Eva didn't deserve any action that would have given her the wrong idea.

They exited the car and headed for the sliding doors. Jonah froze in his tracks. Eva bumped into him from behind.

"Jonah? What's wrong?"

Jonah didn't even hear her. His full attention was on the woman he thought he'd never lay eyes on again.

Mary Anna.

"*Jonah?*" She nearly dropped her purse. "Fancy seeing you here, darlin'!"

SEVEN

EVA MCRAYNE

JOEY LAWSON HAD USED ME. His lover had used me. I couldn't get past those thoughts in my mind. Not when I was being sewed up. Not when I was in the hands of the NYPD and then, the Networkers. It wasn't the gunfight that had sent me into shock. It had been the realization that a man I had seen as my brother had used me so horribly. He'd stashed drugs on the plane? How many times had he done that? How many times had I been the unknowing idiot who trafficked drugs from state to state?

Jonah should have just left me to rot. As numb as I was, I couldn't speak to him about everything. He claimed it was a truth serum given to me by the Networkers. I knew it was because my heart had been broken once again, but I couldn't face the pain of it yet.

Joey was here. I had to talk to him. I had to stay by his side until he woke up and I could ask him the single question that had plagued me since I realized what was happening on that airfield.

Why?

Despite my current emotional state, I bristled when I saw the excited expressions on both Jonah and the woman's face. I tried to get a look at her in the dark. All I could see was a mass of dark curls around a smooth face. The blue and green uniform she wore fit snug against curves I would never have. No wonder Jonah's face lit up. She was exactly his type. Exactly like Lola had been.

The exact opposite of me, I started to step around my friend and the woman when I realized the green and blue uniform belonged to the hotel.

"I'm sorry to interrupt, but do you work here?" I glanced at the small nametag attached to her chest. "Mary Anna, is it?"

"Oh my god." The woman gaped at me. "You're—"

"Yeah. I know. Eva McRayne. I'll sign something for you later." I was too tired to play nice tonight. "Look, if you're busy, then I'll just go on inside."

"No." The woman shook her head. "Follow me."

She led us through the glass door engraved with the name of the hotel. I barely saw Reena standing by the front desk, but I didn't miss her when she jogged over to us.

"Evie, what the hell have you gotten into this time?" Reena must have noticed the expression on my face because she fell in step with the rest of us. "I saw the news. They are saying the guy committed suicide."

"He was going to shoot me in the head." I muttered. "Shot himself instead."

We stopped in front of a massive wooden door. Mary Anna knocked before the door flew open. Jonathan stood on the other side with his standard stoic expression, but I barely nodded my greeting to him. I crossed the room as quickly as I could. I dropped my bag in the chair next to the bed and bit my lip as I took in the sight of my informal brother in the bed.

No, I couldn't call him that. Not anymore. How many times had he lied to me? How many times did he shove me into situations that I never would have been in otherwise? Like a jail cell?

Joey was tan thanks to all the time he spent outdoors, but I could see how pale his face was. Someone had taken off his shirt to wrap his chest in thick white bandages. I looked him over as my tears burned in my eyes. I stayed silent simply because Joey wouldn't hear me. I had a million questions running through my mind but he wouldn't be able to answer them like this.

If he ever answered them at all.

Joey's eyes cracked open, and he looked at me. Then his eyes went to the ceiling.

"My boyfriend is gone, Eva," he said. "I'm not up for a lecture."

I stared at Joey. I knew that Jonah and Jonathan were nearby. I had heard their whispers to one another. But those whispers stopped when Joey spoke.

"Joey, I'm sorry about-"

"Don't. Just fucking don't."

"Joey, I'm not going to lecture you."

"Why didn't you save him?" He jerked against the bed but fell back on the pillows with a choked sob. He covered his face with his hands. "You could have saved him. You could have taken that bullet and lived! You killed him, Evie! Pedro..."

I stood as Jonathan came over to the bedside then waved his hand over Joey's face. Joey slumped down on the mattress.

"I think it would be best if Joseph remains incapacited." Jonathan cut his eyes over at me. "Do you wish to go somewhere else, dear child?"

"No," I whispered. "No. I need to talk to him. I'll stay here until he wakes back up."

"Eva?" Jonah looked at me, his hazel eyes blazing. "Why the Hell did you just apologize to *Joey*?"

"Because he lost someone." I swallowed. "That's why."

"Eva," Jonah said, "This dude happily put you in harm's way. If anything, he should apologize to *you*."

"Jonah-"

"No, Superstar. Not this time. You are not to take the blame for what happened, you understand me? They did this. You ain't gotta pay the price for it."

I looked down at my hands as Jonathan spoke.

"Jonah, perhaps now is not the time."

"Jonathan, I apologize, but that's not right," Jonah insisted. "Eva has been gaslit her whole life. I'll be damned if Joey does it. He and

Pedro started this. They rained down this hell on Eva. I'm sorry, but I can't bring myself to feel pity here. Play stupid games, win stupid prizes."

"I am sure Joey will be dealt with when the time is right, son. All I am saying is that now is not that time." Jonathan moved over to me. "Eva, what do you remember about the men who attacked you?"

"Nothing."

"No auras?"

"Only the one, and it was a flash. Red. Dark red." I frowned. "Their leader. Didn't see anyone else use their auras."

"And how did he use it?"

"He grabbed me to use me as a shield during the gunfight. Pressed a gun to my chin. That's when I saw the flash."

"And he is the one who shot you?" Jonathan continued.

"No."

I looked over at Joey then back at Jonathan. I couldn't face Jonah.

"No. Joey realized Pedro was dead, so he unloaded on the man who had me in front of him. I got hit by one of the bullets. Passed," I rubbed my forehead. "I'm so sorry. Passed. Not the other word."

Jonah growled, and Jonathan raised a hand to quell him. His eyes remained on Eva. "What else happened, my dear. "

"I ducked when I got hit. The leader pulled the trigger," I frowned as I tried to remember. "He shot himself instead of me. Fell on me though. That's the last thing I remember before I passed out."

Jonathan tapped at my chin to examine underneath. He pulled back after a moment.

"Your wound is an ethereal burn. It will heal in time."

"Why was his aura so dark?" I kept my focus on Jonathan. "I've never seen an aura look like that. No one at the estate-"

"Eva, the leader - as you call him - was a spirit reaper." Jonathan explained. "Their auras are tainted. They become darker."

"Why can I still see him?"

"Psychologically, you have survived a traumatic-"

"No, sir. Not in my mind. He's here." I pointed to the corner where the spirit leered at me. "He's right there."

Jonathan and Jonah looked in the corner. The guy glared at me, angry at me for revealing his presence. Jonathan raised a gold-gleaming hand.

"Begone," " Jonathan glared at the corner. "Leave this space, you reaper swine!"

The Spirit opened his broken mouth to scream and then he faded. Jonathan looked at me once more.

"Is he still here?"

"No," I stared at the now empty corner then to Jonathan. "Can you teach me how to do that?"

"No," Jonathan gave me a soft smile. "Tell me, has he said anything to you in spirit form?"

"No. Just stares."

"Eva, did Joey or Pedro ever say anything to you about these men? These spirit reapers?"

"No."

"Not even when Albertson came to the house?" Jonah asked me. "Or the condo?"

"All Joey would tell me was that Pedro's client was stopping by. I figured it was a lawyer thing and kept to myself. I never imagined..."

I let my voice trail off. Jonathan patted my knee.

"Did the Networkers treat you well?"

"I suppose so. I've never been detained before. The one who got me in New York? Dubois, I think. He was kind to me. Very patient."

"Seriously?" Jonah raised an eyebrow. "That guy was a world class dick to me. Katarina tried to make excuses for him."

I glanced up at Jonah. "Yeah, but I'll say something to him next time I see him."

"Why would you see him again?"

"When the investigation is over and he announces his findings to the Curaie. I have to be there."

"I appreciate it, Superstar," Jonah smirked. "The next time I see Marlon and he shows his ass unprovoked, I'll happily tell him off myself."

"They will discover the truth, Eva." Jonathan stood. "But I have been tasked to warn you. The men who attacked you at the airfield are still free. And the Networkers want to search your residences in search of more stolen narcotics. You will not be allowed home until it is safe."

"Not even the estate?"

"Not while the investigation is underway. It is a provision put into place by the Curaie to ensure that estates such as Grannison-Morris do not harbor fugitives."

I felt sad at Jonathan's words. No matter what had happened, I had always been allowed to come and go as I pleased. But things were so different now. Painfully different.

"I understand, Jonathan." I gave him a sad smile. "Maybe I can come back sooner rather than later."

"That's definitely my plan for you," Jonah said. "Since we all know who the criminal is here. He's out of his mind, blaming Eva for his mistakes.

"Eva, I'd be amiss not to ask you how you are." Jonathan took a step back, but not too far. "Mentally and emotionally speaking. This has been horrible experience for you."

I didn't want to talk about my mental or emotional state. I wanted Joey to wake back up and talk to me.

"I don't know," I finally spoke. "I just want some answers, that's all."

"How are you feeling towards Joey at this moment?"

"I don't feel anything. I've been around long enough to know that people use me then throw me away. I'm simply surprised it took Joey this long."

Jonah knelt in front of me. I noticed that the dead numbness in me was briefly filled with life at his closeness.

"*Assholes* use you, Eva," He said in a voice that dared me to argue with him. 'Not people. I would never be as presumptuous as to tell you I know exactly how you feel, but I *can* tell you that your friendships didn't end with Joseph. You've got us."

"Joseph?"

"Yeah," Jonah said. His voice had that iron note again. "Joey denotes he's a boy. A snot-nosed knucklehead whose behaviors can be defended or explained away. Nah. That boy is going to be treated as accountable, responsible, and as *adult* as he is."

All I wanted to do in that moment was to throw my arms around Jonah's neck and beg for him to never let me go. But I kept my hands down. I kept my distance.

I forced myself to meet Jonah's eyes. The sincerity in them was enough to make me want to believe him.

"I know."

That was enough. Jonah stood then focused on Jonathan. "Any word on that keeper Apollo is sending in?"

"No," Jonathan folded his hands before him. "Not at this time."

"The Networkers assigned Eva to my custody, but I need to make sure that the rooms are straightened out."

"I don't need a room."

"Superstar, you can't sleep in a damn chair."

"You're assuming I'm going to be able to sleep." I stood as well. "I don't need a room. I'm going to stay right here until Joey wakes up."

"Eva, I don't get why you're so damned worried-"

"I just want answers, Jonah," I let my shoulders drop as the numbness returned. "I want answers. And he is the only one who can give them to me."

Jonah gritted his teeth, and glared down at Joey.

"If he gets cute or decides to be an ass, come get me," He crossed his arms over his chest. "He tries to be a bastard and I'll show him one."

I said nothing as a knock filled the room. Jonah pulled the door open so that Reena and the woman from the parking lot came inside.

"I set ya'll up with two of the Milverton's finest rooms," The stranger beamed at Jonah. "Least I could do. I put you and Reena together. She said ya'll were roommates. Thought you'd be more comfortable that way."

"Thanks, Mary Anna," Jonah gave her such a warm expression I had to look away from them. "I was just coming to check on how that was going."

"Miss McRayne, I got you a room-"

"Thank you, but no thank you. I'm going to stay here."

"But-"

"No, thank you."

"Well then, can I show you two where to go?" Her accent was so damn twangy, it rankled me. "I'm sure Miss McRayne won't mind."

"Of course not."

"Sure. Jonathan? You need anything else from me?"

"No, son. We are finished for the time being."

"Alright." Jonah nodded before he turned back to Mary Anna. "Give me a second."

"Sure, darlin'."

Jonah came back over to me and clasped my shoulder. I looked up at the ceiling to blink back my emotion as he spoke.

"We'll get through this, Superstar. We always do."

"Yeah." I nodded. "Of course, we do."

Jonah gave me another small smile then followed the women out. I could hear Mary Anna's voice chattering away even after the door was closed.

"Evie."

"Yes, Jonathan?"

"Do not be so willing to harden yourself that you lose sight of your heart."

"Thank you, Jonathan," I lowered back down in the chair. "But my heart has been shattered so much that the pieces are tiny, I'm pretty sure it's powder by this point."

"Tiny can be enough," Jonathan told me. "Even the faintest amount of light can illuminate the darkness."

He came over to my chair and I closed my eyes when he placed a single hand on my head.

"The Green Aura tasked with tending to Joey's wounds will be back in the morning. Do you wish for me to stay?"

"As much as I enjoy your company, Jonathan, I just need to be alone right now. Please, don't put me to sleep. I know that's what you're planning."

Jonathan gave me a sly smile and removed his hand.

"Am I so easy to read, my dear?"

"To me, you are. I know you are worried about what this

could mean. I know that - despite the circumstances - you feel a loss with Pedro no longer in the physical. He was one of your own. But I know you are also worried about the estate. About what the Curaie will do. I won't allow them to sanction the estate, Jonathan. No matter what I have to do to protect it."

"What do you know of sanctions, Eva?"

"Only that the Council uses them to ensure order in organizations like the Agema, the Keepers, and the Greens. I'm sure the Curaie have their own version."

"Indeed, they do. Yet, allow me to handle such matters. I believe you have enough on your shoulders."

With that, Jonathan vanished. I sat there and stared at Joey's prone form until another knock filled the room. I started to ignore it. I wanted to be alone to wallow in my heartache. Two more knocks, and I heard Jonah's voice through the wood.

"Evie, I know you ain't sleeping. Open the door."

Dammit. I forced myself to stand and cross the room. I pulled open the door to see Jonah and the strange woman standing on the other side. Jonah held up a keycard.

"Just in case you change your mind."

"I won't." I took the keycard from him. "But thank you. Good night."

Jonah seemed to hesitate, but he caught my hand then pulled me towards him. I was surprised that he held me so tight, but I relaxed against him to see Mary Anna over his shoulder.

Was she glaring at me? What the actual hell?

"I'll be back in a few hours," Jonah released me only to hold me by both arms. "Me and Reena are in 203, so come get me if you need me. Ok?"

"Yeah. Good night."

I closed the door behind them and pressed my hand against the wood. I could hear them talking just on the other side.

"I thought you lived in the country! It was a surprise to see you again so soon."

Jonah's voice lost its tired edge as he spoke. I tilted my head to the side and bit the corner of my lip. No, he didn't sound tired. Did he sound...flirtatious?

Of course, he did. There was something between them. I racked my brain and tried to remember if Jonah had told me about her before. I drew a blank.

I pushed away from the door as my stomach tied itself into knots. I hated myself for my reaction. After Lola, I'd told myself that it wouldn't be long before Jonah found someone to take her place. Someone who wasn't me.

Looks like he found her less than two days later.

"Rome ain't exactly the city, is it, darlin'?" She giggled, but there was a hardness to her voice that was unexpected. "And you are just full of surprises yourself! Imagine, the man who changed my tire hobnobs with celebrities like Eva McRayne!"

Nobody wants you.

I shook my head as I filed the thought away. I couldn't allow myself to be hurt. I had no claim on Jonah. There was no romantic connection between us except for a frantic kiss and an apology that had set me on the path I was on today.

I had to let it go. I had to let my feelings for Jonah go. I had been so close to doing just that when I allowed him to get in my head. It still stung that Hestia had refused to let me take the oath. If I had, I could have handled Joey's betrayal with ease. And witnessing Jonah's romantic encounters with other women wouldn't feel like I had been kicked in the gut.

With that thought in mind, I went over to the bed. I dropped down into the chair and rested my head against the mattress next to Joey's arm. The exhaustion from the events of the day had started to seep into my bones until I could barely keep my eyes open. But I managed one last promise before I dozed off.

"I'm waiting, Joey. I'm waiting."

———

I woke up around three, shivering thanks to the crick in my neck. I sat up and began to move my head from side to side to work it out when I caught sight of movement by the window. I froze when the shooter stepped out into the faint light with a look of anger on his face. What was left of it anyway. His jaw hung askew, his left eye was gone, and the top of his head was blown open.

"I want my life." His voice rasped in my head. "I want it back."

"What..." I turned the chair away from the bed so that I could stand up. "You can't be here! Jonathan-"

"Stole it!" The man hissed. "You stole it! Give it back!"

After the day I had, I wasn't in the mood to deal with this. Anger rose from the hurt in my chest. It was strong enough to bring the steel back to my voice.

"I am done with you," I willed my sword to appear. I didn't use it though. I kept it down by my side. "As the Daughter of Apollo, I demand you return to the Underworld."

The man vanished. He just vanished. I shook off the chill running down my spine before I marched over the window. The air was ice cold. Cold enough to make the hair on my arms stand up. I whirled around to see the room was just as it had been. There was no Spirit Reaper. No man.

My words had worked. He was gone.

I allowed my weapon to disappear when I remained alone for a few more moments. I crossed the room and adjusted the air conditioner when I heard a loud squeaking noise come from the bathroom.

It was the most annoying sound. Like fingers on a chalkboard, but worse.

"Stop it!" I snapped as I stormed over to the bathroom door. "Dammit, leave me alone!"

The squeaking stopped just as suddenly as it had started, so I dropped my hands from my ears and threw open the bathroom door. I flipped on the lights and almost choked on the scream rising in the back of my throat. The spirit had carved a message in red on the glass. I watched as the letters began to drip and I knew his words had been written in blood somehow.

I want it back.

EIGHT

JONAH ROWE

"I still can't believe you live in Rome, Mary Anna," Jonah said for the second time. "It's a crazy coincidence!"

Mary Anna chuckled. "When I said that, my daddy lent me his truck. I never said I *lived* with him, Jonah. I haven't lived with my parents for a while. I'm putting myself through L.T.S.U. I'm the first in my family to go to college!"

"That's awesome," Jonah told her with sincerity. "What's your major?"

"Hospitality Management." Mary Anna said it without skipping a beat. "I plan to have a whole bunch of hotels like these! I want them to be the direct opposite of my palace—"

Mary Anna abruptly ceased. Her eyes went wide, and her face went white. Jonah looked at her, curious and worried.

"Mary Anna, what's up? You scared of palaces or something?"

Mary Anna blinked several times. It made Jonah wonder just what the hell frightened her so much. "I-I believe in the power of visualization," she said at last. "I envision palaces in my mind because they are so far removed from my parent's farmhouse. I always wanted my future hotel chain to feel like palaces 'cause I imagine people never wanna leave 'em then."

"Wait a second," Jonah said with a frown, "you want your hotels to be like palaces? But you just said that you wanted them to be the *direct opposite* of your palace. What does that mean?"

Mary Anna slowly brought her eyes to Jonah again. "I didn't say that, Jonah. My palaces are in my mind. Mental. I want them to exist in real life for everybody to see. Direct opposite to what they are now."

"Oh." Jonah almost laughed. "*That's* what you meant. But why were you so scared? You lost all color, and I thought your eyes were gonna pop out."

Once again, Mary Anna looked fearful. "Letting that slip was a risk," she admitted. "I try not to reveal my dreams to other folks. Know too many dream killers, see."

Jonah shook his head. "I wouldn't do that, Mary Anna. I've been through the same thing, so I'm not too inclined to perpetuate the cycle."

"Have you, now?" Mary Anna looked intrigued. "What, pray tell, is *your* dream, Jonah?"

"Books," Jonah answered instantly. "My ambition is to be an author. A prolific one. But it ain't happening. I have a mental block. I have half a dozen unfinished manuscripts and I have no idea what to do with them. So, I'm probably better off just letting that ship sail."

Whoa, thought Jonah. Did he just share that with a woman he'd known not even a whole day? It just came out so easily. How did he feel that comfortable with her so quickly?

The worry and fear faded from Mary Anna's face. "Don't you dare let that ship sail, Jonah." Her voice was resolute and firm. "You can be and do anything you like. If there is one thing I know, it's that when a dream consumes you, you need to adhere to it. It's what I'm doing now."

Jonah laughed. He'd heard that before in various shapes and forms. "So, there you go. Nobody's crushing anyone's dreams."

He raised his hands to her shoulders with a smirk. She raised her eyebrows.

"I gotta ask, darlin.'" Mary Anna's expression carried a bit of scrutiny, "Dear Eva wouldn't have an issue with this now, would she?"

Jonah dropped his hands, taken aback. "Huh?"

Mary Anna shrugged. "Just sayin'... I hope it ain't too forward, but the way y'all just fawned over each other—in the same room as her *man*, no less—he sick or somethin'? I doubt he would approve of such affection if he'd been awake. But Eva wouldn't get mad that you were out here talkin' to me and grabbin' my shoulders, would she?"

Jonah caught Mary Anna's meaning. "You—Joey and *Eva?* Oh God, no! Joey is like a brother to Eva! And we're just friends, she and I."

"Mmm." Mary Anna crossed her arms. "Well, the two of y'all got an interestin' way of showin' friendly affection."

Jonah's eyes narrowed. He wasn't about to get into his feelings about Eva. Not when he was trying to get over them. "Alright, woman," he said in a voice meant to deflect, "that *was* too forward."

Mary Anna's eyes widened, and then she grumbled under her breath. "Darlin', I am so sorry. I got nosiness from my family; they are *always* in everybody's business. I didn't mean nothing, I promise! Look—"

She reached into her uniform and pulled out a pocket-sized *New Testament.* "I declare it on my Bible!"

Jonah's mild indignation diminished. The gesture was almost hilarious. "It's cool, Mary Anna. Whatever. I imagine you need to get to work now. 'Night."

"You'll see me again," she promised.

Jonah looked at her curiously. She raised her hands like it was obvious.

"You're staying here for a couple nights, right?"

"Oh! Oh, yeah," murmured Jonah, feeling idiotic. "Right. Well, see you later, Mary Anna. For real this time."

"'Night, darlin'!"

Jonah slipped the keycard into the slot on the door and stepped inside the room that Reena took care of. He had mixed feelings about that, but he had been taught never to question a gift. Just appreciate it and keep moving.

It was a neat room, but a far cry from the Apex Suite that Eva was enjoying.

"Enjoying." Jonah might want to use that term loosely concerning her.

Conversation with Mary Anna assuaged his tension, but now that he'd lowered himself into a chair and massaged his eyelids, the damned feeling reared itself once more.

Jonah felt for Eva. He knew how close she had felt to Joey- no, Joseph. He wasn't going to call him Joey anymore. Not after this. He'd explained his reasonings to Eva. Joseph was going to survive this. The fact that he had woken up was proof enough of that. So what was going to happen when Joseph was back on his feet? Would he be arrested for *his* part in all this? Would he survive this only to be taken out by the cartel he had screwed over? That is, if Jonah didn't take him out first.

Of all people, Joseph *knew*. He *knew* what Eva had gone through. He'd had a front row seat since he'd known her. So to use her as a damn drug mule then shoot her? That was a mon-starter for Jonah. He didn't care how emotional Joseph had been when he first pulled that trigger. He'd done it and he was going to pay the price for it. It was only a shame that damn Albertson hadn't taken him down first.

Victor Albertson. Jonah racked his brain, but he couldn't recall ever hearing that name before today. Then again, he wasn't one with the drug crowd, so no surprise there.

Eva confessed that she'd seen him since the gunfight, but Jonah couldn't assist her in that regard. Elevenths couldn't see the spirits of other Elevenths.

But why could *Eva* see him? She'd seen the Spirit Reaper multiple times. It took Jonathan to banish it. At least, that's what Jonah thought he had done. He'd never seen Jonathan do such a thing. He hadn't stuck around long enough to find out the details.

"Who was that woman?"

Jonah sat up in the chair. Reena sat across from him.

"What woman? Mary Anna?"

"Yeah. That one. You two seem pretty damn chummy tonight."

Jonah relaxed. "Her name is Mary Anna Greene. She works third shift here and is working on a Hospitality Management degree at L.T.S.U."

"Wow." Reena snorted. "Quite informed! But you didn't just meet her at this hotel. You were too shocked when you bumped into her. When did you first meet her?"

Jonah frowned at Reena's tone. "When I was on the way to D.C. to get Eva. I came across her on the side of the road. She needed help with a flat tire."

Reena's eyes narrowed. "Really." It wasn't a question.

Jonah looked at her. "Yeah. Really. She even gave me a rose."

"Touching," Reena said with indifference. "And she happened to be in undergrad at L.T.S.U. *and* happened to work at Milverton?"

Jonah rolled his eyes. "Reena, coincidences do happen. Rarely, of course, but they aren't impossible. And besides, Mary Anna is harmless."

"Astute assessment," Reena said calmly, "Seeing as how you reached after knowing her half a day."

Jonah gritted his teeth. "Did you read something that was off in her essence, Reena?"

"Didn't bother trying, because I don't give a shit about her," Reena snapped. "I am more concerned with you."

"Oh, are you?" Jonah had an idea where this was headed. "Why is that?"

"Jonah, you were sharing *personal* information with that woman!" said Reena with heat. "I heard you! You've known her for *hours*! It's not wise to get so friendly with her so fast, and right in front of Eva? What's wrong with you?"

That stopped Jonah in his tracks. "Eva? What are you talking about?"

"Jonah, you're not stupid. I know you aren't. So don't pretend to be." Reena folded her legs beneath her. "We all know how you feel about Eva. What we don't get is why you're so damned afraid of those feelings."

"Don't." Jonah didn't mean to sound so cold, but it was what it was. He wasn't about to get therapy from Reena, seeing as how what was in his mind was none of her business. "Eva and I are friends, Reena. That's all we're ever going to be."

"You won't even be that if you keep flaunting other women in front of her." Reena shook her head. "You just...you don't realize it, J."

"Realize what?"

"When you're with Eva? You change. You become...I don't know. Calmer. More at peace. Terrence says it's because Eva brings out the man you're supposed to be. I don't know if that's true, but you have to stop this, Jonah. You have to. Otherwise, you're going to keep pushing her away until she won't come back."

Jonah sniffed, irritated. Where the fuck did Reena get off telling him what to do? His own *mother* didn't even have that right!

"My God, the way you make it sound, I just need to be wary of *everyone*," He snapped. "Maybe I should stop talking to you, too. And Liz and Nella. And Maxine and Magdalena. And Katarina. Hell, while I'm at it, maybe I should stop saying sweet words of communication to Nana. You're all women, see. I don't know what you consider to be a trigger."

Reena leered at Jonah. "You need to put that asshole back in the box."

"And *you* need to put that maternal bitch back in the box," Jonah shot back. "I ain't had a mom, don't need one now."

"Jonah, I'm not trying to be your goddamn mother. I'm trying to help you!" Reena glared at him. "You may not like what I have to say, but your reaction proves that what I'm saying is true. You don't want to admit it!"

"Jesus Christ, Reena! Where the hell are you getting off, telling me what I should or shouldn't do! I can talk to any damn woman I please. I can make any arrangement I please! I ain't out here trying to get married. I'm having my fun-"

"Just like Vera."

Jonah froze at her words. "Excuse me?"

"You're out there, just having your fun." Reena met his eyes with her own. "But turned around and told Eva you didn't want her to take Hestia's oath because it would destroy your future. Yeah, Terrence told me about all that. Why is that? Is Eva supposed to wait on you to make up your mind like Vera expected you to do?"

Jonah folded his arms, momentarily irritated that Terrence told Reena everything. Why the hell did he have to go snitch like that?

"Reena, don't you *ever* compare me to Vera. I'm not a manipulative, self-centered asshole who thinks only of himself. To be honest, I'm a little annoyed at Terrence for running his mouth and not giving you the whole story. If he had, you would have known that Eva would have not just been cut off from romantic love, but love in general. No familial love. No friendship. No camaraderie. No nothing. Just a void. A cold automaton. While it seems right that *you* would totally be cool with that, I'm not."

"That didn't answer either of my questions, Jonah." Reena's eyes flashed, but she lowered her voice. "Is Eva supposed to wait or not?"

"I don't care what Eva does, Reena! I have no claim on her. Maybe if she did find somebody else, she wouldn't be so hung up on me!" Jonah ignored the lash of pain that went through his chest as he said those words. And the second one that followed when he continued. "Hell, I hope she does so that ya'll will get off my ass about her!"

Reena's eyebrows raised. "You don't mean that, Jonah."

Jonah felt a sneer tug at his lips. "Don't presume to think you know my mind, Reena. Because I promise you that if you think you know what's in my head, you'll be wrong one hundred percent of the time. Now if you'll excuse me."

He pushed past Reena and headed out of the door. He needed some air. He'd been judged and scolded in the past. More than a little bit.

But for some reason, it was doubly irritating tonight.

He reached the door when Reena's next words stopped him.

"Eva was poisoned by Albertson's gun. Jonathan spotted traces of a foreign subject in that burn on her face. Thought you might want to know that. But hey, I don't know your mind, right? Maybe you don't."

Jonah paused for just a second. Poison? By a gun? How the Hell did that happen? But Reena's delivery nettled him even more.

"Obviously, I'd want to know *that*, as it's pertinent to this whole mess." Jonah's voice was quiet for acknowledging the poison thing, but hard for Reena's tone. "There you go again, assuming you know my mind. Go to bed, Reena. Your judgment and assumptions are in rare form tonight. Get some rest."

"You're in rare form tonight," Reena narrowed her eyes at him. "Are you ok? Did something happen in D.C. that we don't know about?"

"Nope, everything was A-Okay," Jonah replied with a shrug. "Or as A-Okay as could be expected. See you later. I need some weed."

Reena didn't try to stop him this time. He headed out then downstairs. Jonah was at the exit when he caught a glimpse of gold disappear down a flight of stairs.

Eva? What was she doing? Jonah thought she said she wasn't going to leave Joseph.

He looked at the glass doors then went to check it out. Jonah headed downstairs then saw Eva slip through another door. He followed her until he realized where she had gone.

The Milverton had a small gym in the basement. Jonah didn't realize that. He stopped in front of a glass wall that separated the room from the hallway to see Eva climb up on a treadmill. She punched a few buttons with a scowl.

Despite everything, Jonah laughed. Eva hated treadmills with a passion. Her reaction to this one would have been exactly what he expected. He watched her punch at the buttons again and the treadmill went faster until Eva was running as hard as she could.

Jonah didn't want to interrupt her. He knew what she was doing. She was trying to outrun her own mind. That was the whole reason she'd started running in the first place. But he couldn't seem to stop himself as he entered the gym. Eva spotted him, but she didn't stop. She didn't even slow down.

Jonah sat on a weight bench and just watched her until she finally punched the buttons to slow down enough to speak. She didn't stop completely.

"You ok?"

"Yeah," He responded. "Saw you come in here. Thought hell froze over."

"I don't know. What's the temperature outside?"

Jonah smiled a little. "Did Joseph wake up or something?"

"No. I, um. I just needed to run. Since I can't leave this damn building, I had to come down here."

"By all means, don't let me stop you," Jonah said. "Gym is my therapy, too, so no shade here. I won't ask you to go into stringent details just so you can focus on breathing, but at least tell me is the running working?"

"It helps," She tilted her head to the side. "Why were you up? I thought I wasn't going to see you until tomorrow."

"Reasons." Jonah wasn't about to share his little tiff with Reena. "Why the need to run? Joseph?"

"Not quite."

"What does that mean?"

"Um," Eva took a minute before she responded. Could have been a pause to catch her breath, but it wasn't. Jonah knew her too well for that. "The spirit is back. I needed to pretend I could get away from it."

Jonah shot up. "I thought Jonathan got rid of him."

"He's back."

Jonah grimaced. Some spirits couldn't catch a damn clue. "I'll summon Jonathan--"

"No, Jonah." Eva bumped the treadmill down to a leisure stroll, to converse better. "Don't. I'll handle it."

"Eva--"

"You know how I am about coddling, Jonah," Eva said with a wave of a sweaty hand. "I don't need someone swooping in and cleaning all my messes. Let Jonathan relax. It shouldn't even be his job."

"We're here for the long haul." Jonah studied her. She was flushed. Her skin gleamed with sweat, but she'd just been running. "However long that takes."

"I don't expect you to put your life on hold. I'll be fine, you know that."

"You don't want me here?"

Eva's face softened and she looked past his head to the far wall.

"You know I'd be lying if I said I didn't. Because I do, Jonah. It's just one more catastrophe, that's all. It'll get handled."

"Eva, I told you I was all but grounded." Jonah sat back down. "Everyone's watching me like I'm some national treasure, some precious cargo. It's maddening. So, to be sequestered in this fancy place? Actually, a good and refreshing thing."

"Really?"

"Really."

She shut down the treadmill and grabbed the towel she had thrown over the rail. Eva wiped her face as she sat next to him.

"This is where the Landry mess went down, isn't it?"

"Why do you want to talk about Landry?" Jonah raised an eyebrow at her. "He's old news."

"Because whenever you do that impression of him, it makes me laugh. And I need that desperately right now."

Jonah laughed. "Yeah. He had your suite. Did I ever tell you that he invited Reena to bed?"

"I'm sure that went over well." Eva smiled. "What happened? Did she break his face?"

"Sadly no," Jonah said with mock sadness. "However, once he found out he had *no* chance, he tried to call security. Reena caught him with her speed and sprained his wrist. Nicer than I would've been myself."

Eva laughed and Jonah smiled. He loved hearing her laugh like that. He reached over to take her hand and squeezed it. She made a face.

"You shouldn't touch me right now. One, I'm disgusting. And two? Considering the death glare your friend gave me when you hugged me earlier, she might shank me in my sleep."

"Mary Anna?" Jonah scoffed. "It's a coincidence that I know her at all. On the way up to get you, she was on the side of the road with a flat tire. I helped her out, she gave me a rose in lieu of payment, and I went on my way. Had no clue I'd run into her here as an employee."

"That was sweet of you."

"What?"

"Helping her with the flat." Eva went back to drying her face. "But you don't have to explain your connection to her, Blueberry."

"Oh, it's not like that," He waved it off. "Just pointing out how you won't get shanked or anything."

Eva cut her eyes over at him then shook her head. "Sorry. Bad phrasing on my part. I'm just too jaded, I guess. Too superstitious. I wasn't trying to imply anything."

Jonah leaned forward to take in the small gym. It wasn't much, but it was something. Nothing compared to what he had access to at the estate.

"Have you thought about the future?" He asked at last. "Like, the aftermath of all this?"

"What do you mean?"

"Joseph can't stay with you anymore, Eva," Jonah couldn't help but notice the sadness in her face at his words. "He can't. He can't be trusted to travel with you, either. He could end up in prison."

"He won't." Eva bent over to adjust the bottom of her yoga pants. "NYPD didn't believe me about the drugs. They think we were being robbed. So no charges will be filed against Joey. Not even for the shooting because it was seen as self-defense."

Jonah blinked slowly as all the light was extinguished from him. "That motherfucker is getting off scot-free. Are you serious right now?"

"Legally? Yes. No drugs, no possession charge. Gunfight where his loved one was murdered? Stand Your Ground doctrine. As for Theia, his contract is as ironclad as mine is for the next year. I'll just keep a closer eye on him."

Eva glanced towards the door as if Joseph would walk in at any minute. She closed her eyes and rubbed her forehead.

"So, I don't know about the future, Jonah. I just don't. I have to clear things with the Networkers first. Then I can think about moving forward."

"But..." Jonah struggled to find the right words. "But he shot you!"

"Accidental injury. It's not considered a crime because I was in the way."

Jonah threw up his hands in frustration. "Eva, that's bullshit! Joey got you mixed up in some serious shit, using Theia private property to do it. He got Pedro killed, shot *you*, and you get stuck holding the bag? In what world does that make sense?"

"The real one." She stood. "I better get back. You gonna go smoke?"

"Yeah," Jonah grumbled, still pissed off. "How'd you know?"

"You have a joint stuck behind your ear."

Oh.

"Come with me." He stood and stuck his hands in his pockets. "Some air will do you some good."

"I can't, Jonah. I'm not allowed to leave, remember?" She turned towards the door then held it open for him. "You smoke one for me. I'm going to shower. Try to sleep."

Jonah didn't like it, but he nodded. "This mess will blow over, Eva. I'll personally do whatever I can to get you out of this quarantine-style shit."

"I hope so," She stopped by the stairs leading to the first floor. "Good night. And thank you. For everything."

"Always, Superstar."

Jonah watched her go and shook off the chill that ran down his back. For a fleeting moment, he was sure he saw a shadow following Eva up the stairs. But it was nothing. Tricks of the mind.

NINE

EVA MCRAYNE

I SPENT the next two hours trying to scrub the damn blood off the mirror. I had hoped that it would have vanished by the time I returned from my run. I had hoped that it had been a figment of my imagination.

No such luck. I was down to the final washcloth before I took a step back to see the result of my hard work. The glass was still covered in red. The blood was now smeared in circles on the glass. I took a deep breath, flipped the cloth over on the other side, and stuck it under the water faucet. I watched the water turn red as it swirled down the drain before I glanced up at the mirror again.

The words were back as if the past two hours hadn't happened. The blood I had smeared everywhere had reformed into the hateful words that made my heart stand still.

"Gods dammit!"

I threw the washcloth into the sink and pressed my fingers against my eyes. I should have talked to Jonah about the message when I saw him at the hotel gym. I knew that there was a very good chance he could explain to me what was going on. But I didn't want to seem too dependent on him.

I didn't want Jonah to leave me, too. Not like Joey had done.

I needed him to hold me. I needed him to tell me everything was going to be alright. It was never going to happen. The only person who could calm me down now was myself. I needed to get a grip on myself before I really did go crazy.

I needed him to hold me. I needed him to tell me everything was going to be alright. But most of all? I needed to get a grip on myself before I really did go crazy.

It took another three renditions of counting to ten before I felt calm enough to leave the bathroom. I marched over to the phone and hit '0'. A woman answered on the first ring.

"Front Desk."

"Hi. Sorry to call so early, but I'm out of towels. There's been an accident in the bathroom. I used them all to try and clean it up."

"An accident? Do you need maintenance?"

Yeah, lady. Maintenance. They would do a world of good against the vengeful spirit who has decided to drive me insane.

I was good. I bit my tongue and shook my head; despite the fact she couldn't see me. "No. Nothing like that."

"Very well. I will bring your towels shortly."

I hung up the phone then turned to Joey. He hadn't moved an inch since we had arrived. I plopped down in the chair I'd pulled next to the bed and rested my chin against my hand. Joey had been by my side for six years now. Six years of danger. Threats. Hateful violence.

Long enough to figure out I was a gullible idiot. Long enough to stab me in the back and land my ass in a jail cell.

"Why?" I whispered to his prone body. "I just want to know why, Joey. Why would you set me up to take a fall like that? I thought you loved me."

I jumped when I heard a knock. I crossed the room and opened the door to see the night clerk I'd heard flirting with Jonah standing there with a stack of towels in her hands.

"Ms. McRayne." Mary Anna gave me a slight smile. "I hope these are enough to help your bathroom calamity."

"Thank you."

I started to take the stack from her, but she pulled them away. She gave me a once-over and clicked her tongue against the back of her teeth.

"No, allow me. I can't have an A-list celebrity cleaning up my hotel. It just ain't done."

Mary Anna practically pushed me aside as she entered the room. I watched her as she headed to the bathroom. The woman was almost to the door when I remembered the mess I had left behind.

"No, don't!" I whirled away from the door and grabbed her arm. "Please, you don't want to go in there."

"Don't touch me," the woman hissed as she jerked away from me. Her eyes flashed a strange shade of purple as she glared at me. "You have no right to steal—"

She didn't finish her sentence as she opened the door. I dropped my hand down to my side in confusion. What the hell was that about? Mary Anna looked almost frightened. I held my breath as she crossed the threshold. I was expecting to hear her scream. I expected her to run out of the room as if her hair were on fire. Instead, she flounced out a few minutes later with an expression of pity on her face.

"I'm sorry about the mess," I managed. "I'll figure out a way—"

"There's no mess in there." Her pity turned to confusion. "What were you talking about earlier?"

"Wait, what?"

The frown on my face was heavy as I moved past her. I leaned into the room to get a good look at the mirror. It was spotless. No words. No blood. No smears.

"I don't understand." I sagged against the doorframe. "How … what is happening to me?"

"There, there." Mary Anna patted my arm. "Honey, I've seen the news. You've been through hell in less than a day. Come over here. Let me take care of you."

I let the woman lead me over to the chair. She pulled out a small bottle of liquor from her back pocket and winked at me as she poured it into a plastic water cup. When Mary Anna passed it over to me, I held it up to the light.

"What is this? Liquor? Lady, it's not even 6 a.m."

"Oh, what's time matter to a girl like you?" Mary Anna giggled. "Now go on. It's Vintage. Good for your nerves."

My nerves, huh? I lifted the cup to my lips and eyed her before I tossed it back. The liquor burned worse than Cyrus' whiskey. I handed her back the cup and she refilled it again. Three shots later, I felt as if my very soul was on fire. But my courage was back. The fear and frustration over the events of the past day were gone.

"Now, then." Mary Anna poured me another. "Tell me what you know about my Jonah."

"*Your* Jonah?" I narrowed my eyes. "Bitch, he is not *your* Jonah."

"Yes," she growled, "he is." She folded herself up in the chair across from mine. "We will be closer. And I'm gonna make sure you don't get in the way."

"Mary Anna," I giggled at the sound of her name. "You sound like you should be on some sixties sitcom with that name."

"Jonah. Now." She snapped her fingers in my face, and there was that flash of purple again. "Tell me what you know."

"What can I say?" I heard my words slurring but couldn't stop them as they tumbled out. "He's my best friend. I've been in love with him since I met him almost a year ago, when I was filming the Covington episode."

"You're in love with him?" Her eyes narrowed. "Does he love you?"

"No. No, Jonah doesn't love me like that. Told me himself." I took the cup from her again, but almost missed it entirely. I felt my fingers slipping along the ridged sides as I drank it down and almost gagged for my efforts. "What is this stuff? It's too damned strong."

"Oh, poison." She waved a hand and grinned at my look of confusion. "Now, tell me. Since Jonah has absolutely no interest in a trollop like you, how can a simple girl like me win his heart?"

A wave of dizziness hit me. I dropped the cup and rested my head on the mattress. I heard the woman stand up. I felt her fingers press against the burn beneath my chin. I winced at the shock of pain that went through my jaw.

"Not yet, brat of Apollo." She leered at me just as the stalker had done. "I will allow you to sleep, but not until you tell me what I need to know."

So, I started talking. I told her about Jonah and the Eleventh Percenters. I told her about how Jonathan was his mentor. How they were a family bonded together by their abilities and how they had adopted me into their fold. I told her about how much I loved him. I confessed words to this stranger that I'd never told another living soul. Finally, Mary Anna did the most blessed thing she could have done for me.

With a smile, she brushed her hand over my eyes to close them. I was asleep within seconds.

————

"Jonah, Reena, thank God you've come!"

I could hear Mary Anna clamoring to talk just before I felt Jonah's hands on my shoulders. She was still talking when Reena knelt beside me. There was another woman with them who looked to be in her twenties. This must be Akshara.

"I found her this way when I came to drop off the linens." Mary Anna sounded as if she were seconds away from panicking.

I wanted to sit up. Tell them to leave me alone. But I couldn't speak. I could barely open my eyes as they began to talk around me.

"She promised she would go sober." Reena, this time. She rustled around beneath the chair I was in before she spoke again. "Vintage? How could she have gotten a hold of this stuff?"

"Eva took the shooting hard." Jonah sounded pissed. "I didn't think she'd go back to the bottle though. Akshara, can you tell you if the Vintage has fucked with anything?"

"Alcohol, as a general rule, causes disturbances in most situations, anyway," Akshara explained.

I saw a flash of green through my eyelids and knew that she was hovering her fingers over my face while they gleamed with the green of her aura. "But Evie here is in a heavy alcohol haze. Thanks to her regenerative abilities, she doesn't have alcohol poisoning. She will be in a bad way for an hour or two."

"Dammit, Eva," I heard Jonah grunt. My heart hurt from the disappointment in his voice. "Mary Anna, which room is in her name?"

"Forty-two." The woman still sounded frightened. "Is-is she dead? So many celebrities today end up overdosing in hotels. I don't need that kind of publicity for Milverton."

"No, she isn't." Akshara's friendly voice had a note of impatience. "I literally just said that she needed to rest the alcohol off."

"You needn't worry, Mary Anna," Jonah snapped before he turned his attention back to me. "Eva won't be another hotel statistic. She's got me."

"Does she, now?" There was something in Mary Anna's voice that was borderline frightening. Like a quiet danger.

"She has *us*," Jonah amended. "Get the doors for me. Akshara, if you need any help at all with Joseph, let us know. If he wakes up and gives you any problems, let *me* know."

"Appreciate it, Jonah," said Akshara. "He is in excellent hands with me."

I was jostled from the chair before Jonah picked me up as if I weighed next to nothing. He wrapped one arm beneath my knees, then lifted me until I was pressed against his chest. "Mary Anna, I know you just got off work. Can you hang around a bit? I'd like to talk to you."

I wanted to scream at him. Tell him this weird woman was the one who got me so fucked up. Instead, I ended up whispering against his shirt as he took me out of Joey's room.

"Blueberry ...something is wrong with me."

"Uh-huh. Ninety-proof liquor will do that to you." He adjusted his grip on me. "Sleep it off, Superstar. Then, you're back on the wagon. Non-negotiable."

"No. Listen. Please."

I tried to speak, but my tongue was too thick. My throat felt as if it were going to close in on itself any second. I felt another wave of drowsiness hit me before Jonah lowered me down on a strange bed. He brushed the hair away from my face. Gave me a lingering kiss on my forehead that made tears spring up in my eyes. Why? Why would he do such a thing? I didn't matter. He squeezed my hand before he stood.

"Did Jonathan find out anything about the poison?"

Poison? What poison?

Reena took a minute, but she responded. I could hear the strain in her voice as she spoke to Jonah.

"Jonathan was really troubled by the poison on that gun barrel that was on Eva's face," She said. "Not to go around Akshara, but I wanted to consult Liz, of course, but Jonathan said it wasn't necessary."

"He did? But she is so gifted at all of that!"

"Well, he said she wouldn't know *this* one, nor would Akshara," said Reena. "He said it's called Venaré."

"What does it do?"

"Oh, so you give a damn now?"

"Reena, this is not the time." Jonah spoke low, almost too softly for me to hear. "So, what does it do?"

"It's chameleonic," Reena sounded troubled by her own explanation. "Alterable. The poison reacts to lifeblood in all humans, Tenth and Eleventh. But that's where it gets tricky. You can poison twenty different people with Venaré, and it will have a different effect on each one of them."

"Are you kidding me?"

"Wish I was, Jonah," Reena said.

Jonah made a noise in the back of his throat. "So, you're telling me this poison could have one effect on say, me, and a completely different one on Eva?"

"That's exactly what I'm saying, Jonah," Reena said. "Jonathan said he hasn't seen it used in decades. I don't know where that Spirit Reaper got it, and now, we can't ask him."

Jonah looked away. "Convenient."

"That's one way to put it," Reena said. "All I know is that there isn't a damn thing in the Greek sphere of existence that can help them. This is ethereal poison."

"Does Jonathan know an antidote?"

"Like I've told you before, Jonah—Jonathan doesn't know everything."

"Great," Jonah responded. "Eva gets her first experience with dark ethereality, and it's a substance that no one knows about."

"I'll stay with her," Reena offered. I wanted to tell her to leave. I didn't want any of them to see me like this. "Go. I know you have a lot of things to figure out right now, Jonah."

I cracked open my eyes to watch them leave the room just before a shadow fell across my vision. The man who had started this whole mess glared down at me.

"Give it back," He hissed. "You stole what is mine!"

He reached down and grabbed my face. I felt as if my skin was on fire. When he released me, he snorted.

"Stupid, stupid girl. You had no idea who you were fucking with."

TEN

JONAH ROWE

JONAH COULD HAVE PUNCHED SOMETHING.

Why did Eva keep doing this to herself? And *where* did she get a bottle of Vintage? That stuff would take down a rhino, and she drank an entire bottle of it!

She'd promised Reena that she'd go sober. She'd promised *him* she would drop that habit. Now, she was shit-faced off a bottle of Vintage.

Jonah loved that woman to death. But he couldn't get her need to get lit. Did she figure that cirrhosis and alcohol poisoning weren't issues to her because she was 'immortal'?

But Jonah never really put much stake in that. Life never ended, so Eva's immortality didn't impress him. Besides, it always seemed to fail her when she needed it the most. There was the thing with Athena's Blade, which had caused a wound that hadn't even fully healed when they first met. Then there was Hera's Grave Endowment. That *almost* worked. Eva couldn't even be in Rome without the jewelry that Jonathan made for her afterward. Then there was that thing that Hera and Hades—dear God, the Olympians were like a divine Springer episode—had concocted. Eva almost wound up in the Underworld for eternal torture.

Jonah sighed. It seemed like Eva's 'immortality' put her *more* at risk of losing her physical life than anything else.

And then she compounded that with alcohol.

Jonah glimpsed redness on his shirt. He looked down, assuming it was spilled Vintage.

But it wasn't Vintage. It was blood.

He didn't get the chance to bandage the cuts from the thorns and must have aggravated it when he carried Eva to her bed. They were small wounds, but he didn't address them. Now he had blood on his hand and shirt.

"Dumbass," he muttered to himself.

He pulled off the shirt and headed for the bathroom. The cuts were so small that they only took minutes to fix. That was done.

Then another realization hit him. It made him swear out loud again.

He had this nice room with Reena, but he hadn't packed a travel bag. It wasn't like he knew he'd be a patron at the Milverton when he woke up that morning.

Terrence was busy, but Bobby might be able to use the *Astralimes* to bring him a few polos, maybe some extra jeans. He headed out of the bathroom, eyes on his phone.

And froze. Again.

Mary Anna was in his hotel room, gaping at his bare chest.

"What the—? Mary Anna, what are you doing here?"

"Y-You told me to come here!" Mary Anna said defensively. "You said you had to talk to me!"

"Aw, damn." Jonah rolled his eyes at no one in particular. "Right. I *did* say that, didn't I? 'Course I had a shirt on at the time. Listen, Mary Anna—just forget it. I'll just talk to you later."

"But Jonah, I'm already here," Mary Anna said. "Not havin' a shirt on don't affect your mouth. We can talk right now."

"Very true," Jonah said in a dry voice, "but we haven't even known each other for twenty-four full hours, and you're already seeing me shirtless. Don't you think we're moving just a little too fast?"

Mary Anna grinned. "I don't think we're movin' too fast at all, darlin.'"

Jonah blinked. "That was a joke, Mary Anna."

Mary Anna blinked herself. "Of-of course!" She laughed. "A joke! I was just playin' along!"

Jonah frowned. It sure didn't sound like she was just playing along. Or maybe his brain was just in overdrive. Wouldn't be the first time.

"Jonah, seriously, let's just sit here and talk," said Mary Anna, who lowered herself into a chair. "I'm a country girl, so I ain't easily shocked. If you still feel that strongly about it when we're through, I'll go downstairs and get you an old Milverton polo or something.'"

"That's fine," Jonah told her. "Just let me turn off the sink. Be right back."

He hurried to the bathroom and turned off the sink. He fogged up the mirror, so he couldn't see how red his face probably was. That was good. But the mirror on the open door gave him a clear view of Mary Anna.

She'd closed her eyes and released the most protracted sigh he'd ever seen.

Jonah frowned. So, he hadn't been dense, or in overdrive. She *had* been staring at him.

Hey, it was what it was.

He wasn't ripped like Bobby, or lucky like Terrence. He was far from a cover on *Muscle & Fitness*, but the combination of Reena's eating plan, ethereal training, and gym time had given him a much more improved physique than he'd had in years past. The beard didn't hurt things, either. If she liked what she saw, then who was he to deny her the sight?

Jonah shook his head. Hard. Where the hell had this heightened confidence come from? He never acted like this. He wouldn't ever have shown off his upper body to impress girls as a kid. Granted, he was chubby back then, and many things had changed since that time. But he hadn't ever done things like this.

Well, times changed. And people changed right along with them.

He forced himself to focus. Joey was injured thanks to his illegal dealings, and Eva was in a drunken stupor. Those thoughts put him back on track.

He stepped back out to where Mary Anna was seated. Thankfully, she had composed herself. Or Jonah assumed as much.

"Now Mary Anna, I need you to give me an honest answer to this question," he said. "You said you went to deliver linens to Eva's room and discovered her like that. At this hour, linens are only taken to rooms if requested. Neither Eva nor Joey was in any condition to request anything. He is out, and she is smashed. So, explain yourself."

Mary Anna was silent for a moment, which made Jonah sense guilt. It almost made him want to prepare for the worst.

"Jonah, as you can see, I ain't rich," she said at last. "I don't know if you know, but it's no secret that a lot of the clientele here are either well-off or flat-out loaded. They come here to be under the radar, at least for a little while. So, on occasion, I do extra work. Bring extra toiletries, and all that. Sometimes, it results in big tips."

Oh.

"So—you were hoping Eva would give a huge tip?"

"One can only hope, darlin'," said Mary Anna. "I'm a college student. Every little bit counts."

Jonah could understand that. He'd been there. "I wish that she hadn't gotten drunk like that," he muttered. "I wish she cared more about her well-being."

"*You* seem to care plenty about her well-being, Jonah." Mary Anna's eyes narrowed. "As I told you before, it sounds to me like ya'll are a bit more than friends."

Jonah breathed deeply. "Let it go, Mary Anna. We are just *friends*."

"She is in love with you," Mary Anna interrupted. "There ain't no doubt about it."

"I—what?" Jonah frowned. "How did you know that?"

"Oh—um—how she was looking at you," answered Mary Anna. "I read faces better than any book, darlin'. And she was giving you googly eyes from the moment she saw you!"

Jonah was so thrown off by that response that he laughed. Mary

Anna joined in soon thereafter. It was such a refreshing, calming thing. But there was still a bit that stayed with him. He'd had a crush on Eva since the moment he saw her. There was the bitch mask they had to get past, but the seed was planted. Then, when he was possessed by Ares, he'd physically accosted her. Eva responded with excitement; the encounter would have clearly ended in sex right there in the Rover had they not been interrupted.

Jonah remembered everything. The feel of her. Her scent. The softness of her lips—he clearly recollected how they'd been reddened by their wild kissing, but Eva hadn't cared. It was an alluring thing, even under possession. But he had chalked that up to Eva being heavily deprived by Cyrus. Anything could happen in the heat of the moment. A notion not worth entertaining. He wasn't ready for the chains that came with a relationship. Not when there were so many women out there who couldn't be bothered with labels. He got what he needed when he needed it. Eva couldn't provide that.

Mary Anna's words broke him out of his thoughts.

"Let me have the floor now, Jonah." The mirth left Mary Anna's face and she looked businesslike. "From what I gather, you done made it your mission to save everybody. Well, everybody don't wanna be saved, darlin'. That's a huge burden. Somebody ought to save *you.*"

Jonah laughed lightly at the thought but shook his head. "I don't have time to be saved. Too many responsibilities. People count on me, and Eva is one of those people."

"But what about you, Jonah?" Mary Anna asked him as she rose. "Who is there for you?"

"Plenty of people!" Jonah exclaimed instantly. He was on his feet himself; it didn't seem right to go to bat for his friends from a seated position. "My family would do anything for me. I just need to be there for them more. I'm the Blue—"

He froze. Mary Anna's eyes gleamed.

"Blue?" she said. "I don't understand. Blue what?"

"Forget you heard that," Jonah murmured hastily. "Just know that it's up to me to handle a lot for other people's well-being."

Mary Anna walked into Jonah's personal space and grabbed his wrists. "Jonah, don't you ever get tired of adherin' to other folk's fantasies of you? I did that for … for a long time. I still ain't free of it. Not fully. But I'm breaking out of it now. Whatever I want, I'm goin' to have it. Whether it's handed to me, or I have to grab it myself. I refuse to be anybody's puppet or trophy. I deserve more. You do, too. You deserve far more than to be 'protected' while everyone around does whatever."

Jonah's brow creased. Persephone told him something a couple of months ago. Now he heard it again from a farm girl that he'd known for a collection of hours. That couldn't be a coincidence.

"I know that look, darlin'," Mary Anna said quietly. "You know what I'm tellin' you is the truth. Don't you?"

Jonah regarded the woman. "I don't get it, Mary Anna. I feel like I can tell you anything, and you wouldn't judge me."

Mary Anna smiled. "You won't get judgment from me, darlin'. When you've had the life I've had, you learn that patience and understanding are much more helpful."

The door opened, and Reena walked in. Her eyes surveyed the scene: Jonah, bare-chested, hands clutched within Mary Anna's. No explanation on earth would explain this away.

Plus, Jonah's voice didn't want to work. Convenient.

Reena pointed a finger at Mary Anna. "You. Out. *Now*."

Mary Anna laughed quietly. There was something in that laugh that Jonah didn't like. It seemed like she was a stone's throw away from attacking Reena. He was certain that Reena could kick her ass, but … there was something about that laugh.

"No problem." She released Jonah's hands and headed for the door. "'Night, y'all. Or should I say, 'Mornin'?"

ELEVEN

EVA MCRAYNE

I STRUGGLED to remain conscious this time after the spirit sat next to me on the bed. He was making horrible rasping noises through the hole in his face, so I forced my voice to work around my dry mouth.

"Re, you have to listen to me." I could hear the plea in my voice, but I didn't care. "I didn't mean to do this."

"Drunks never do." Reena stood over my bed with her arms crossed over her chest. "You broke your promise, Eva."

"No." I shuddered as the spirit began to grab at my arms. He was checking my jewelry. My fascas. "Please. Tell me you can see him too."

"Who?" Reena studied me. "Who are you talking about, Eva?"

"The shooter. He's here." I swallowed the nausea that threatened to overwhelm me. "Been here. Left blood."

"Ok." Reena started to turn away from me. I could hear the disgust in her voice when she spoke again. "Jonah's right. Sleep it off."

"I want it back." I was damn close to crying again as I forced myself to lean up on my side. "Written in blood on my mirror. Wouldn't come off."

"What did you say?" Reena whirled around. "Blood that wouldn't come off?"

"It moved. It moved back into the words no matter how many times I washed it." I buried my face in my hands. "She gave me the liquor. To calm me down. I … can't …I couldn't stop myself."

"Who?" she snapped. "Who is *she*?"

"Mary Anna. Called her to get more towels to clean off the mirror." I rubbed my face with the back of my hand. "Re, I'm so, so sorry."

"Wait. You said she gave you the liquor?" Reena was back beside me. "And there is a spirit in here?"

"Yes," I whispered. "I'm not crazy. And I'm not a damn drunk. Today was the first time I'd had a drink since I saw you last. I swear it."

"Tell me about this blood," Reena barked, but I could see her face had softened. "You said it just appeared."

"Where is it?" The man whispered in my ear. "Take me to my life or I will take yours, Sibyl."

I shuddered again as another cold chill ran down my back. "Reena, please. The spirit is looking for something. Something that was stolen. He keeps saying I have it, but I don't know what he wants."

"You're not answering my question, Evie." Reena decided to change tactics on me. She sat down on the bed and took my hand. "Start from the beginning. I'm listening."

So, I did. I told her about the attack. I told her about seeing the spirit after we left the Networkers. When I described how the message had disappeared when Mary Anna appeared in the room, Reena closed her eyes.

"Lifeblood," she whispered. "Dammit."

"Re, I am sorry." I could feel the liquor burning itself out of my system. The cloudiness in my mind, the sleepiness, was dissipating. "I don't break my promises without reason. Please. Believe that."

The spirit growled from his spot behind me.

"Reena, what am I going to do?" I closed my eyes. "He's going to drive me crazy. And then, there's the fact that Joey damn used me as a drug mule. There's my trial with the Curaie-"

"Stop." She squeezed my arms. "This isn't you, Eva. The girl I know would storm in, kick ass, and laugh about it later. You know how strong you are." Her mouth was set in a hard line as she continued. "I believe this is the poison. It's eating away at you. Your confidence. Your control. Do you feel up to walking?"

"Yeah." I ignored the spirit as he stood behind me. "I have to get back to Joey, Re. If he wakes up, I want to be there. I need to talk to him. Maybe he knows what Albertson is looking for."

"I really think you need to sleep." She was back to frowning again. "Eva, did Mary Anna say anything strange to you?"

I started to respond before I shook my head. "I don't remember. But I think I recall her eyes flashing purple."

"Really." Reena moved over to the sink, filled a cup with water, and passed it over to me. "I don't trust her. She's too quick on the trigger with Jonah."

I took the water and sipped. It took a few more sips, but the dry mouth was finally gone. "I thought so, too. She doesn't like me very much."

"I see the pieces." Reena was talking more to herself than to me as she began to pace across the rug. "But damn if I can't fit them together. One, Joey gets caught up in a drug ring led by a spirit reaper. Two, the shooter now wants something that was stolen from him. Three, some strange bitch shows up out of nowhere to fawn all over Jonah."

"I don't know what to make of it, either." I shifted around on the bed to stand up. I ignored the head rush that accompanied the movement. "You said the poison was affecting me by eating away at my control. What did you mean?"

Reena launched into a long-winded explanation of the ethereal poison. She told me how it affected everyone differently. She told me how Jonathan didn't know the origin, or how to treat it. My friend started to open the door to lead me down the hall when I stopped her.

"Wait. You said that this poison affects everyone differently, right?" I scrunched up my face. "Could Jonah be affected too?"

"No. It has to enter the bloodstream. And Jonah hasn't been in contact—"

"But Reena, Jonah is acting so weird." I leaned against the door-jamb. "Think about it. He's hanging onto this Mary Anna like some love-sick puppy. You should see the way he looked at her when they were here."

Reena pursed her lips together. "Eva, you know how affectionate Jonah is with the women he is interested in. You saw how he was with Lola."

Yeah, I knew. I knew that all too well. Just as I knew that I had to let what happened between us go. Those stolen moments had meant nothing to Jonah. Even now, they meant everything to me.

"Just ask him. Please." I stood up. "I'm going to head back just in case he wakes up."

"Alright." Reena gave me one more look that told me I was still in serious trouble with her. "We'll come check on you guys in a little while."

We walked back in relative quiet to the Apex suite. I pulled out the keycard and turned to my friend. I whispered my next words. "Thank you, Re. For everything."

She pointed a finger at my nose. "No more drinking."

"Yes, ma'am."

I gave her a small smile as she went away. I pushed open the door to feel a rush of cold air rush around me. Joey's bedroom door was shut, and I didn't hear Akshara at the moment. Given the hour, she may very well have dozed off. That was fine. I had my own issues.

I squared my shoulders, then stormed into the room. Reena was right. I was stronger than this. Liquor or no, I would defeat this thing.

One way or the other.

"What the hell do you want?" I called out to the silent room. I moved to stand at the end of the bed. "Give me that much."

"My life," the spirit whispered into my left ear.

I whirled to see him standing behind me with a smirk across his hateful face.

"Jonah told me about you being a Spirit Reaper," I snarled. "You're a pretty weak excuse for an Eleventh Percenter. Even then, that doesn't explain why you are here. How you're here."

"You stole what is mine!"

He reached out, but I was quicker. I jumped back and kicked up. The man howled as my boot connected with his knee.

"Bitch!" he screamed. The spirit lunged forward to slam against me.

I hit the wall with a grunt. The liquor was leaving my system, but I was still slow. Still sluggish. I dropped my sword to get my hands around his arms when he grabbed my face. The fire returned as the room began to glow in a strange red light. His power rushed through me as my mind seemed to shatter. I felt my eyes roll back in my head before the world shifted.

I blinked twice and grinned as I let my head fall forward. The threat was gone. She had stolen my life. I took hers as payment.

I laughed. The sound was so strange to my ears. The girl was a goddess in the flesh. Even her voice rang like music in my ears. No. My voice. She was mine. Now and forever. I moved over and picked up her sword from the carpet. The Ceremonial Sword of the Sibyl. A weapon the girl used time and time again to vanquish her enemies. I examined it with a snort. Guns were so much better. Gunpowder was so much easier to charge.

I was so close. So close to retrieving what was mine. There were only a few more souls to destroy. I focused my energies onto the sword and grinned again when my hands began to glow their trademark red. This was going to be easier now. The girl was mine.

I moved to the room where the boy lay. Damn Lawson would fade away within hours. He'd turned on me. Him and the worthless Columbian. Stole product. Stole my life. I was sure of it.

Perhaps I could do a little something to nurse along his demise. Nothing could stop me now, after all.

I opened the door, but when I tried to cross the threshold, I hissed as my flesh burned.

What the hell?

I tried to step in again, but the burning of my flesh became unbearable. Some of my mirth at my successful takeover faded. What was going on?

Then I saw her.

The girl sleeping near Lawson in a chair. The one who'd been nursing him. She was a Green Aura. A being of healing and purity.

I was a product of darkness. Impurity. I could go nowhere near Lawson so long as she was so near to him.

Fucking hindrance.

I forced myself away from the room. The boy would expire soon enough. That Green girl? I'd deal with her, too.

But neither of them mattered at the moment.

I had to find it. The Sibyl had friends here. The man she loved. Did he have it? Had she given it to him?

I marched down the hallway to the room where the Blue Aura was. I knew the Yellow one would be there too. Wonderful. Two birds with one stone. I knocked on the door as my grin widened.

"Eva?" The Yellow Aura was standing there with a look of confusion on her face. "What are you doing here? I thought—"

The girl never got the chance to finish her sentence. I slammed the hilt of the sword across her cheek with all the strength my Eva possessed. The one called Reena collapsed in a heap on the carpet.

"Reena? What the hell?"

The Blue Aura stepped out of the bathroom as I shut the door behind me. I stepped over the bitch on the carpet to point the sword at him with a laugh.

""She gave you my life, asshole," I tilted my head to the side to get a better look at him. "Where is it?"

"Eva, if this is the liquor talking—"

I watched him back up to the nightstand. I knew he fought with batons. I had to make damn sure he never got a hold of them. I rushed forward and tackled him to the ground.

"No!" I slammed my fist into his nose. "Give it back!"

The Blue Aura snarled as he grabbed at my sword hand. When

his flesh came in contact with mine, the fire in my blood erupted. He gritted his teeth and held on long enough to throw me off.

"Who are you? What have you done to—"

Another sentence he couldn't finish. I rose to a crouch and landed two blows against his side. The girl's knowledge of fighting was going to come in handy. I grinned as he fell to his knees with a grunt. I grabbed his hair when I felt a sharp wind rush past me. I barely heard the hard crack as a baton smashed into my shoulder. I released him with a growl. My opponent wrapped his arms around my waist to pull me down onto my back, but I was ready. I let enough of the girl come through to show the fear in her expression when the Blue Aura raised his fist to strike back.

It worked. Jonah Rowe, the great Blue Aura, hesitated long enough for me to wrap my legs around his waist. We rolled in one smooth motion as I brought the sword down to rest across his throat with another giggle.

"She stole it from me." I flashed her dazzling smile down upon him. "Now, I will take your head as payment!"

I started to finish the job. I lifted the sword to chop his damn head off when I felt another arm wrap around my waist to throw me aside. I rolled until I found my footing to see a man in a suit standing in front of my opponent. His expression was cold as he pointed his own sword in my direction.

"Release the girl, Albertson," he snarled. "I will send you down to the depths of Tartarus for the horrors you have put her through."

"The depths, huh?" I wiped my arm across my mouth. "Fuck you."

I shoved myself up, smashing into him to knock him off balance, with the sword poised to strike. I would win this.

The Blue Aura and the new asshole be damned.

TWELVE

JONAH ROWE

IT WASN'T the near decapitation that made Jonah the angriest. It wasn't the fact that Ulysses had just gotten knocked back on his ass. It wasn't even the fact that Reena lay in a heap near the door.

It was the fact that he had been played. Again.

And his best friend was now possessed.

Eva still looked like Eva, but everything was different. And her ceremonial sword gleamed red, like she was an Eleventh Percenter.

But she wasn't. She was possessed by the spirit of Victor Albertson. Because of that bastard, they now had to deal with the powers of the Sibyl *and* those of an Eleventh Percenter.

This just kept getting better and better.

Ulysses returned to his feet. Jonah didn't know the man well at all. He'd helped save Eva once before, when Cyrus had decided to throw her off a cliff. Seemed like a good guy based on that act alone. Jonah pushed his thoughts away when he looked back at the woman before them.

Eva looked at them with amusement and contempt. "Look at the two of you," she rasped. "To think that *I* was supposed to be the bitch here!"

"Oh, make no mistake, Victor," Jonah said coldly, "You are

indeed a bitch. I just wonder who gave you the right to possess an innocent woman."

Jonah willed the air in the room to yank his second baton from the floor. It flew towards Eva's head, but she dropped her sword and snatched the baton from the air with a laugh.

"I have the Sibyl's memories, Rowe," Eva snapped. "You did this same trick several months ago in Nemesis' dressing room. Did you really think it'd work twice?"

Jonah smiled. "Actually, no."

He kept Eva's attention long enough for Ulysses to run in and punt Eva's dropped sword away from her. He swung the blade of his short sword at her, but she blocked it with a wave of dark red ethereality. Jonah threw his whole body's weight into Eva's back, and she slammed into the wall.

"Bastard!" she roared as she punched Jonah in the face.

Jonah made himself oblivious to the pain the punch caused and used his wind ethereality to constrict Eva's oxygen. He hated to do it, but after Eva caught him with that graceful roll that almost resulted in his decapitation, he'd dispensed with finesse. He had to fight dirty.

Eva's eyes widened, and she grabbed her throat. Jonah only needed a few more seconds, and Eva would be unconscious—

She kicked him in the groin. He'd been so focused on rendering her unconscious that he didn't block it. It hurt like fire—it was pain beyond pain—but Jonah wasn't incapacitated. He'd been through too many injuries for a shot to the balls to make him useless.

Eva must have thought that that would have defeated him because she went for that trademark head-butt of hers. Jonah swung himself out of the way, connected with a knee to her midsection, and flung her toward Ulysses, who attempted another flat-sided strike.

Jonah roared in frustration. "Stop holding back, Ulysses!" he barked. "Vic will *drop* you!"

"Whatever injuries you cause, Jonah, be rest assured that Albertson won't feel them. Eva will."

"We have to stop her!" snarled Jonah. "Knock her out, at the very least!"

At that moment, Eva emitted a dry sob. "Ulysses," she gasped, "he's so strong—help me, please—"

Pity and surprise crossed Ulysses' face once more, and he lowered the sword.

"It's a trick!" Jonah warned, but it was too late.

Eva undercut him, and the Keeper took a nasty spill on the floor. She drew her legs into her chest and kipped up like she'd been doing the move for years.

"Give it back!" She yelled. "Give it back!"

She grabbed her sword off the floor, but Jonah had another surprise for her. When she made contact with the metal, her flesh hissed, and she screamed.

"Long-distance heat!" Jonah willed his hands to burst into flames, revealing that he had Apollo's blessing once again.

Eva's eyes widened. "How—?" She gasped in shock.

Jonah didn't understand for a few seconds, but then he saw it.

Ulysses, his face full of anguish, had stabbed Eva with a small dagger, his secondary weapon. Eva ground out a sound of agony as she worked the dagger out of her side. With painstaking effort, she straightened to her full height. Jonah knew she was in serious pain and hoped that the wound would make her pass out.

No such luck.

"I am immortal now, idiots," she growled. "What did you expect that little blade to—?"

Someone grabbed Eva's left shoulder and spun her around.

"I owe you something, bitch."

Reena threw a vicious right uppercut at Eva's face. She rolled across the table and crashed to the floor on the opposite side, bleeding and out cold.

"Goddamn, Reena," commented Jonah.

Reena shook out her right fist. "Well, that sword hilt hurt, damn it."

"She's possessed—"

"By Victor Albertson," Reena finished for Ulysses. "That's why Jonathan called Apollo, since danger of possession with the spirit stalking her."

"Which is why Apollo sent me here. To assist in protecting our Representative. It appears I am too late."

"Sucks that you had to do that, Ulysses."

Ulysses stared at Eva's unconscious form then up at Jonah and Reena. "I am disturbed at how easily you both attacked Eva."

"Dude, we weren't attacking Eva!" Jonah stared at him. "We were attacking Albertson! What'd you expect me to do? Let him stab me?"

"No. But know that whatever injuries you caused? Eva felt them. She will feel them when she is freed from this beast."

"You said that already." Jonah grumbled. "But I wasn't gonna take the risk."

Reena moved to Eva, conjured ethereal bonds, and bound her from her feet to her chest.

"The Venaré poisons people differently," she said again. "And the poison diminished Eva's control and will. It made her that much more susceptible to Albertson's possession."

"I can see that" Ulysses responded as he knelt by Eva. "Who has been affected by it?"

"Eva is the only one we know for sure. Beyond that, unknown." Reena turned to Jonah. "You ought to know that Eva said some disturbing things about your new friend, Jonah."

"New friend?" The Keeper asked. "To whom are you referring, Reena?"

No one answered him, but Jonah raised an eyebrow at Reena. "Such as?"

"She said that Mary Anna was the one who got her drunk on the Vintage," Reena told him. "She said she took advantage of her. She mentioned seeing flashes of purple around her, too, which may suggest she could be an Eleventh. She also speculated that you might be poisoned as well."

Jonah scoffed. Seriously? "With all due respect, Reena, Eva is *possessed*. Would you really take her words as truth right now? Mary Anna, an Eleventh? God only knows what else she told you that might be suspect!"

Reena lowered her gaze back to their friend. "Fair point. But I still don't trust that woman."

"You don't trust most anyone nowadays, Reena," Jonah said dismissively. "None of us do."

Reena gave him a shrewd, suspicious look, but made no comment. Instead, she asked, "Ulysses, how do you know about Albertson?"

The keeper glanced up from his inspection of Eva's injuries. "Apollo notified me of the events which occurred in New York when Eva was in the custody of the Networkers. I came as soon as I heard the news."

"What the hell took you so long?" Jonah interrupted, "If you knew about Joseph and Albertson-"

"No, Jonah," Ulysses looked Jonah's way. "That is the problem. None of us knew about Lawson's dealings with the Spirit Reaper. He was considered inconsequential until Eva was involved in the altercation at the airfield."

Jonah shook his head. "I never would have suspected Joey would get wrapped up in Spirit Reapers. He is a nobody!"

"Never underestimate a so-called 'nobody', Jonah," Ulysses warned him. "Odysseus referred to himself as Nobody when he blinded Polyphemus. When the other Cyclopes asked him what happened, all he could say … was 'nobody'."

Jonah sighed. "Point taken. I just want to know how he did it."

"Me too," said Reena, who was watching Ulysses as he inspected Eva's face. "We may have found out how he did it, Jonah. But first, we need to figure out how to do an unbinding for Eva."

"A *what*?"

"An unbinding," Reena repeated. "It's not called an 'exorcism' in the ethereal world."

THIRTEEN

EVA MCRAYNE

I WATCHED the group standing around the end of my bed with a bored expression. Reena was there, as was the Green healer who thwarted my plans against Lawson. Two more men had joined Rowe and the Greek. One I heard called Jonathan and the other I knew to be a god.

Apollo, the great Lord of the Sun, was staring at me with such hatred, I was sure he would strike me down the moment he had the chance. The damned Greek mirrored his master's expression to perfection. Rowe and his mentor kept their faces stoic, but I could just imagine the shit storm circling in their thoughts.

The Green girl regarded me with curiosity. I tugged at the ethereal ropes the bitch had looped around my entire body when she knocked me out. Someone had managed to attach me to the bed, as if they considered me a threat.

They were right. I *was* a threat. A damned strong one that would rip them all to shreds.

"This has happened before." Rowe broke the heavy silence in the room. "Montana, right? How was she freed from the possession then?"

"Cyrus Alexius fought her." The Keeper stood stiff while he

147

looked at the Blue Aura. "Most spirits fight during a possession, but their hold is fleeting."

"Most?" Rowe again. "What if they hang on?"

"The girl's physical body must be killed." Apollo seemed to be speaking through gritted teeth. "We can retrieve her soul from the Underworld, but there is still a chance that we would lose her down below. Especially after Hades' little show, when you saw him last."

I grinned at them through the veil of blonde hair that had fallen over my face. I knew I had them at a crossroads. Kill the girl for the chance to save her. Kill the girl for the chance to save her. Or leave me to get what was mine.

"You're too late," I whispered. "Much, much too late."

"Silence," the great god hissed. One snap of his fingers was all it took for me to fall silent. "Damned reaper. Your soul will burn for the crimes you have committed against my daughter."

"Daughter. Politician. Starlet." I croaked the words in a song to fight the spell he had cast. "The girl is gone. Yet I remain."

"Not for long," the Blue Aura all but spat in his anger. "Tell us about the poison you concocted."

I laughed. I couldn't stop myself. The sound was dry. Raspy. I felt my lips curl up in a cold smile as I tugged against the restraints once more.

"Idiots."

"Answer the damn question!"

Rowe took a threatening step towards the bed before the bitch with him grabbed his arm to hold him back. I threw my head back and laughed once more.

"You truly believe you can save her. It would be cute if it weren't so damn annoying." I rested my head against the headboard as my laughter died down. "When worlds collide, you are left with nothing but pieces. Parts of a whole that no longer exist."

"Lord Apollo, if I may."

The mentor known as Jonathan sat down on the bed next to me. He took hold of my chin as I growled at him. I tried to jerk away. I tried to ignore the pain shooting through my face. But the old leader held strong. He examined the burn mark that remained, despite the fact some three days had passed since I pressed the gun to the girl's head. I felt a strange pull against the hold I had on this body that caused panic to fill my heart.

"No!" I started to thrash against him. I continued to thrash against the bed as I pulled against the ethereal rope so hard, it drew blood from my wrists. "I will not lose this. She stole my life! She stole it!"

Each of them stood back as I struggled to break free. By the time Apollo approached the bed, I had begun to grow tired. He drew a series of circles over my head until the fight left me.

"You!" I gasped as I rested my forehead against my arm. "You are next, you golden bastard. I will usurp you. I know how. The girl knows ... too much."

Apollo ignored me. He turned his back on me as I struggled to sit up once more.

"The gods fear this girl. The gods fear me!" I lunged forward as far as I could. "I will steal everything. Every thought. Every power. You *will* fear me!"

"I need answers." Apollo refused to look at me. "Jonathan, if you please, tell me about the damned Reaper."

"Victor Albertson. Forty-three years of age. Well, he *was*." The damned traitor also ignored me. "Discovered what it meant to be an Eleventh Percenter, as well as a minimal ability to manipulate heat, at the age of twenty-six. Became involved in the *Los Muertos* cartel at that time. Worked his way to the head of the Los Angeles division. He became twisted by his abilities. Darker. Crueler. Albertson became a full-fledged Spirit Reaper at the age of thirty."

"And he discovered Lawson, how?" Apollo questioned. "Keeper, this is where you come in."

"It was Lawson and his lover, Pedro Garcia, who discovered Albertson." The Greek made my name sound as if something rotten had died in my mouth. "The two men became involved in Albertson's narcotics operation just over a year ago. It is believed they used Theia's private jet as well as rental cars to transport narcotics all over the world."

"With Eva present?"

"Indeed, milord. The inspectors of the jet trusted her given the time she has been with Theia. They would allow her to sign the inspection forms to verify the contents being shipped."

"Did Eva know about this then? Apollo stiffened. "Or was she an unwilling victim?"

"A victim, according to our own investigation." Ulysses responded and I sneered. Pretty good of Lawson to use the bitch's reputation to move product. "It is unfortunate that Eva trusted Lawson. He would hide the cocaine in the equipment cases. Tell her he made sure they had everything they needed. Albertson would have men staged at the airfields as technicians who unloaded the cocaine from the cases without Eva ever being the wiser."

"Until Joey fucked up." The Blue Aura crossed his arms over his chest. "So what did he do?"

"He stole a very powerful artifact from Albertson as well as cocaine for personal sale. I believe it is the artifact that Albertson is so desperate to obtain."

"Damn right I was!" I snarled. "The sooner I have it back, the sooner I can return to my life."

The group looked at me. I leered over at them.

"Maybe I'll keep the girl. Serves fuckin' Lawson right. He stole my life. I steal his nest egg."

No one spoke. The god once again turned his back on me as he addressed the others.

"What has occurred since Eva was brought to this wretched hotel?"

A recount of events followed. I let loose another low chuckle at the shock on the Blue Aura's face when the bitch described the lifeblood I had left on the girl's mirror. Even the great Jonathan seemed to be taken back at her words.

I was so focused on their conversation, I let my grasp on the girl's soul slip. I felt my body fall against the mattress as she took hold of my voice.

"I can't fight him. I can't stop this. Please."

"Eva?" Rowe pushed past the others before he knelt on the floor beneath me. "Fight him, Superstar. Fight the hold he has over you."

I struggled against her determination. Her renewed strength as the man she loved spoke to her. I began to curse as I regained control.

"You know what you gotta do." I twisted her face into a look of hatred while I peered past Rowe to the Greek. "Kill her, asshole. Or give me what is mine!"

The Keeper's eyes hardened but he didn't move to strike. I grinned at his weakness while the Blue Aura stood.

"You said before an unbinding would have to take place." Rowe's words were lined with steel as he turned towards the others. "We gotta try it. For Evie's sake. Letting her go is not an option."

"We must depart for a time," the mentor told the group. "Preparations must be made."

———

It was well after midnight when the woman slipped into the room. The others had left me alone under the pretense of sleeping, but I knew better. I wasn't worried about that as the woman glared at me, her fingers sparking purple as she got in close.

"Fool," she hissed. "You did it too soon. You were not supposed to take the girl until after Jonah had sealed my salvation. Then you can reclaim your precious life back."

"The girl's lifeblood is healing itself," I broke in. I had no time to listen as I felt my hold once more slipping. "The poison is almost gone."

The woman glanced around as if she could be overheard. "So, you need more of it, then?"

"Yes, I need more," I snapped. "I know you have it on you."

"Mind your tone, filth," the woman growled. "I won't be spoken to like some piece of meat you've violated in the past. Know your place, and don't forget what I can do to you."

She raised her hands, which sparked violet once more. I blinked as fear grounded me.

"I apologize," I said hastily. "Mouth got away from me. Perhaps I got some of the bitch's sarcasm in this possession deal."

I chuckled, but the beauty at my side did not as she pulled out a bottle from the apron she wore. She glanced around once more, and I found myself wondering how she had survived as long as she had. She poured the poison into a plastic cup and held it to my lips. I sucked down the liquor that contained the Venaré. I relished the fire as it returned to my blood. I grinned when she pulled the cup away.

"Better than a rose, that." I smacked my lips. "Any luck with the bastard you've claimed?"

"I need you to hold on for a bit longer." She took a step back to sit the cup on the table beside me. "I can't stay here."

"Mary Anna?"

I heard a voice break through the darkness just before the lights flicked on. Rowe narrowed his eyes at the scene unfolding before him.

"What are you doing in here?" he demanded as Apollo stepped up behind him. "I want an answer. *Now*."

FOURTEEN
JONAH ROWE

MARY ANNA SPRUNG UP, frightened. Her eyes bulged so much that she resembled someone who'd suffered oxygen deprivation. Eva snickered, like this would be a magnificent show.

Mary Anna moved away from the bed, which brought her features more into the light. Jonah couldn't help but notice that with her hair pulled back like that, she seemed like the sweetest, most beautiful Southern belle. All those old movies he used to watch with his grandmother were to blame for that attraction.

Don't get distracted, he warned himself.

Mary Anna pointed at Apollo. "Who are you?" she asked. "You new in town or something? And why are *your* eyes gold; is there a man-Sibyl, too?"

"Dodging won't work, Mary Anna," Jonah told her. "You owe one hell of an explanation right now, so you'd better hop to it."

Mary Anna swallowed. "I-I thought that the Sybil could help me."

"With what, woman?" Apollo demanded. He was so tightly wound that he looked seconds away from attacking her.

"This was a bad idea." Mary Anna shook her head. "I'm just gonna go—"

"Like *hell*, you will." Apollo moved to block the door.

Jonah started; wasn't that a bit excessive?

"Who are you?"

"Dude, calm down!"

"I will do nothing of the kind! I want to know why she is here!"

"Look at you two," Eva grinned. "You're like a married couple."

"Silence, dilettante!" Apollo swung his hand through the air, leaving a shower of gold in its wake.

Eva was struck dumb. She almost looked like she gagged on something.

"What the—?" began Jonah, but the god cut across him.

"We're still waiting, girl—why are you here? Why do you require Eva's assistance?"

"Look, she was in here by herself when I came in here. And I'm not crazy." Mary Anna still looked frightened. "But something's happened. Scared me half to death."

"What happened?"

"When I got home, I went straight to bed," Mary Anna began. "I had this scary dream, soon as I got to sleep. A man was chasin' me. He had these red hands—dark red, like he'd been bleedin' or whatever. He kept goin' on and on about how some little lady was his. He was behind me sayin' it: I want what is mine'."

Jonah's suspicion turned to alarm. He glanced at Apollo, who looked equally troubled. What the hell was this? Had Victor projected himself into Mary Anna's dreams? Why would he do such a thing?

Jonah almost asked Apollo to reverse the whole silence thing, but he decided against it. Wasn't like they'd get a straight answer out of Eva-Victor, anyway.

"I must ask something," said Apollo in a slightly warmer tone. "How exactly was Eva supposed to assist you with this?"

Mary Anna licked her lips. "I panicked. My mind went to all the worst-case scenarios. So, I came back here to talk to her, hopin' that she could … make the man leave me alone. Isn't that what she does?"

"Um, not quite, my dear." Apollo looked rather awkward about his overreaction now. "That's not how the Sibyl works, exactly."

Mary Anna looked foolish. "It doesn't matter, anyway," she said. "I tried to ask her for help, but she was babbling like a ten-year-old. Couldn't make heads nor tails of it. Is she sick? Like, in the head?"

Apollo didn't answer.

Jonah didn't blame him. He noticed that Eva regarded Mary Anna with wide eyes, but he didn't think much of it. She'd already accused the poor woman of getting her drunk on Vintage during this possession.

"How did you sneak in here, Mary Anna?" he asked. "*Why* did you sneak in?"

Mary Anna looked embarrassed and a little ashamed. "To answer your first question, I *work* here, Jonah. I know how to not be seen when I want to avoid people who might give me more work to do. As to the why, well ... I was raised to be a strict Southern Baptist. If my daddy knew I was talkin' to the Sibyl from the television, with all her talk about a bunch of gods and monsters and Olympus and all that, he'd disown me."

Jonah sighed. This was all a huge misunderstanding. He didn't know how Eva-Victor transferred himself into Mary Anna's dreams, but he would personally consult Jonathan and Apollo to make sure that it didn't happen again.

Apollo caught his eye and gave him a look that clearly said, "*Get her out of here,*" and he nodded.

"Mary Anna let's talk somewhere else," he said. "Eva's had um — had a long day — um, well, let's just talk somewhere else."

"Where, your room?"

"No," Jonah replied firmly. "Reena's in there. I don't want to cramp you in my car —"

"I know a place," Mary Anna said, grabbing Jonah's arm. "It's one of my hangouts when I need to get away."

Jonah allowed himself to be pulled away, noticing that Apollo gave his new friend a wary glance. Just like Reena had. Why were they so certain Mary Anna was bad news? What was it — Gang Up on the Country Girl Day?

155

Minutes later, Jonah and Mary Anna were in the ballroom. The same ballroom, Jonah noticed, where Turk Landry had made a fool of him and Reena once. But he filed that away. He took a savage pleasure in the fact that Eva was dominating him in ratings.

Now, there was just the simple matter of unbinding her from the spirit of Victor Albertson.

Mary Anna looked so ashamed about her actions that Jonah almost pitied her. "Jonah, I feel so stupid right now," she grumbled. "That damned dream got me so discombobulated; could I have been any more foolish and naïve—"

"Mary Anna, stop," Jonah told her in a stern voice. "Dreams have a way of messing with you. Hell, *life* has a way of messing with you. Sometimes you just want to escape."

"I wish I could," Mary Anna lamented. "I wish I could so bad."

Jonah frowned. Mary Anna had that same wistfulness in her tone that Reena had had when she flirted with becoming a Tenth Percenter. "What do you mean by that?"

Mary Anna, who'd had her face toward the far wall, turned to face him. "Jonah, I'm a liar."

Jonah stiffened. "What are you talking about?"

"I'm a liar," she repeated. "My granny used to say somethin' that I never forgot: 'When we don't obey what's in our heart, that's when we stop being real people. We're just characters in somebody else's story.'

"Well, I'm a character, Jonah. The woman who spent more years than she should have on her daddy's farm, just to make him happy, was a character. The woman that wears this uniform on the third shift is a character. The woman you saw earlier driving her daddy's raggedy truck, because her car broke down, was a character. And I'm so sick of it, Jonah. So sick of it."

Jonah could relate to the feeling but couldn't help the feeling of confusion. "What brought that on, Mary Anna?"

She shook her head. "Just thinkin' about the Sibyl, I guess. She is so beautiful, glamorous, famous ... gets to see so many places. Then, you got someone like me, who has to spend all my time not bein' myself because I'm s'posed to be some good little Christian girl who pleases everybody else."

Jonah just looked at her. How could he have suspected that she had done something to Eva earlier? "I don't think that Eva's life is a perfect as you made it sound," he said. "But let's not talk about the Sibyl. Let's talk about you. If what you are is a character, then who is the real Mary Anna? Could she have been that woman who told me that I could do or be anything earlier?"

Mary Anna smiled. "That was a glimpse of her," she confirmed. "She is also the woman who finally decided to make something of herself. She's the one who wants to buck tradition and get out of her domain—"

"Domain?"

"That's what I call my daddy's farm, darlin'," said Mary Anna without hesitation. "But most importantly,"—she walked into his personal space again— "she is the woman who doesn't feel anything like a character when she's around you."

It was too good an opportunity. Jonah couldn't pass it up. He kissed her. It was weird, but not a negative thing. Jonah had felt a bit out of sorts earlier; like he might have let Mary Anna get too close. Like he hadn't been himself around her. But the second his lips were on hers, that feeling dissipated. There was no need for caution. She wasn't dangerous at all. She was just a sweet woman, with lips that were soft as hell.

They parted, and Mary Anna chuckled.

"I may have enjoyed that just a bit too much," she confessed.

Jonah snorted. "Why do you say that?"

"Because I'm willin' to shuffle your reservation so that Reena can have the room she's in alone, and get us a room to ourselves."

Jonah's eyes widened. "Are you serious?"

Mary Anna regarded him. "Wholeheartedly. Hell, forget the room, you can have me right here if you want—"

"No," Jonah interrupted. "I can't do that."

"Why not?" Mary Anna asked in a provocative voice. "I'm not new to sex, darlin'. You've never given in to temptation?"

"You misunderstand," Jonah told her. "You're worth more than a fuck in the ballroom."

Mary Anna's slightly crestfallen expression cleared instantly, and her eyes widened. "You said that because you actually respect me enough to have me in privacy. But you still want me?"

Jonah frowned. "Of course. Call me old-fashioned, but—"

"No, no it's fine." For some reason, Mary Anna looked giddy. She looked like she'd won the Powerball. "It's—it's just refreshing."

Jonah's desire was colored a little by puzzlement. "I take it that you haven't met many decent, respectful men, then."

"Not a single one, until you." Mary Anna looked near happy tears, which was odd. What had this woman been through? "Here."

She handed Jonah a card from her pocket.

He took it and regarded it.

"It's a key card, programmed to room 592," she explained. "Go there. I'll be there soon. I promise that I won't keep you waitin.'"

Jonah gave her a sly smile. "You had this on you already?" he asked shrewdly.

Mary Anna answered him by grabbing his shirt and kissing him once more. Her lips were intoxicating. It was nearly enough to make him say forget the room; they could stay in the ballroom after all. But he surprised himself by showing restraint.

They parted, and Mary Anna looked at him, trying to catch her breath.

"Room 592," she breathed. "You won't be waitin' long."

It was all Jonah could do to hide the fact that Mary Anna had made him weak in the knees. "I better not be."

———

Jonah was in room 592 quicker than breathing. He hadn't bothered to tell Reena what he was doing. He'd turned his phone off. He still had concern for Eva, but she'd be unbound from Albertson. All would be well.

He dispensed with his shirt. He wouldn't need it, anyway. It was just a matter of waiting now. Mary Anna said that she wouldn't be long. He had to take her at her word and hope that it was true.

He heard the lock activate to a card, and then click as the door opened. Mary Anna entered, and quietly closed the door. Her hair was no longer pulled back. Her brown curls hung in casual grace around her face. She had also put on lipstick, magenta in color. In Jonah's mind, she didn't have to freshen up, because she was beautiful already. But now that he saw what she had done, he couldn't help but feel that her alterations, though minor, had greatly accentuated something that was already perfect.

They regarded each other without words for several seconds, then Mary Anna slowly, almost methodically, approached Jonah. As she did so, she grabbed at her shirt and pulled it open, indifferent to the buttons that spilled over the floor.

Jonah looked over her slightly pale upper body, idly observing her black bra as he was more focused on the tattoos dispersed across her torso. Clearly, this Southern Baptist girl was not as strait-laced as her parents wanted her to be.

That was fine by him.

When she was in Jonah's personal space, he raised his hands to touch her, and she did the same. He noted her shaky intake of breath at his touch. Jonah couldn't argue with that reaction; it was as though Mary Anna's flesh had an undercurrent of electricity beneath its surface. There was no mirth, or girlish laughter in her eyes now. She looked intense, almost hungry, as though she hadn't had sex in a long while.

But those thoughts were like white noise. Somewhere on the edge of his mind, largely irrelevant to the present time.

Jonah couldn't get enough of Mary Anna's touch or her scent. This must be what it was like to be under a vampire's thrall. Jonah had to admit that it wasn't so bad at all.

It was only after they'd nearly driven each other insane with touching that they kissed again. Mary Anna's kiss was as ravenous and intense as her gaze. Jonah could have sworn that he saw a flash of purple in her eyes, but he thought nothing of it. Desire made your mind see crazy things.

He brought his hands to her bra and freed her of it in seconds. He then did the same thing with her pants. The moment that Mary Anna was liberated of those articles of clothing, she climbed him. Holding her was no trouble at all, but Jonah lowered her to the bed anyway. No point in wasting a good king-sized bed.

It was time to give this day, a day that had had such a tumultuous start, an exceptional, gorgeous end.

FIFTEEN

EVA MCRAYNE

THE DAMN golden god closed the door behind the traitor and the bitch. I watched him through the hair that had fallen in my eyes as he turned the lock before he faced me. Even here, in the darkness that only midnight could provide, I could see that his eyes gleamed the strange gold of the sun.

He reminded me of a wolf. A wild animal meant to be taken down with as much force as I could muster.

Apollo took a seat in the chair across from me. He then leaned his elbows against his knees as he studied me. I will admit, I was surprised. I was expecting more threats. More violence. Instead, he went silent.

"What?" I snapped. "Are you finally coming to accept me as your new Sibyl? Your new daughter?"

"No." The god shoved himself up to grab my chin. He tilted my head back until I was forced to look into those strange eyes. The bastard leaned in then inhaled. "Vintage," he muttered as he dropped my face.

I pushed myself further away from him as he picked up the cup Mary Anna had left behind. I began to curse aloud as he sniffed it.

"Tell me something, Reaper. How is it that you could stand to stomach this piss water from the Middle Ages?"

"What?" I narrowed my eyes at him. "Release me, dammit. I command it."

"I'm sure you do." The god returned the cup to its spot. "But I'm more curious about how you were able to get a hold of the liquor, drink it, and hide the bottle all while bound by ethereal bonds."

"I am more powerful than you will ever know." I grinned. "More so, now with my new abilities."

The god didn't make a sound. He continued to stare at me with those hateful eyes until I was forced to break the silence once more.

"Ah, does it hurt to know your darling little girl is gone? Does it break your heart to see her like this? She hasn't been this powerless since she was in the hands of her mother. And you did nothing! Nothing to save her then. Just as ..."

I didn't finish my sentence. The god cold-cocked me across the jaw. I felt her head snap back. I felt the resurgence of pain in my freshly healed bones as my teeth clamped together.

"I gave you time to speak, Albertson. Now, it is my turn —"

"You are far outside your domain, Greek," I sneered. "My powers are ethereal. They have coursed through my veins far longer. We are more powerful than you in every way."

"You were a smart man, Reaper. And I will grant you only this. Never has a spirit attempted to usurp the Sibyl in such a fashion. It was a bold move on your part to use the Venaré to weaken Eva."

I knew from the girl's memories that the god tended to pace when he was thinking. But he did nothing of the sort. He stayed still as he continued.

"You see, the Protector Guide, Jonathan, has informed me of many things. Venaré is a powerful poison, yes. But it tends to wear off, depending on the type of lifeblood it is affecting. A poison that fades in time is no better than water unless it is mixed with another, stronger ingredient."

"The girl is alone, ancient one. She has always been alone." I leaned forward as much as I could with my binds. "She believed you had abandoned her. Just as everyone else has abandoned her —"

"Now, as I said," Apollo ignored my attempt to goad him, "you're a smart man, but you're not that smart. I believe you had assistance in this plan of yours. What did they promise you? Fame? Power?"

"You're damn right it was power!" I snapped before I could contain my voice. "But I had no help. I didn't need anyone else to take you down."

"Oh, but I believe you did." Apollo gave me a cold smile as Ulysses of Athens appeared in the shadows behind him. "I have been in contact with the Eleventh Percent world for centuries. I understand the inner workings of your power more than you could ever realize. But my knowledge isn't important. The issue now is what to do with you. A spirit with ethereal abilities who had the balls to possess the daughter of a god."

"Nothing." I grinned wider this time. Colder. "There is *nothing* a Greek can do against someone with my abilities."

"Ah, but that is where you are wrong." He matched my smile with a vicious one of his own. "You see, you attacked a hallowed soul, precious to many powerful gods in our realm. Not just to me. They insisted you pay for this insult with whatever price I demand. A quick meeting with the Networkers has sealed your fate. Your crimes cause you to fall under our jurisdiction. Not your own."

"You cannot—"

"I'm not finished." The god waved his hand in front of my face and I fell silent as his power took my voice away. "Now, I am not an unjust being. I am willing to allow you assistance to pass over to the Other Side in exchange for information. If you are unwilling to participate ...? Well. There will be no unbinding done by Jonathan. No Protector Guides to assist you."

I began to struggle against the binds as the shadows in the room began to move. The first to step forward was Jonathan. The second was a god I was unfamiliar with. He tipped a black ball cap at me as he flapped his silver wings against his back.

"You see, Eva is an immortal. One only needs to watch a single episode of her television show to see that. But, as with all immortals, she is vulnerable. There have only been two weapons ever crafted to take her power away. The first was Athena's Blade, which was

163

broken into pieces and burned at my command. The second? The sword of her Keeper."

Ulysses took a step forward as Apollo detailed the options I had. Turn against my benefactor, whom I had sworn my allegiance to. Give him the information he wanted so desperately. Or he would kill his own beloved daughter to free her from me.

"Your answer," he growled. "Now."

The god released the hold he had on my voice. I began to scream in earnest, struggling against the ethereal binds. I would not lose this. Not after I had come so close to finally mattering as a Spirit Reaper.

"No! You wouldn't dare kill her! I was promised her body, dammit! Promised!"

Ulysses leaped onto the bed as his short sword flashed into view. I attempted to throw my head back with the hopes of breaking his damn nose when his arm snaked around my throat. He forced my head back as he held me tight against his chest. Ulysses leaned in to whisper in my ear.

"Time to go, Albertson."

I released a small cry of shock as he plunged the blade deep into my side. The fire granted to me at birth began to seep out, along with the girl's lifeblood, as chaos erupted around us.

"Hermes, now!" Apollo yelled as Ulysses released me. The room was growing dim as the god with the silver wings stepped forward to grab my face.

"Oh, I am going to have fun with this one. Come on now. Let her go." The god grinned as I felt my hold on the girl snap. "That's a good boy."

I shifted back into the world of shadow as I watched Apollo rush to the girl's side. I saw that her eyes were still open wide from my shock. Her patron god and Keeper encircled her body as Apollo lifted her shirt to slam his hand against the wound made by the ancient one.

Was he healing her? Impossible. The girl was me. She was promised to me. I made a move towards the bed to rejoin with her body when a strange fog began to surround me. I was frozen in place as I heard a voice speak behind me.

"Quite the show, that." The one called Hermes grinned at me through the mist. "Time to go, Reaper."

"Wait," I choked. "I am an Eleventh Percenter. No, I am a Spirit Reaper! I demand—"

"Tell it to the guards of Tartarus. I hear that my brother promised you would burn for eternity. A fitting end, given your powers from this life."

"No!" I screamed as I tried to push through the smoke. "My Eva. My body! I won't let go."

"Why must they always make this more difficult than it has to be?" Hermes sighed. "Can't I get one cooperative spirit?"

He appeared right in front of my face. He tapped me once between the eyes and the world I had known—the world I had risked everything for—was gone.

SIXTEEN

JONAH ROWE

JONAH COULDN'T GET Mary Anna out of his mind.

There was something about her that he just couldn't place. Something intriguing, something complex, something to be nurtured. Beneath her calm, demure nature, there was strength. And edge. A sense of determination that couldn't be diminished. She desired improvements in her life, and she'd make them come to pass. Come hell or high water, she'd get what she wanted.

But there was something underneath the strength, serenity, and quiet beauty. It was sadness. Hurt. It flowed beneath her attributes much like an undercurrent. She'd seen things. Survived hardship. It wasn't just from her words; the moment Jonah kissed her, he knew. It was like he'd absorbed just a glimpse of her emotions.

Absorbing things from others ... something about that was familiar ... but it didn't matter. He was certain that it didn't matter since it was something that distracted him from his thoughts of Mary Anna.

And now, he could add her luscious body to the growing list of things he thought about.

Jonah had almost declined Mary Anna's advances. He had more respect for her than to treat her like a one-night stand. He initially wondered if he needed to be cautious with her. He had a feeling that her sadness, or at least a portion of it, had something to do with a guy.

But in the end, he couldn't. She was too damn irresistible.

Whatever notions that Jonah had that he needed to be gentle with Mary Anna were dashed the second they were in bed. She was a completely different woman once they were engulfed in darkness, when the moonlight and her pale body were the only sources of illumination. She was the personification of unparalleled pleasure and passion. It was the most perfect bliss to experience that in the night.

Four times.

When they'd ceased, Mary Anna had to leave, mentioning personal business to attend to, and promising him that she'd see him again that day. With another one of those addictive kisses, she was gone. As her scent faded, one thing came unbidden into Jonah's mind. And once it was there, he knew he'd follow it through.

He wanted to save her. Wanted to rescue her. When she said that he could be or do anything, he took heart. He believed it.

How did he feel *this* secure and at ease about this woman so quickly? It was a weird thing, but it was also a weirdness that he didn't mind. With all that had happened in the past couple months, it'd be nice to have a positive occurrence for once.

Jonah returned to the room he shared with Reena. He didn't need her permission to live his life, but he had no time or patience for the scrutiny he'd encounter if she woke and discovered he wasn't there.

He flopped on his bed and was out in moments. It had been a long night, after all.

He was in a place he'd never seen, that smelled of dirt and stale breath. It was dark, save for torches lodged across the walls. He wondered what the place might be but was distracted by two voices.

One was a guy who resembled a distant runner. His outfit made him look as such, anyway. Strapped to his waist was a baseball cap that had wings on it, and he looked to have a face that was made for smiles and grins, though neither were present at the moment. His current countenance made him look as though he wanted to punch someone.

"Escaped?" he asked in a fierce whisper. "How is that possible?"

"I-I'm not sure, my lord," sputtered the second person. "It must have been due to his ethereal nature."

"I was told that that was not an issue!" the track star hissed. "I was informed that his crimes placed him in our jurisdiction!"

"I don't know what happened, my lord," said the spirit, whom Jonah was surprised to see was a spirit. "This whole situation troubles me."

The track star got in close to the spirit. "Look," he said, "you know that I have no power in Hades' domain. This is why I deal with *you*. This is why I grant *you* my blessings. This was a delicate matter. The Underworld was not our stop. Tartarus was. I had to work the machinations from a distance because Hades' anger burns still for the Sybil—"

Suddenly, dark shadowy people—Shades—appeared in a circle around the spirit and the track star. The spirit yelped and vanished, but within seconds, his image flashed back into view. From the look on his face, it had been against his will.

The track star scoffed. "Is this a jest?" he demanded. "I can extinguish you as easily as those torches—"

"You have no business in my domain, Hermes."

Jonah knew that voice. Even though this was a dream, he still had to fight the urge to recoil. It was Hades.

The lord of the Underworld walked into view, his pale mask of a face pulled into an expression of coldness and intrigue. The Shades parted to clear a path for him to walk to Hermes and the other man.

"You will not touch the Shades," he continued. "As a matter of fact, if you touch any of my charges whilst in my domain, your current situation will even graver than the one of this idiot next to you."

He turned his gaze to the spirit, who didn't resemble a spirit anymore. He simply looked like a flesh-and-blood being. "Did you not think I'd find out what you've been doing, Clavius? Did you think that I wouldn't notice your actions because you masquerade in spirit form, projecting from a different location?"

Clavius swallowed. "I can go anywhere I want," he advised. "I am a demigod."

"You're a fool," Hades said. "Let's see how defiant you are when your flesh has been seared off."

He waved his hand, and Clavius caught fire. He screamed in horror and anguish, and attempted to beat away the flames, but they didn't budge. Collapsing on the ground and rolling didn't help, either.

With another bored wave of his hand, the agonized and burning demigod vanished.

"How I do loathe treachery." Hades returned his gaze to Hermes. "That is one imbecile down; now, what to do with *you*, Hermes?"

Hermes didn't show the slightest hint of fear. "If you knew what was good for you, Hades, you'd leave me be and let me carry out my goal."

Hades' eyes narrowed. "You dare threaten me in my own domain? Titans have fallen for lesser insults."

Jonah would have recoiled at that statement, but Hermes rolled his eyes. "If the posturing is meant to frighten, you've got the wrong one," he said. "I'm an Olympian, same as you."

"An Olympian who, unless I am mistaken, was given ironclad strictures regarding matters such as this," Hades told him. "The Fates were quite clear with their orders."

"Those strictures are not applicable," Hermes snapped. "At least, not regarding this. Tartarus was my destination. I wasn't transporting just any spirit. He was a prisoner who escaped my grasp—"

"No one escaped you." Hades sounded bored again. "I took him the second I discovered Clavius' backdoor dealings with your spiritual transport in my domain. And now, the bastard burns."

"Clavius is your nephew!"

"As are *you*," said Hades. "In regard to your prisoner, well ... whom you call prisoner, I call guest."

Hermes' eyes widened. "You would do well to give him back to me, Hades. That prisoner is no mastermind; he is trash. A mangy mutt in search of a master."

"True." A small smile crossed Hades' face. "But that mutt hails from the world of the ethereal. And he has shared a most fascinating tale with me during his time in my court—"

A bang on the front door knocked Jonah out of the dream and onto the floor. He'd jumped so hard that he rolled completely out of bed. The urgency in the knock distracted Jonah from his confusion about that dream. He untangled himself from the covers and ran to the door to see Reena on the other side of it.

"Where the *hell* were you all night?" Reena grabbed his arm. "You know what, forget it. You need to come with me to Eva's room, now!"

"What's wrong, Re?" Jonah asked. "Is something up with Eva?"

"Yeah!" Reena answered. "She's free of Albertson's spirit!"

Something cold formed in Jonah's gut. It was a feeling that made it clear to him that what he'd seen while asleep was no dream.

But he also had the feeling that the time to reveal that suspicion would present itself soon enough.

SEVENTEEN

EVA MCRAYNE

I WOKE up to the sound of whispers. Not the frenzied, desperate ramblings of the dead. These were quiet. Concerned. I started to speak up and tell them to stop being ridiculous when I heard Jonah's voice rise above the noise.

"How do you know she has been released from the possession? Are you sure we shouldn't keep her bound until we know something?"

"I know without a doubt," Ulysses responded from his seat on the bed to my left. "Eva will return to us when she is ready. The Spirit Reaper is gone."

Return to them? I was already here. I frowned as the past few days rushed to the forefront of my thoughts. The barbeque. Jonah and Lola. Hestia denying my request to become a Bestial Virgin. The gunfight and the drugs. I was in trouble. I needed answers from Joey to get me out of it.

I sat up with a cry at the last thought. Ulysses caught my arms to keep me from smacking into him. I jerked away from him as panic filled me once more.

"Don't touch me! Where's Joey? Did he wake up?"

"Easy, Eva. You shouldn't move too fast so soon."

"Stop it, Ulysses!" I jerked away from him a second time and tried to throw the covers back. "Where is he, dammit?"

"Superstar, calm down." Jonah came up on the other side of the bed then reached for me. "Akshara is with him now and he isn't awake. We just spoke to her before we came in here."

I threw my arms around Jonah's neck to bury my face into his shoulder. My best friend mirrored my movement as he crushed me against him. He was whispering words of nonsense against my hair, but I had no idea what he said. I was too busy trying to figure out why Jonah smelled like roses. There was an underlying feminine scent on him.

Mary Anna.

I froze at the pang in my heart, then pulled away. I looked over at Ulysses, then got my first good look at the group standing around my bed: Apollo, Jonathan, and Reena. The latter two were staring at me with obvious suspicion.

"What?" I croaked. "Ya'll act like you've never seen a possessed Sibyl before."

That broke the tension in the room. Reena began clamoring, asking me questions about how I felt and just how the hell I got possessed in the first place.

"God, you have a mean right hook, Re. Remind me not to get on your bad side, ok?"

Reena laughed. "Yeah? Well, I'm not used to being knocked out, Evie. It was a retaliatory move."

"Eva." Jonathan cleared his throat. "If you don't mind, I would like to check your essence to ensure that every trace of the Spirit Reaper is gone."

Reena shifted from her spot to give Jonathan room. He put his hands on each side of my face in a strangely familiar gesture. I felt my skin begin to tingle before he released me.

"Your plan worked, friend." Jonathan turned to Apollo. "She has been released."

Plan? I tilted my head toward my father. I started to ask him, but there was no need. My memories were slowly seeping back. I shuddered as I remembered the sensation of Ulysses' sword slicing through my skin. Before I could respond, my father joined our little group by the bed. He brushed a hand over my filthy hair as he studied me.

"You may return to your duties as soon as you are able."

"What do you mean, when I am able?" I shook my head. "I'm fine. Or I will be as soon as I get a shower and coffee."

"Let us leave you then, for the time being." Apollo took a step back as Jonathan and Reena stood up. "We will speak of what has occurred soon enough."

I watched as they filtered out of the room. I couldn't help but notice how Jonah had held back. He was almost out the door when I called out to him.

"Hey, Blueberry." I gave him a weak smile when he turned around. "Next time I roll you? Go the other way. It'll throw me off balance."

He snorted. "There's no chance in hell you'll ever roll me like that again."

I laughed as the final bit of tension seemed to leave the room. He crossed the room in three large strides to wrap me in his arms a second time.

"You're such a brat, scaring me like that," he muttered into my shoulder. "Glad to have you back, Superstar."

Jonah stood up, squeezed my hand with a nod to Ulysses, and left us alone. I waited until the door closed behind him. When I heard the lock click into place, I studied Ulysses in silence.

"You're my new keeper."

"Officially, yes." Ulysses ran his hand over his beard. "Apollo was insistent I accept the position after Alexius was thrown into Tartarus."

"That means you can kill me."

"I have the ability, yes, but not the desire. I have known you for a very long time, Eva. I don't want to harm you."

"You have?"

"Indeed," He gave me a small smile. "I was the ghost from your childhood."

I widened my eyes as my memories of a man in the shadows

came to the surface. He would simply stand and watch me whenever I was following Janet's demands.

"I called you John," I whispered. "You would always raise a finger to your lips because you didn't want Janet to see you."

"That is correct," Ulysses chuckled. "I truly questioned my abilities as a Keeper after being outed by a three-year-old child."

"But you weren't around after a while." I frowned. "Nor did I know you through the whole Cyrus mess."

"I was forced to leave my post after your mother spotted me one afternoon during your piano lesson. Due to her agreement with Apollo, none of us were supposed to check on you."

I didn't say anything for a long while. Ulysses didn't, either. I appreciated the fact that he didn't try to fill the silence with meaningless words. And while, yes, I was caught up in the horrific memories of my mother, that wasn't the topic I broached when I spoke again.

"Why did Jonah smell like cheap perfume?"

"Pardon?"

"Jonah. When he hugged me, he smelled like drugstore perfume." I frowned. "I am just curious as to why."

"Darling girl, perhaps now is not the time—"

"Do you know something? Something I don't?"

Ulysses released a sigh, then offered me his hand. I stared at him for a good minute before I accepted the comfort, he had to offer me.

"Eva, Jonah and the Green woman are together."

"What do you mean 'together'?" I bristled. "He doesn't even know her."

"Aye. Jonah was spotted going into her room last night. He did not emerge for quite some time."

He slept with her? While I was possessed? I felt as if someone had dowsed me with ice water as I repeated the words in my head I kept trying to believe. Jonah didn't want me; he never wanted me.

"Are you—"

"Fine. I'm fine," I interrupted, desperate to change the subject. "How is this new keeper arrangement going to work? Because I don't want a babysitter."

"Good, because I have very little experience in watching children." Ulysses smiled. "I believe you have proven yourself capable, so I will only come to you when you request my assistance. Apollo agreed that you did not need a shadow following you around twenty-four hours a day."

I released a breath I didn't know I was holding. "And if I *do* need you?"

"I am a simple text message away. If a situation arises and you cannot contact me in time, I will be able to feel your fear and will come to your location."

"Is it bad that I am really liking this arrangement so far?"

"No," he laughed. "You are a grown woman, Eva. A hero. It is time you are treated as such."

"Thank you, Ulysses. I mean that."

"That being said, I do plan on sticking around until we are certain Albertson is no longer a threat."

I shuddered and Ulysses squeezed my hand.

"We will discuss the details later. For now, why don't you rest? I will remain right here."

"Ok."

Ulysses stood and I stretched back out, on my side. When I closed my eyes, all I could see was an image of Jonah and damned Mary Anna. They were together. An item.

I ignored the new lash of pain in my heart and told myself to stop being stupid. He wasn't mine and he never would be.

———

Ulysses was not pleased that he wouldn't be allowed to attend my trial before the Curaie. There was nothing I could do about that. I considered it a miracle they agreed to hold a trial at all.

I smoothed out the front of my skirt and slipped on my heels when Jonathan appeared in my room at the Milverton. He greeted me by clasping my hands into his and then bowing to Ulysses.

"Are you certain I cannot attend, Jonathan?" Ulysses stood upright to face the protector guide. "Surely the Curaie-"

"No, I am sorry. The structures of these matters are too

embroiled in tradition to change now." Jonathan gave me a soft look. "Yet, they are not unwise. They will see the truth for what it is."

"I'm not even sure if the truth matters anymore." I grabbed my suit jacket to slip it on. "Are you taking Joey as well?"

"Due to Joey's injuries, he will be tried in absentia." Jonathan took my hand again. "Jonah and I can escort you to the entrance. From there, you must face the conclusion of the investigation on your own. When it is done, we will return you to the earth plane."

"I don't think Jonah is coming."

"Pardon?"

"I haven't seen him since I was freed from Albertson," I cleared my throat. "It is better this way."

Jonathan sighed. "Are you ready then? We must depart."

"Yes." I bowed my head towards Ulysses. "I will see you soon."

"Indeed. May our Lord Apollo be with you."

Jonathan initiated the Astralimes and the hotel room became a grand room of wood and carved walls. I would have been impressed, but my heart wasn't in it. A woman dressed in purple robes gilded towards us and I resisted the urge to hide behind Jonathan.

"Protector Guide, you bring the accused?"

"I do."

"Then we shall proceed." She turned away from me without so much as an introduction. I watched as her aura sparked the same shade as her robes and she beckoned me forward.

"Go forward."

I didn't say a word as I stepped through a gate and into another grand room. There were spirits residing behind a very large desk. I heard another woman speak.

"Eva McRayne, blood of Apollo. Step forward as we address the crimes levied against you."

I kept my hands folded before me as a familiar face appeared to stand just to the right of me. The Networker who had taken me into his custody in New York.

"Agent Dubois. What did your investigation find?"

"In regard to Miss McRayne, she had no knowledge of the relationship Pedro Garcia and Joseph Lawson had formed with the Spirit Reapers. She is not guilty of conspiracy."

"The narcotics?"

"Of that, McRayne is guilty of possession and trafficking. She was on the aircraft that transported the cocaine. She was the representative who signed the documents certifying that the equipment cases were to be transported on the aircraft."

I wanted to scream at him. I wanted to scream at the spirits who sat in judgment of me. I knew better than to speak out in these hallowed halls. I was a stranger here. An outsider. The accused and now, convicted.

"McRayne, do you admit that you signed these documents?"

"Yes, but I had no knowledge of the contents in those equipment cases."

The spirits began to whisper before the woman held up her hand. The leader studied me with a scowl.

"Eva McRayne, we the Curaie, do find you guilty of possession and trafficking narcotics meant to enrich our enemies."

I felt sick at her words. I felt lightheaded. I waited for the floor to rise up to meet me as I fell. I remained standing, somehow.

"That being said, we are not completely ignorant of your plight. Jonathan has spoken quite passionately on your behalf. So, we will spare you from the Plane with No Name."

The relief that lifted off my shoulders was so great, I felt them drop. I stiffened once more as she continued.

"Yet, we must enact some punishment. Your actions would have been beneficial for our enemies had you been successful. Thus, you will not be allowed on ethereal lands for the period of two years. Your homes are being released back to you, however. They were searched and nothing of use was found."

If I had been relieved before, I was frozen now. I couldn't go to the estate for two years?

"We have been in contact with the Olympian Council. They were less than pleased at our actions but agreed that Spirit Reapers fall under our jurisdiction." The woman continued. "Thus, along with your banishment, you will be imprisoned in one of our detention centers for a period of six months. There will be no contact with the outside world nor can you contact any ethereal beings during this time. You will be given five days to get your affairs in order. After that period, Agent Dubois will come to collect you at dawn."

Imprisoned? Did she really just say that? I stared at the woman as she lifted her hand as if to wave me away.

"Wait. Please. Allow me to speak, great spirit."

"What are your words, girl? We have much to accomplish?"

"Ma'am, please. Do not banish me from Grannison-Morris. Please. Jonathan and the Elevenths who reside there are my family. The estate is my second home. A place of solace and refuge. As far as imprisonment, I can't be taken away from my life for so long. My duties to the Olympian Council demand that I be available at any given moment. I understand your position. I understand the Networkers findings. But surely, there is something else that can be done."

The woman stared at me before she shook her head.

"Be grateful your imprisonment is only for six months and your banishment two years, girl. We had considered the Plane for you and your friend."

I couldn't move as the room shifted and I was returned to the great entrance. Jonathan crossed over to me and grabbed my arms.

"The verdict?"

"Banishment. Imprisonment." I whispered though I could barely believe my own words. "I have been banished from ethereal grounds for two years. I can't...I can't go home again for two years."

Jonathan's expression was one of sadness and anger. It was the first time I had ever seen those emotions so starkly on his face.

"Imprisonment? I was told the Plane-"

"Not the Plane. One of the detention centers. Six months." I explained in broken sentences. "I won't be allowed contact with anyone outside of it for six months."

"Eva," Jonathan tightened his grip on my arms. "I am sorry, dear girl. This is a terrible injustice. I was so certain they would release you."

"I was on that plane." I didn't recognize my own voice. It

sounded too flat. Too dazed. "I was technically in possession of those drugs. Technically trafficking. They had to do something. I have five days before the Networkers come to take me away."

"Come. Let us get you back to the hotel."

"I can go home." I forced myself not to choke up at my next words. "The Sullivan House. It has been released back to me."

Jonathan initiated the Astralimes and the grand foyer became my kitchen. I caught myself on the counter as I tried to breathe. Six months of my life was now slated to be spent in an ethereal prison. I would have no choices. No control.

"Eva, allow me to convene with Apollo and Ulysses." Jonathan spoke. "Perhaps, I can send Reena to stay with you."

"No," I shook my head. "No. Don't bother her, Jonathan. I...I need to be alone."

The Protector Guide squeezed my arms again and vanished. I moved on automatic. I slipped off my heels and walked through the house. Nothing was out of place. Nothing was out of the ordinary. It was as if I was coming home after being on the road.

I knew better. I knew the Networkers had torn this space apart then put it back together. Little things were out of place. The papers on my desk were askew. Drawers not fully closed. Everything was normal until you looked a little closer. Then, you could see the mess that truly remained.

I went to my bedroom and stripped out of the suit. I took my time changing clothes because the more I thought about the trial, the more I started to shake. I wanted to scream at the walls. I wanted to lean out the window and yell that it wasn't fair. That none of this was fair.

Nothing in my life had ever been fair. Nothing.

I went back downstairs when I heard the backdoor open. I found Jonah in the kitchen with a frame under his arm.

"Jonathan told me I'd find you here."

"Yeah." I studied the frame that looked so familiar. "What's that?"

"I wanted to give this back to you. Don't seem right to keep it now."

Jonah sat the frame on the counter, and I recognized it instantly.

Inside the frame was a photo that Jonah and I had taken together in London. He had his arm around my neck, and I had my face all scrunched up as he gave me a kiss on the side of the head. Jonah had loved it so much; I'd had the picture developed and framed.

The fact that he was giving it back to me now was like a knife to my heart. It was enough to take my mind off the trial. At least, temporarily.

"You don't want to keep it?" I crossed my arms over my chest. "Let me guess. Mary Anna. Is she so damn jealous that you can't keep a photo of me anymore?"

"Watch it, Eva. That's my girlfriend you're talking about."

"Girlfriend?" My eyebrows shot up. Was he serious? "I didn't realize the two of you had gotten so serious so soon."

"Yeah, well, I finally found the right one. I won't have you talking bad about her."

I studied his face for a second as I felt a sharp pain fill my heart at his words. The right one. He'd finally found the right one. Someone who wasn't a quick lay. Someone who wasn't me.

"I have to go. Mary Anna is waiting in the car."

"She's here?" I narrowed my eyes at him. "Fine. Then I'm going to ask her what the hell her problem is over a damn picture."

Jonah shoved my shoulder as I approached the door. It wasn't hard, but it was enough to catch my attention.

"If you ever, and I do mean *ever*, try to hurt her, I swear I will knock the shit out of you, Eva."

"Excuse me?"

"Jesus," He ran his hand through his hair. "Is this about what happened between us in the garage? Are you jealous?"

"No!"

I started to speak before but he cut me off.

"We're *friends*. There is nothing beyond that. I know you've been holding onto hope and all, but it's never going to happen."

"You think I've been holding onto hope?" I gaped at him. "Are you kidding me? How could I hold out hope when you-"

"Come on, Eva," Jonah sounded exasperated. "You know good and damn well that I'm not in love with you. So, let it go."

"Let it go," I released a laugh that sounded as broken as my heart. "You're right, Jonah. I've let it go. I let it go the second you told me about Lola. I let it go when you made it perfectly clear that I was not good enough for you."

"I knew that staying friends with you was a mistake."

I felt something break inside of me. Something that had been carefully mended back together cracked wide open. The pain was so sharp, I whispered my next words.

"I was a *mistake*?"

"Yes, Eva. Being friends with you was a mistake."

"Then why —-"

"Because I felt sorry for you! Because you were running around with your sob stories of Janet and Cyrus! I thought that you needed a friend, but your negativity is constant. It's fucking constant and it's not worth my peace."

I swear, if Jonah had hit me with one of his batons, it wouldn't have hurt as much as his words now. I felt the wall I had been tearing down around him fall back into place as I stared at him.

"I'm leaving. Don't call me, Eva. I'll call you."

I stayed rooted in place, when I heard the door slam shut a second time. I stayed still long after I heard Jonah's car leave the driveway. I was still standing there when Ulysses reentered the room.

"Eva? Are you alright?"

"Fine."

"Perhaps you should sit down. You look like you're about to pass out."

I let Ulysses wrap his arm around my shoulders, then lead me into the media room. He lowered me onto the couch next to me as I tried not to cry.

"Eva, what happened?

It wasn't the memories of my fight with Jonah that broke me. It wasn't the trial that had banned me from the estate or even my impending imprisonment. It was the kindness in Ulysses' tone. I buried my face into my hands and began to sob in earnest. The Keeper said nothing as he shifted to wrap his arms around me.

Ulysses said nothing as I buried my head against his suit and sobbed as if my heart were broken.

In truth, it was. I would never have expected that Jonah could have said those horrible things to me. How he was only my friend because he had felt sorry for me. It took a while, but my thoughts began to center around an idea. Jonah wasn't acting like himself. That gave me the clarity to calm down enough to speak.

"Ulysses, I am so sorry." I took the handkerchief he gave me and pressed it to my eyes. "Truly. I'm a mess and I ruined your suit and—"

"I do not care about my clothes, princess, but I do care about *you*." He kept his hand on my arm as I sat upright. "What happened between you and Jonah?"

It was hard but I went through our conversation again. When I was finished, I dabbed the tip of my broken nose with a wince.

"I think Jonah's been poisoned."

"Poisoned? Like with the Venaré."

"I think it's Mary Anna." I picked at the pillow next to me to hug it against me. "And I think Mary Anna is Persephone."

"Explain your reasoning."

"I can't."

"Listen to me." Ulysses studied my face again as if to convince himself I wasn't possessed. "I believe you. But if you are going to save Jonah, you need more than belief. You need proof. Why Persephone?"

"Because she has appeared to him more than once since I was taken to the Underworld. Jonah told me once that she praised him and even left a note saying that she would see him soon." I hugged the pillow tighter and closed my eyes. "I need more time. I only have five days before the Networkers come to get me."

Ulysses' expression darkened. He said nothing, so I continued.

"For Jonah's sake." I sighed. "He's so wrapped up in her, he won't listen to me. When Reena told me about the poison last night, she said it has to be mixed with something. What ingredient could be used?"

"Roses," Ulysses answered without hesitation. "On occasion,

they are red, but most often, they are black. The black rose, after all, is Persephone's symbol as the goddess of springtime. Yet, she was tainted by her forced marriage to Hades."

"Alright." I nodded. "And if the base ingredient — Venaré — is mixed with black roses, what happens?"

"It would depend on the victim." Ulysses rubbed a hand over his face. "The potion would have to be continuously introduced into their system for them to stay under its influence."

"It won't kill you?"

"No. It is not a poison meant to kill, but to change." The Keeper frowned. "Or drive insane."

"Do you think Persephone is Mary Anna?" I frowned. "She came to Jonah once that I know of. But as herself. Why go through this whole facade of being someone else? And why poison me?"

"It's quite possible." Ulysses explained. "Persephone is known more for her madness than her reasoning. As for Albertson, he has a connection with her."

"What connection?"

"As a leader of Los Muertos, he would have worshiped her due to her status as Queen of the Underworld."

"He would know about the Venaré poison? As a follower?" I stood up to pace in front of the fireplace when it came to me. "Why would he have that knowledge?"

"To make sacrifices to Persephone using her preferred method of murder." Ulysses had shifted around to watch me. "Eva, Albertson is not in Tartarus."

"What?" I frowned. I'd barely heard him as the pieces began to fall into place. "Where did you send him?"

"Tartarus." Ulysses caught my hand to stop me. "I received word from Hermes. The damned Reaper escaped his grasp in the Underworld. He is now a guest of Lord Hades."

"A guest?" I raised my eyebrows as I let my sarcasm drip off my words. "How lovely! I wonder if he'll be shown the torture chambers. The room of mirrors was my personal favorite."

"Eva, this is serious."

"So is Persephone. And her little excursions going around

poisoning people." I gritted my teeth as I realized the true damage of what she was doing. "So is her breaking my Jonah's heart."

"To be fair, your Jonah just broke yours."

That stopped me faster than when Ulysses grabbed my hand. I studied him for a moment, then whispered, "I don't matter, Ulysses."

"I disagree. I believe you matter a great deal."

"Please. Just help me get Jonah set back to rights. Then, I will deal with everything else."

"Such as the ramifications of the trial?"

"I don't want to talk about the goddamn trial. I want to help Jonah."

Ulysses released my hand with a sigh.

"Persephone is a mistress of poisons. There are only two goddesses who are more knowledgeable in the art. Demeter and Hera."

"So, I'll talk to Demeter."

"You cannot. She is enjoying her allotted time on the earth plane."

"Then, I will talk to Hera."

"Given your history with her, I do not believe that is a good idea."

"I have to try, Ulysses. I have to."

Ulysses stood and looked down at me. "You are sure about this?"

"Yes."

"Keepers are not allowed into a goddess' domain unless expressly invited. Are you willing to be alone with her?"

"Yes."

Ulysses looked up to the ceiling then extended his arm. I latched onto him and within seconds, my new media room became the foyer of a California estate. I knew that Hera would be here somewhere. Zeus had banished her here for a while after she lost our last fight.

Maybe she was supposed to win that one. Maybe the Fates were punishing me for my victory and that's why everything was so fucked up now. Worse than before.

A thin man dressed in a black suit appeared in a doorway.

"Can I help you, Representative?"

"I need to see Hera right this moment."

"She is not taking visitors."

"Oh, she'll see me. Where is she?"

The man hesitated for a few moments before he finally bowed his head in my direction.

"Follow me."

I started after him before I realized that Ulysses wasn't following me. I remembered what he said about Keepers being banished from a goddess' domain, so I turned towards him.

"I won't be long."

"I'll be right here."

With that out of the way, I headed after the butler. We moved through corridors that were lined with windows, but I barely saw my surroundings. I was too wrapped up in my head. My worries about Jonah.

The butler stopped in front of a room and knocked on the door. When he opened it, I pushed my way past him.

"Ricardo, what now? I told you —"

Hera fell silent when she realized I was standing there. Her aggravation at her servant became outright rage as she leaned forward in her chair. Even in this room of glass and gardens, she had the appearance of a witch in a fairy tale. Gnarled and twisted. Hateful and ugly.

"What are you doing here? You are not welcome in my house! Have you come to take this from me too?"

"Ricardo, is it?" I turned to the butler. "Leave us, please."

"Do not tell him what to do!"

The man looked between us before he ducked out of the room. Hera sneered at me once we were alone.

"If you've come to exercise your rank, bastard of Apollo —"

"I want you to help me. I will pay any price you ask in exchange for your assistance."

That shut her up. I knew it would. I crossed my arms over my chest as she stood.

Hera leaned on a cane before she responded. "Any price, you say?" she cackled. "The only thing I wish for now is your death. Surely, you aren't willing to pay for my assistance with your life."

I should have seen that coming. Hera didn't need money. She

needed me dead.

"Fine."

"Pardon?"

"Fine. If you help me, then you can kill me however you wish."

Hera narrowed her eyes at me before she snorted. "You want to set me up. If I murder you now and rid the world of your cancerous influence, I will be thrown in Tartarus."

"Will you? Or will your supporters rally around you? Will they demand that you are put back on the throne?"

She smacked her lips together as she held onto the cane with both hands. Finally, Hera narrowed those hateful green eyes at me.

"I no longer have the power to strike you down. Even if I did, how would I know you haven't done this to get your revenge?"

"What good is revenge if I'm dead?"

"You are serious, then. You are willing to pay the price of your life for this man?" Her lined face twisted into a horrible grin. "When?"

"As soon as this job is done."

Hera hobbled over to a small workshop and began muttering to herself. She leaned the cane against the bench before I heard glass clinking together. I didn't move as she worked. Instead, I told myself that what I was doing was for myself. For peace. I told myself that Jonah had nothing to do with this. I was putting the Universe back as it should be.

Hera poured a clear liquid into a vial, then whispered over it. I saw it flash green before she stood.

"This. You will take this."

"What is it?"

"A sleeping poison. One drop, you will sleep. Two will put you in a coma. Three will be enough to rid the world of you."

"Ok. Now, it is my turn."

I launched into the theory I had about Persephone poisoning Jonah.

Hera listened before she began to cackle. "That is true."

"Persephone poisoned Jonah?"

"Indeed. Why, I created that potion myself. Persephone came

here a few weeks ago, wanting a love potion." Hera waved her hand dismissively as she handed me back the poison. "It was nothing."

I blinked as the pieces began to fall into place. The line I had heard before but couldn't place? Persephone had said it to me in the Underworld. How Jonah had helped her change a tire and that's how they met. Hadn't he met another woman like that before? A Renee? No, Rheadne.

"Why did she come to you if she is a mistress of poison?"

"Because the fool she loves is ethereal. His blood would nullify the effects in only a few moments. She needed something to stick."

"Then, I need the antidote."

"Very well." Hera sat back down.

I slipped the vial of poison in my bra and told myself this was the right decision. I was going to save Jonah first, then fulfill my part of the bargain. After all, if I died, then I wouldn't have to hurt anymore. I wouldn't have to bother Hestia with taking her oath. And the negativity that Jonah said surrounded me would be over.

"When will you fulfill your part of the bargain?" Hera passed me another vial of black liquid. "The sooner you give him this, the better."

"Within five days." I choked a little as I turned to leave. "I have to help Jonah first. Then, I will take the poison."

"I would say farewell, but good riddance is more like it." She cackled at my back as I left the room.

I ignored her. I found my way back to the Keeper.

"We've got to go. Now."

"Did you get what you came for?"

"Yes." I took Ulysses' arm. "She was receptive to assisting me."

The Keeper gave me a look of utter disbelief, but I didn't explain myself any further. I refused to let him in on the deal I had made to save Jonah from a life with a goddess willing to drug him into loving her.

When we appeared in my kitchen, I willed my phone in my hand. I had a plan to make and I knew just who could help me with it.

"Reena?" I breathed out her name when she answered. "I know what's wrong with Jonah. We've got to talk."

EIGHTEEN

JONAH ROWE

FOR THE PAST FORTY-EIGHT HOURS, Jonah barely thought about Eva McRayne.

Because, simply put, Mary Anna hadn't given him the chance.

When they'd returned to the hotel room, Jonah was still incensed. It seemed as though Eva was determined not to see him happy. She was determined to believe the worst of Mary Anna. Just what the hell was her deal?

But before he could voice any of it, his darling lady kissed him. As usual, it stopped him in his tracks.

When they parted, she shook her head. "Let's not even talk about it," she'd said. "I'm just as hurt and mad as you are. But I know the perfect thing to get our minds off all of it."

She dispensed with her clothing, and Jonah nearly forgot all about the stressors.

"Let's just take our frustrations out on each other," she said in a provocative voice.

Those couple of days passed in a whirlwind of some of the most breathtaking, astounding, and wildest sexual abandon that Jonah had ever experienced. They ordered room service but didn't go any further than the balcony during that time.

On that Friday morning, the two of them lay in bed, having completed yet another round of carnal pleasure. Nothing had changed—they still didn't want to leave room 592. They were there, in pleasurable silence, until Mary Anna broke it after placing a slow kiss on Jonah's chest.

"It's been so long since I've felt happy, safe, and free like this," she said. "I know I kind of sound like those sappy TV shows, but I can't help it. You are the best thing that's ever happened to me, Jonah Rowe."

Jonah didn't even bother opening his eyes. "Couldn't have said it better, Mary Anna Greene. This is the first time in a long time where I've been in a state of—I don't know, joyous living—and it wasn't fleeting. It's refreshing. I truly do not want this to end."

"Then let's not let it end. Come away with me, darlin.'"

That opened Jonah's eyes. "What? You're serious?"

"Never been more serious about anything in my life." Mary Anna sat up on her shoulder, to look Jonah in the eye. "Let's just go."

"But what about your school?" Jonah asked. "What about your family? What about your *life?*"

Mary Anna scoffed. "None of that matters. I don't care about dropping everything. I just want you."

Jonah sighed. "Mary Anna, I've got responsibilities, I've already told you that—"

"And I have already told *you* that it's time to live for yourself, and no one else," Mary Anna interrupted. "Jonah, I know everything you've said. Remember it all. But at the end of the day, have you gotten any closer to peace? Have your 'responsibilities actually done anything for *you?* They can't have. Because since we've been together, you look like someone took a thirty-pound bale of hay off your back. You've been free. Finally. Just like me."

Jonah shook his head with a laugh. "None of this makes sense."

Mary Anna grinned. "Nope," she agreed. "Not a lick of sense. That's kinda the reason that I think we're on the right track."

Jonah couldn't argue with her. The past week had almost been like someone else's life. Never in Jonah's life had everything fired on all cylinders like this. Like they had with Mary Anna.

His family would be fine. They had Jonathan. Reena. Terrence. All the people that had been at the game a lot longer than he had, anyway. He imagined that it'd be nice for them to not have him along, needing explanations for ethereality they already knew. They were a formidable group, always had been. They could handle the ethereal world without him.

"Okay," he said.

Mary Anna regarded him. "Really?"

"Really," said Jonah. "I'm ready to leave all the bullshit behind, anyway."

Mary Anna looked at him, and then the most illuminating grin was on her face. She freed herself of him, found her skirt, and reached into one of the pockets.

"I know this goes against all tradition," she said, "but this isn't a normal situation. I want to give you something."

She produced a ring. A black-stoned ring. Jonah stared at it.

"Mary Anna," he said, "is that what I think it is?"

Mary Anna climbed back on the bed. Her naked body was almost enough to take his mind off the ring. "It could be," was her cryptic response.

Jonah chuckled, a little stunned. "I—"

His phone rang. He grabbed it and saw Reena's picture. Mary Anna saw it, too, and her face darkened slightly. Jonah waved her expression away.

"Don't let this color the day," he said. "This will be quick." He put the phone on speaker. "Hey, Reena."

There was a brief silence, and Jonah thought he knew why. He hadn't masked his aggravation over this interruption.

"Hey, Jonah," She responded at last.

Jonah exhaled at length. "I'm busy. What do you want?"

"Yeah, well, since you haven't come home, I wanted to see how you were doing."

"Fine." Jonah's answer was abrupt. Terse. "Whatcha need?"

There was another bit of tense silence before Reena answered. "We're holding a dinner at the Sullivan House tonight to say goodbye to Eva."

"Goodbye? She is going back to L.A.?"

"No. The Curaie trial was yesterday, Jonah. Eva was sentenced to six months in an ethereal detention center. The Networkers are going to come get her on Friday."

Jonah felt a pang of anger and worry, but then Mary Anna kissed his cheek. Within moments, the bitter feelings vanished. How could he have any negative feelings while Mary Anna was here, so beautiful and reassuring?

"That sucks," He said. "But I'm guessing you want us there?"

"I would think you'd want to be here. You realize that Eva won't be in contact with us for six months, right? Even then, once she's released, she'll be banned from the estate for two years."

"Obviously I know of the banishment," Jonah muttered. "That's standard Curaie protocol when someone is convicted of a crime. It's just real life, Reena, and that isn't always fair or pretty. Just one thing. No big crowds. Don't bring everyone over. Mary Anna gets anxiety over large groups and I don't want her palms sweaty the entire time. That's the deal. Take it or leave it."

"Fine." Reena breathed out. "Ulysses will be here. Me. I'll make sure that nobody else shows up."

Jonah looked over at Mary Anna as she took his free hand and kissed the back of it and smiled at him. He smiled back. "Sounds perfect, Reena. See you then. Bye."

"Good." Reena sounded troubled by his responses, but hey, what did she expect? He was over Eva. Completely done. "Six o'clock. See you two then."

Jonah had his eyes on Mary Anna. "What do you think of that?" he asked her.

Mary Anna regarded the phone coldly, as though Reena was still on the other line. "I can't call it, baby," she said. "But I have a perfect idea. Let's go there this evening and get it over with, and then hit the road."

That made Jonah's eyes gleam. "Tonight?"

"Yep," Mary Anna nodded. "Just leave. We don't have to tell anyone we're gone … until we're gone."

191

Jonah grinned. "Sounds like a plan to me. If only we didn't have this fuckin' dinner, we could go now."

Mary Anna snorted. "It won't take forever, darlin.' Here. Hold on to this."

She pressed the ring into Jonah's hands. He surprised her by putting it on his ring finger. Her eyes widened in glee at that and, for an infinitesimal second, there was that flash of purple. But Jonah thought nothing of it. It was a part of her now. An alluring piece of a gorgeous whole.

Mary Anna pushed him down on his back and straddled him.

"Now, before we head out there for dinner," she murmured, "let me give you a morning appetizer."

Somewhere in the back of his mind, Jonah was suspicious of Eva. She hadn't said anything positive about Mary Anna, and now, Eva was all smiles when they'd reached the kitchen, with hugs all around. That made Jonah's suspicion swell even larger. She had dared insult his Mary Anna and now she wanted to present her with the questionable gift of black roses? Was this a fucking funeral?

It was almost as crazy as when the former vice president, Dick Cheney, shot his best friend in the face while hunting, and then *that* guy went on live television and apologized to *him*. That didn't make sense.

Neither did this.

But Jonah wanted to believe that Eva could be happy for him. How many people successfully found their perfect match in so short a period, after all?

He thought about their argument in the kitchen and shook his head. Classic Eva. She tended to make a martyr of herself. Maybe exposing herself to his love for Mary Anna was an attempt at that?

Eva mentioned something about a text from Apollo, and then dashed upstairs. Jonah returned his focus to Mary Anna.

"You okay, baby?" he asked. "You seemed shocked as hell by those black roses. Do they mean anything to you?"

Mary Anna's response was instant. "No. You … you just never know the forms kindness will take. The gift was unexpected was all."

"Some gift," Jonah remarked, looking at the roses again. "Why black roses?"

"Black roses are … gorgeous, Jonah," Mary Anna said quietly. "No different from red or white. It's just a different flavor of beauty, but beauty nonetheless."

She pulled out her lipstick and touched it up.

Jonah gave her a curious look. "Baby, you don't have to do that," he said. "You couldn't be any more perfect if you tried."

Mary Anna just grinned. "See, saying things like that will get you rewarded for hours on end."

Just then, Eva returned from upstairs, heading outside. She threw a golden glance at the ring on Jonah's finger, and her expression dimmed somewhat. Within seconds, though, she recovered with a provocative smile.

"You guys coming?" she asked. "The fun will be outside."

"Um, yeah," Jonah attempted to get his head screwed on straight. Mary Anna couldn't say things like that and not have him get distracted. "We'll be out there."

"Good," Eva said as she gave Mary Anna an appraising look. "Now, hurry up!"

She headed out. Jonah put one foot on the threshold, but Mary Anna caught his hand.

"Jonah. Wait."

"Two seconds, people!" he called.

Jonah saw the salty looks from Reena and Eva outside, but he ignored them and stepped back inside the kitchen to face Mary Anna. "What's up, baby?"

Mary Anna kissed him. It didn't seem quite as passionate as the other kisses they'd shared, but more … controlled. More precise, if Jonah had to put a label on it. It was heart-stopping and knee-jerking nonetheless.

They parted, and Mary Anna ran a finger under her bottom lip. "That should be enough," she murmured.

"Huh?" Jonah asked. "Enough? Enough of what?"

Mary Anna smiled slyly. "Enough for you to remember why you're with me. Why we're hitting the road tonight."

Jonah snorted. "I'd never forget that. You don't have to worry."

"Oh, I'm not worried. Not now, anyway."

Mary Anna's smile was now radiant. Not devious, like the prior one. Jonah loved that smile. She cast a suspicious look at Jonah's friends outside the door, and then looked back at him. "No matter what happens ... no matter what any of them say out there tonight, particularly that Sibyl, just remember what we have. What we've shared. It'll never change."

She kissed him again.

Jonah hadn't cared for the disdain in Mary Anna's voice towards Eva. The moment she kissed him, however, all doubt, all apprehension, all *everything*—just faded. It was truly something to behold, how one of Mary Anna's kisses could correct the entire world—

"Alright, that's enough."

Reena appeared out of nowhere and physically parted them. "The Allies didn't use their mouths this much when they discussed D-Day. Now get out here."

Jonah didn't appreciate that, but he did as his sister asked.

They all seated themselves around the fire pit. Even though it was late summer, there was a chill in the air, so their spots around the fire were very comfortable. It felt like the family setting that Jonah had missed in the time since his home had become a quasi-police state. The dynamic was present once more, complete with the addition of Mary Anna. He wished that Terrence could be there to meet her because he didn't know if there'd be any chances for introductions once they hit the road.

But that was fine. Jonah had to do what was best for himself.

Eva passed around *hors d'oeuvres*, while Ulysses sipped on a flask. Jesus, what was it with Greeks and alcohol? Mary Anna took water. Jonah saw Eva give Reena a poignant look before she gave him a rather large cup of citrus drink.

"What's this?" he asked, leery of the look.

"You don't recognize Tampico?" Eva asked. "You swear by that stuff, so I stocked up."

"Oh, of course!" Jonah sipped on his favorite sweet drink. "If this were available in L.A., I'd drink it at your condo!"

Eva grinned, which made Jonah lower his guard. Eva seemed to be Eva again. Maybe her impending imprisonment was enough to get her head back on straight.

Now if only he could expedite this so he and Mary Anna could get going. Their bags were already in his car.

Mary Anna sipped some water and shook her head. "You have a very fancy life, don't you, Eva? Condo in Los Angeles, this new McMansion you just bought simply to get away from the Milverton? I tell you—it's somethin'!"

Eva glanced at Reena again and then smiled at Mary Anna. Jonah didn't care much for that look, but he didn't have a chance to address it before she spoke. "I'm not defined by possessions, Mary Anna," she said. "I tend to let my life and actions do that."

"You've done some wild things, darlin'," Mary Anna commented as she sipped more water. "Are you sayin' that you define yourself by livin' on the edge?"

"That's right," Eva agreed. "But it's only when we live on the edge that we know who we truly are ... beneath the surface."

Jonah raised an eyebrow. That was an odd response.

But something else was odd, too. The more he drank the Tampico, the more it felt like some type of fog was lifting from his head. It was a strange thing. Maybe citric acid was great for the brain?

"You're a farmhand, Mary Anna, is that right?" Reena asked.

Mary Anna moved her eyes in Reena's direction. "Guilty."

"Nice." Reena munched some ice before she continued. "Jonah told us all about how he assisted you on the road when he was driving to D.C. to get Eva. What were you doing the day the tire blew out? If you don't mind my asking, of course."

Mary Anna frowned. "Why would I mind you asking?"

Reena kind of shrugged. "It might be misconstrued as nosy. But I assure you, I only want to know more about the lady in my brother's life."

Jonah regarded her. It seemed harmless enough, but there was something off about the way Reena said what she said. Was he being paranoid?

"I was taking roses to Ms. Millie's house up the road," Mary Anna responded in her quiet tone. "Yeah, that was it. She's always been so nice to my family."

"Ms. Millie." Ulysses piped up. "Her name wouldn't happen to be Millicent Harper, would it?"

"Okay." Jonah had to speak up now. "What is the deal with these questions?"

"Drink the Tampico and let her answer, Jonah." Ulysses' voice was one step above cold. "Am I right, Mary Anna? Millicent Harper?"

Mary Anna looked at Ulysses with alarm. "That's odd, darlin', but you're right! How'd you know her name?"

Ulysses calmly placed his hand on the arm of his chair. Jonah swore that he saw the air ripple near the Keeper's hand. Was he summoning a weapon? It was too dark outside to be sure. "I know her name," Ulysses said, "because a close friend of mine and I had a nice conversation with her. On the Astral Plane. She truly is a sweet spiritess."

Jonah blinked. What?

Mary Anna blinked herself. "I—I don't understand. What is a spiritess? Is that another Sibyl thing?"

Eva laughed. "I've never actually witnessed a train wreck before," she said. "It's kind of fun."

Mary Anna's eyes darted at Jonah, and then back at everyone else. "I'm sorry, Eva, are you trying to be funny?"

Eva's momentary mirth faded, and her ceremonial sword appeared across her lap. "Tell Jonah about that the night you got me drunk on Vintage," she urged. "Tell him all about how you got me shit-faced, so you could get inside information on him."

"Wait, what?" Jonah lowered the Tampico and looked at Eva with doubt. "I've heard that already. But Eva, you made that accusation when you were possessed."

"Wrong, Jonah." Eva rose from her seat. "That's when *you* heard that I'd made the accusation. But I told Reena that before Albertson possessed me."

"That's true," Reena said without hesitation.

Eva looked as if it was all she could do to keep from pointing her sword at Mary Anna. Jonah had seen that look on her face many times. He didn't know what was up, but she would *not* assault his girlfriend. He slipped one hand into his pocket so as to grab a baton. He tried to free his other hand from Mary Anna's grasp so that he could get the other one, but Mary Anna's grip tightened.

"This is Persephone, Jonah," Eva told him flat-out. "She has been playing all of us. Her eyes kept flashing purple whenever she got emotional, so I thought she was a Purple Aura. You call them Gate Breachers, right? But no. She is dear Persephone. Albertson was a distraction of hers. She wants you. She's wanted you ever since that night she appeared to you that night in my condo."

"Are y'all touched in the head?" Mary Anna finally released Jonah's hand, rose out of her seat, and shrank away from them. "Here I was, willin' to make this work for my Jonah's sake, but all of y'all are crazy!"

"We're crazy, huh?" Reena removed a socket wrench from her pocket, which gleamed with the yellow of her aura. "You met Jonah on the road when you had a flat tire—"

"I already told you that!"

"Shut up," Reena snapped. "I'm talking to Jonah now. Think, Jonah. *Think.* Your head should be pretty clear now. The Tampico's almost gone—"

Jonah shot up and glanced at the nearly empty cup in alarm. "You drugged me, Reena?"

"Nope." Reena's eyes were on Mary Anna. "Your little girlfriend did. Eva just provided you with a cure for it. The Tampico was spiked with an antidote that Eva got from Olympus."

"Mary Anna poisoned me, huh?" Jonah jumped to his girlfriend's defense. What was up with this elaborate plan to throw her under the bus? "How exactly would she have done that?"

"You got trapped, Jonah," Reena explained. "Like I told you

before; you need to think. You met this woman on a roadside and aided her with a flat tire? Didn't that seem just a little familiar?"

Jonah racked his brains. Mary Anna threw him a look.

"Jonah, don't you dare listen to this horseshit—"

"She recreated a specific event from your past, Jonah," Reena interrupted. "Go back into your memory bank. Who else did you meet on the side of the road where a flat tire was involved? You can't have forgotten that situation. Vera didn't speak to you for weeks."

Something fired in Jonah's head. It felt like a pinprick in his mind. Reena was right: that *was* a familiar event. But what did it mean?

"Mary Anna, Reena is right," Jonah said, confused, "what is going on?"

Mary Anna flashed a look at him. "Don't listen to them, Jonah! Remember what I told you earlier? Ignore what they say and think about how I make you feel. Let's just go; I can promise you heaven tonight—"

"You're a fucking goddess," Reena said. "You provided the Venaré to Albertson for the Los Muertes' assassinations, who then used it against Eva when he pressed the barrel under her chin. Eva began losing control of herself and her mind, which made her easy pickings for possession. But Jonah—you poisoned him in a way that wore away his resolve and caution. You wanted him to fall hard for you, just like he has!"

"You need Jesus, woman!" Mary Anna cried. "Why would I poison Jonah? *How* would I poison Jonah?"

"I've given you the why," Reena said. "But the how ... I have no issue revealing your plan. You poisoned Jonah by seeing to it that he pricked himself on the thorn of a black rose. Then, you continuously reinforced it by kissing and fucking him every chance you got."

"Reena, wait." Jonah was confused as hell, and at a complete and total loss. But he knew *that* much. "You mean the rose that Mary Anna gave me in lieu of payment for her tire? That was red, not black. It's still in my car!"

"This one?" Eva lifted a wilting rose.

A wilting black rose.

Mary Anna made a choking sound. Jonah frowned at it.

"I checked out your car while we were at the Milverton, Jonah," Reena revealed. "I had a feeling you hadn't removed that rose because Eva told me that it was in your backseat when you guys got back from D.C. You can also tell by the state it's in that it's not one from the bouquet in the house. The red was a deception. Nothing more. This is Persephone, Jonah."

"I'm not Persephone, I am Mary Anna Greene!" Mary Anna roared.

But everybody's eyes widened. Even Jonah's. Something was horribly wrong, and it scared the hell out of him.

"Mary Anna," he said in a numb tone, "what happened to your accent?"

"What?" Mary Anna asked in her usual drawl. "Jonah, baby, what do you mean?"

Jonah stepped away from her. The heavy southern drawl with the sexy girlish flavor to it was back. But in her words before that, her accent was sharp. Crisp. The diction was so pristine that it almost sounded European.

And familiar to Jonah.

It was at that moment that Eva raised her sword. Ulysses did the same, and Reena lifted the yellow-gleaming socket wrench.

"Jonah is right, girly," she whispered. "You went from Pioneer Woman to Helen Mirren and back again in the past ten seconds. Why is that?"

Mary Anna looked petrified. Her skin resembled ice milk. "Jonah, tell me you love me."

"Excuse me?" Jonah demanded, wide-eyed.

"No, Jonah!" Ulysses barked. "Don't you dare!"

"Just say it, now!" Mary Anna pleaded. Her southern accent was gone once again. "Please!"

"Don't say it, boy!" The Keeper snarled. "To say that you love her will bind you to her, just like she was bound to Hades!"

Just then, Eva's phone went off, and she snatched it out of her pocket with the hand not holding the sword. Upon checking it, she raised her eyes to Mary Anna with an evil grin.

"Well, now!" she exclaimed. "What do I have, but a message from Apollo? It says that Persephone has been off the grid for quite some time! While this is her allotted time away from the Under-world, ol' Hubby Hades has always been able to keep tabs on where she is. That hasn't occurred lately, and we know why. Because she's been masquerading as a bumpkin temptress, who's been messing with Jonah's head."

"Give me that phone, you invasive bitch!"

Mary Anna swatted the sword away, barehanded, and grabbed Eva's phone hand. A bright light flashed and blinded everyone. When the vision readjusted, Jonah could have thrown up.

The haphazard brown hair was now a lustrous shade of raven and adorned with small obsidian stones. The face, once serene and reserved, was now strikingly beautiful. The pleasant pale skin with a hint of farmer's tan was now smooth and ivory, and the wrinkled blouse and slacks were replaced by a slashed mid-riff and black leather pants.

His perfect Mary Anna was gone. Persephone stood in her place.

She gave Eva a pronounced look of hatred. "I will break you, Sibyl," she rasped. "Your golden father is no help to you now!"

NINETEEN
EVA MCRAYNE

I HAD NOT EXPECTED Persephone to transform. No matter how much we'd pushed her. Maybe it had to with when she touched my father's phone. Olympian power exposed her true self, perhaps?

I also wasn't expecting her to attack me. It wasn't her style. Lying and manipulation? Yes. Physical violence?

Yeah. Not quite. Though I was quickly learning that this goddess was full of surprises.

"Persephone, stop!"

I grabbed her arm as she went for my throat. But I should have known better. The moment I acknowledged her, the very second I made contact with her skin, my mind was assaulted with her memories. Her emotions. I felt the fear just as she had the day she had been taken by Hades. The slow-burning anger she harvested for being forced to remain in the Underworld. But along with those memories came the knowledge only the goddess of the Underworld could possess. Within seconds, I understood how to control spirits. I knew how to manipulate stones, and bend people to my will. I knew about flora of all types; the ones that could heal, and the ones that were deadly. I knew more about poisons and potions than I thought possible.

I will never confess how wonderful the power felt as it ignited my blood. It was a feeling that scared me. I knew better than most that I was susceptible to addiction. And this power was something I could very easily become hooked on. I knew I had to let go. Her energies were diminishing faster than Hera's had. So, with a final groan, I released her arm. The goddess collapsed in a heap at my feet.

She was panting as she glared up at me. I looked up to see Ulysses next to Reena and Jonah. His mouth was a hard line as he studied me. The Keeper knew what I had done. He started forward, but I held up my hand. My fingers were glowing a strange shade of purplish black. Much like the bitch's eyes whenever she got emotional.

"Stop," I swallowed as her accent had overtaken my Charleston one. "We won't hurt her. I wish to hell that we could, but we won't."

"Eva—"

"You knew Joey and Pedro had been stealing from Albertson's. You knew of the attack at the airport before it even happened." I turned my attention back to the goddess. "You knew I'd get tangled up in it, so you bided your time. You had been watching Jonah. Knew when he left. So you recreated the memory from his past to get his attention."

"How dare you." Persephone spat her words. "Jonah, you could be so much more. Strike her down. Take your place as the champion you are."

"Albertson was a willing fanatic, wasn't he? What was it you promised him?" I grinned as the memory came to me. "Ah, there it is. Once he was in spirit, you told him I had stolen a stone that represented life from his altar to you. You told him you could resurrect him if he got that stone back. Didn't quite work out that way for him though."

"Why?" Jonah took a step forward, his hands clenched by his sides. "Why would you do this to me?"

"I was right." I narrowed my eyes. "You wanted Jonah for yourself. He is everything that Hades isn't. Kind. Good. But he was still powerful. Just not as powerful as you wanted him to be. And then there was the recurring problem that I had become. You had to turn him against me. You had to drive a wedge between Jonah and the one woman who would recognize you for what you are. A sad excuse for a goddess who was willing to destroy anyone who dared to get in her way."

I willed my sword to appear in my hand.

"I should hack at your fucking head until it comes off, bitch. But I can look past the pain you put me through. I can't expect anything less from you gods and your fragile egos. But I refuse to forgive you for the pain you have caused Jonah. He deserves so much more than the deception you created."

"Jonah is far better than you," Persephone hissed as she struggled to sit up. "Stronger. He should be the one people fall over. Not some sniveling drunkard who can't keep her hands to herself."

"I won't say you're wrong there," I muttered. "But this sniveling drunkard has knocked you on your ass."

I swung my sword in a slow circle by my side as I prepared to strike. I knew I couldn't kill her. But she deserved an injury. Disfigurement. A muscle tear. Fucking *something* for what she'd done. The goddess was no danger to us. Not in this state.

I wasn't worried about repercussions. Not after I saw the hurt in Jonah's eyes when she transformed. Suddenly, my pragmatic sentiments gave me no comfort.

I just wanted to hurt the bitch. Yet just before I could send her back to the Underworld where she belonged, I heard a roar fill the air. "What the—"

I started before a gust of wind smacked me in the chest. I hit the ground a few hundred yards away from the group. I heard shouting. I felt the winds blow once more, so I forced my head up to see Hades step out of the shadows with a line of Shades behind him.

"You've got some fucking nerve, boy." Hades rubbed his hands together as he approached Jonah. "Not many gods would dare to seduce my wife. Yet, the Blue Aura had no qualms about it. Did you truly believe I would give her up so easily?"

"How stupid are you?" Rage flashed across Jonah's face as his batons appeared in his hands. Reena and Ulysses stood with him shoulder to shoulder as he confronted the god. "I didn't even know who she was!"

"Mmm-hmm." Hades didn't even try to sound convinced. He tapped his finger to his chin. I shuddered as I remembered the gesture from my time in the Underworld. "My sincerest apologies, but I don't believe you. Come now. Where are your armies? Where are the spirits you wished to use to usurp me?"

I shoved myself up. I took a running start towards the group when Hades waved a single hand in my direction. I slid to a stop as a group of Shades surrounded me.

"Albertson." The lord of the Underworld sounded as smooth as silk. "You have done well. The reward for your cooperation awaits you."

I watched as the Shades shifted until the Spirit Reaper entered the circle they had made. I grinned as my sword reappeared in one hand and my dagger from Jonah appeared in the other.

"I will live again," Albertson rasped. "You will give it back to me!"

"I have to say, for a drug kingpin, you really suck." I moved in a slow circle as the Shades closed in on us. I could hear the beginnings of a fight near the house. Reena, Ulysses, and Jonah with their weapons. "You could've offed me from the word go. Joey and Pedro, too. You chickened out."

"You stole it," he said for the millionth time as he tried to lunge forward. I stepped aside just before he could reach me. "Give it back!"

"I wonder if this is what fighting a zombie is like." I leered at him. "Coward. You hide behind a pathetic excuse for a god. You follow the instructions of a goddess who had been weakened by her own desires."

The Spirit Reaper roared just before he shoved himself upwards. He wrapped his arms around my waist to pull me off balance, but I was ready for him. When I hit the ground, I twisted. I forced my body to roll upwards until I was on top. A single sweep of my sword across his throat was all it took. The Spirit Reaper screamed as he disappeared into the darkness.

I stood up and gave my weapon a shake as I faced the Shades. "One down, a shit ton to go."

The group surged on me as a single unit. I caught sight of Jonah's blue batons whirling in the darkness as night descended. I saw Ulysses with his hands full as well just before an arm snaked around my throat. I slammed my sword back and connected hard enough to force the being to let me go. I grabbed his arm and slung him into the next two. The Shades separated enough to give me a pathway. I rushed forward slashing through every enemy who dared to get in my way to get to the others.

"I will not lose this time, Blue Aura," Hades growled. "There will be no forgiveness for the insult you have done to me."

"Dearest, wait!" Persephone was on her knees in front of her husband. "The fault is mine!"

"I will deal with you later." Hades placed his hand on top of her head to shove her aside. "You will not stop me from enjoying this."

"Ulysses, watch out!"

I slammed my elbow against the back of a Shade's head as the creature clawed at the Keeper. I grabbed the being and threw him aside. I pressed my back against Ulysses as I faced the enemies behind him.

I wanted nothing more than to find Jonah. Tell him that everything was going to be alright. But right now? There was no time.

The Shades had surrounded us. Clamoring over each other to tear us to pieces.

It was time to fight.

TWENTY

JONAH ROWE

JONAH HAD BEEN PLAYED.

In the foulest, most fucked-up way possible.

And the messed-up part about it? He didn't even have time to wrap his head around Persephone's betrayal. The Shades didn't see fit to accommodate.

Nothing to do but compensate the adrenaline at the moment.

He also realized something. The Shades that went for Eva and Ulysses were the same old spirit-style ones from the past. But the ones that attacked him and Reena had been Eleventh Percenters once. It was evidenced by their eye colors; the spirit one's eyes were toxic green, like always, but the other ones had various eye colors. Jonah guessed that they were the colors of the auras before they had sold out to Hades. Misguided dumbasses.

As if he could talk.

"Reena—!"

"I know!" Reena crushed the trachea of one of the former Elevenths with her socket wrench, and the thing faded to the shadows before he could even gurgle. "Idiots couldn't cut it as Spirit Reapers, so they attempted to seek greener pastures? Stupid and foolish, just like Albertson!"

"Just like *me*," Jonah muttered.

"What was that last part, Jonah?"

Jonah didn't answer when a red-eyed Eleventh Shade clutched his throat. Without thinking, he dropped his batons, willed Eva's fire poker into his hand, and impaled the thing through the eye. The remaining red eye widened in shock as the figure faded away.

"Don't be so surprised," Jonah grumbled to the open air. "That's what happens when you don't stick to what you know."

He tossed the fire poker away and willed the batons back to his hands. He and Reena took out two more Eleventh Shades with classic blunt force trauma. It was truly satisfying. Eva and Ulysses didn't know what they were missing by using those swords. You just couldn't treasure the agony when you cut someone.

Jonah knew that his anger concerning Persephone's betrayal made him think such savage thoughts, but he didn't care. Anger was a tool, after all.

"Jonah!"

Jonah whirled around, but he'd never raise his hands to intercept the final Eleventh Shade in time. Eva and Reena were too far away—

A sword of gold slashed through its neck, and it crumpled like a broken table. Ulysses had done it.

"Ulysses?"

"You never would have been able to smash it in time." Ulysses gave him a nod. "Besides, I can't let you—"

Ulysses' words ceased as he bellowed in pain and collapsed against Jonah. An obsidian-bladed knife was in his shoulder. It didn't appear to be a bad wound, but that action still drove up Jonah's anger and adrenaline several notches. The culprit, Hades, stood apart from the fracas with a small smile on his face.

"You son of a bitch!" Jonah snarled. "You've resorted to stabbing people in the back now? Are you such a coward that you can't take on a true threat?"

Ulysses, even injured, regarded Jonah with alarm at those words. Eva and Reena, who were in the midst of their own fights, did the same.

"Jonah, my love," Persephone implored from her kneeling position, "you cannot speak to him that way—"

"*Silence*, bitch." Hades pushed her flat on her back, but his eyes never left Jonah. "You are already facing horrors of my choosing in the Fields of Punishment, boy. Is your insolence so strong that you wish to try for Tartarus, as well?"

"I'm done trying to convince you that Persephone mind-fucked me." Jonah shook his head in mock pity. "You ought to take better care of your shit."

Hades's eyes flashed. "You can kiss your life goodbye."

Jonah spat on the ground. "I won't even tell you what *you* can kiss."

Hades roared and charged at Jonah sword-first, but Jonah was ready. He mentally envisioned a cage over his mind and slammed its door. A blue, crackling Mind Cage erupted from the ground and imprisoned Hades. The king of the Underworld laughed.

"Do you think me a wayward spirit, boy?" he demanded. "Or one of those infernal dogs? This iridescent shack cannot contain me!"

He began to break through the cage with his bare hands, but Jonah paid him no attention. He knew that Hades would never be held by the Mind Cage, so his next trick had to be quick. He ran over to Eva.

"Do you trust me, Superstar?"

Eva nodded. "With everything I have, Blueberry."

"Then accept my apologies."

He palmed Eva's face as though it were a basketball and used his ethereality to siphon away her most recent acquisitions. He took away everything she'd just absorbed from Persephone, and a few other things with it. Eva gasped like she'd been doused in cold water, but Jonah made sure she didn't fall.

"Sorry," he repeated.

He hurried to Persephone, who was struggling to her feet. "I don't have to ask *you* for shit," he muttered. "I've earned the right."

He palmed her face much the same way he had Eva's and

siphoned an entire load from her. As expected, Persephone had a lot to give. That was good.

Hades tore free of the Mind Cage at the exact second that Jonah released Persephone's face. He turned to see Hades' black blade coming his way. He lifted both batons in one hand to intercept, which was successful, though the force still upset his balance and knocked him a few steps aside. He righted himself as Hades drew the sword back, dropped the batons, and pressed both hands to the sides of Hades' head, focusing with all his concentration.

Hades looked surprised for only a second, but then true horror and agony twisted his face. He dropped the sword with an anguished cry and collapsed, shivering like he has a fever.

"Jonah," Ulysses winced, due to his injuries. "What did you just do?"

Jonah barely heard him. He only had eyes for Hades. "Doesn't feel good, does it?" he asked the quivering god. "I knew that I couldn't beat you in a straight-up fight. You're a god, after all. So, I had an ace up my sleeve. Turns out all that physical contact with Persephone taught me some things, which I can recall now that the Venaré is out of my system. I just hit you with Persephone's essence. Every bit of it, including what Eva absorbed from her.

"You now feel a millennium worth of pain, fear, hopelessness, desperation—all the bad feelings you've caused her from the day you stole her from Demeter until now. And that wasn't all; I also filled you with the portion of Eva's essence that contained all the pain and help-lessness from when you, Ares, and that damned Incubus, tortured her a few months back, plus the mental anguish you caused me. It's all yours now, asshole. Slightly out of whack. My powers might involve balance, but I can unbalance things pretty well at the same time, should I wish to. You've fucked up people in their heads. Time you try that same flavor."

Jonah regarded Hades' trembling, overloaded form, and then kicked him in the midsection just to let off steam. To see him in this state angered him. It was all too familiar.

"You bullies are all the same," he grumbled. "Dish out every form of hell under the sun to everyone else, but when you get a taste of your own medicine, you become a steaming pile of bullshit. Do you think you're a threat to me? You are nothing to me, Hades. I have enemies in the ethereal world that you can't hold a candle to."

He kicked Hades in the groin this time and then knelt next to him.

"Some free advice? Be mindful of who you fuck with. Because when you aren't, shit like this happens."

He rose and faced Persephone, who was dumbstruck at how he had just owned her husband. "Send him back to the Underworld, Persephone," he commanded. "But *you* stay. I ain't through with you yet."

Still in awe, Persephone waved a hand at her afflicted spouse, and he vanished. Jonah barely noticed his friends as he approached the goddess who'd turned him inside out.

"You know, I always felt sorry for you when I read Greek mythology," he told her. "Hades did you ten kinds of wrong. It was one of the sickest things I ever read. But I never imagined that you, the goddess of goddamned *springtime,* were capable of something like this."

Persephone shook her head. "Jonah, that is such a small part of who I am," she said. "I could have been more, and I *would* have been more if that cruel and abusive bastard hadn't taken me from my mother. I never meant to hurt you, Jonah. I saw a wonderful, powerful man with my same plight and wanted to expand horizons together! With you! The façade was necessary. I never have to return to the Underworld again; all I need is for you to tell me that you love me before the end of my allotted time above ground! I know it's true for you. It's certainly true for me —"

"No, no, *no!*" The last one came out as a shout from Jonah's mouth. "You do not get to say that poetic shit anymore!"

"Jonah, please. You can do so much better than this...this thing. She gets burned by two men, and she wants to take an eternal oath of maidenhood. Now, she's going to be detained in the most lackadaisical imaginable for six months. *Six goddamn months!* I've been entombed for millennia, and I'm not treating the world like it's about to end. Don't you see I'm stronger? Better?"

"This ain't about Eva! *You* screwed with my head, in a disguise, no less! You wanted me to say that I loved you so that you could bind yourself to me! You were literally going to do the same thing to me that Hades did to you!"

"It was the only way, Jonah!" Persephone was so passionate about her stance that she actually stepped closer to Jonah as opposed to away. "You were already leery of me because of our previous interactions. I may have been a little too forthright at those times, but there you are. I had to use the resources that were available to me, even Albertson! If you've read the mythology, then you know my history. I never got the chance to become strong. I'm a long way from a powerful goddess."

"Bullshit, Persephone!" Jonah had no issue whatsoever shooting that one down. "You're a daughter of *Zeus*! You have just as much power as Athena, Apollo, Ares, Dionysus—any of them! You can do and be anything that you want! As a matter of fact, there is no time like the present to be strong. I want you to do some stuff for me. Go on and swear on the Styx."

Persephone's eyes widened. "What do you want? What are you proposing?"

"Swear on the Styx," Jonah repeated.

"Fine, Done! Now, what do you—?"

"Say the words, Persephone."

"I swear on the Styx, Jonah. There."

The fire in Eva's fire pit dimmed for a few seconds, then resumed full height. Jonah knew that she was on the hook now.

"It's binding now, and non-negotiable," he said. "First of all, none of this—and I mean none of it—blows back on Eva. Second, I want you to eradicate every Shade in existence. They are Hera's Frankensteins and have no business existing in the first place. Third, I want you to find that minor god Clavius and end his punishment. Put out the fires, restore him, and free him of the Underworld."

"Jonah—"

"I'm not finished," Jonah told her. "Hermes is still getting the third degree from the Fates when all he did was transport a dangerous spirit. I want you to vouch for him. Do all that you can for him. And finally—"

The pain that this woman caused him threatened to overtake his anger, forcing him to pause. He shook his head and powered through. "Just—just grow backbone, Persephone. You've been hiding behind excuses for way too long. I don't think that you would have ever become this calculating or this ambitious if you hadn't let Hades and everyone else walk all over you for so long. Not that what you did wasn't wrong, but if you'd taken control sooner, none of this might have happened. Hades will be screwed up for quite some time, so you can be strong and make changes now. Just take control."

He had to walk away from her. There was sadness and fear in her face that tugged at his battered heartstrings. He stared into the darkness, which was a pretty accurate assessment of how he felt at the moment.

"Come with me, Jonah." Persephone's voice was supplicating. "Our original plan doesn't have to change. I am bound by the Styx to your wishes, but I can do them so much more smoothly if you were with me. You've seen what my husband is like. He may take a while to recover, yes, but one day he will be the exact same man as before. Besides, you've just proven why I've always needed you with me. You're powerful. Immensely gifted and strong. Truly, a perfect specimen of a man. You don't need that estate; they benched you! You don't need the Sibyl, or this war you're in. All you need is *me*. You relished in me as Mary Anna. The delights we shared were genuine. They will be so much richer if you enjoy me in my true form. I implore you. Let me make this right."

Jonah's eyes stung, and he closed them tightly. No way would tears fall. Mustering all the resolve he had in his body, he returned his gaze to Persephone. "The things that you swore on the Styx to do? Those are in your power. But you don't have enough power to make this right. Goodbye, Persephone. You've got things to do."

Persephone's face was one of stone, but it didn't stop her tears. It was as if it was in that specific moment that she realized just how badly she'd screwed up. She vanished.

Unfortunately, the last piece of adrenaline Jonah had vanished with her, and the anger by itself wasn't enough to combat the hurt. Eva, Ulysses, and Reena all regarded him like one would a fragile jewel or a volatile weapon. Eva hadn't ever seen just how powerful Jonah could be, and the awe in her eyes was beyond measure.

And Jonah didn't give a shit.

"Jonah—"

"No." He let the batons fall from his hands. "Don't. I'm taking one of the bedrooms upstairs."

He turned his back on them and headed inside without another word.

TWENTY-ONE

EVA MCRAYNE

WHAT DO you say to a man who's suffered a broken heart? I leaned my forehead against the sliding glass door to watch Jonah. He had been at the Sullivan House for three days. Mostly in one of the bedrooms, but on rare occasions, I caught him out in the backyard. This was one of those times. Jonah was sitting on the edge of the pool with his feet in the water.

I didn't have much time left. In less than twenty-four hours, the Networkers would be here. In less than sixteen hours, I planned to take the poison to end my life. Funny how it was the man I had agreed to lose my life over had become the reason I wanted to live it.

I wanted to see him through this. I didn't have that luxury. Even if I did, Jonah wouldn't want my help. He may have been under the influence of poison, but his words were based on something. Some subconscious belief that I was a mistake.

"Hermes and Clavius have been set back to right." Ulysses stepped out of the shadows as he pocketed his phone. "As a matter of fact, Apollo has extended an offer to Clavius to become an agent of Olympus. His knowledge of Underworld tactics and elusiveness would be most invaluable. Lord Apollo is grateful to the Blue Aura for the progress he has set in motion."

"Mmm-hmm," I responded, but I didn't look at him. I couldn't tear my eyes off Jonah as Ulysses stopped beside me. I knew that he would be leaving soon. It was part of our agreement. Now that the danger had passed, he would be returning to Olympus. Ulysses had no idea what I had planned for tonight. He had no idea that his tenure as my Keeper would be a very, very short one.

It was for the best. I knew he would try to stop me if he knew. The problem with Ulysses is that he wanted to see the good in me. He hadn't been exposed to how fucked up I truly was.

"The Shades have been wiped out. Not even one of them remains."

"That's a small comfort," I mumbled.

"It also appears Persephone will keep her oath. You have nothing to fear regarding retribution."

"I'm not worried about myself, Ulysses."

"No, I don't believe that you are." Ulysses sighed. "I must go, Eva. Apollo has demanded my presence at Delphi."

"Yeah. I understand." I glanced over at him. "Thank you, Ulysses. For everything. You are a very good friend to me."

Ulysses looked outside then back to me. "You wish to speak to him."

"Of course, I do," I sighed. "But what on earth do I say? Persephone's a bitch? He knows that already. Let's go grind her into the ground? I had my chance to do that, and I blew it."

"No, you showed kindness. Compassion. That makes you a better woman than she could ever fathom being."

He kissed my cheek, then I watched him vanish. I stepped outside. I crossed the patio and plopped down on the poolside next to Jonah. He was staring into the water as if it held all the answers he would never have. After five minutes of trying to figure out what to say, I kicked at the water so that it would splash his knee.

"Hey."

Jonah gave me a long look before he pulled his legs up. He made the move to stand but I grabbed his arm to tug him back down.

"Jonah, if you don't sit down and talk to me, I'm throwing you in the pool."

"Yeah?" he growled. "Try it, Superstar."

"Sit." I patted the tiles. "I'm serious. You won't talk to Terrence or Reena. You won't talk to Jonathan. Hell, you won't even talk to the wall. So now you're stuck talking to me."

Jonah sighed as he lowered himself back down. He locked his fingers together in his lap and resumed staring out at the water.

"Self-pity blows, doesn't it?" I leaned back on my elbows as I studied him. "Admit it. Your heart isn't broken so much as your pride."

I saw the muscle in Jonah's jaw twitch, but I continued.

"You aren't a fool, Jonah. You aren't an idiot for falling for the illusion that Persephone created. In her twisted way, she cared about you enough to come after you."

"Eva—"

"You aren't a fool, Jonah. You aren't an idiot for falling for the illusion that Persephone created. In her twisted way, she cared about you enough to come after you."

Jonah's teeth clenched, and he started to rise, but I grabbed his arm again to force him back down.

"She was a bitch for what she did. To both of us. I'm not an expert on the gods, like Ulysses. Or an expert on the Elevenths, like Jonathan. But what I am an expert in is having my heart battered."

"What are you saying, Eva?"

"I'm saying that hate and hurt have no place within us, Jonah. I'm saying that I held onto the pain others have caused me, just as you are hanging onto how stupid you feel at the moment. But it doesn't do us any good. I want you to be happy, Blueberry. But as long as you beat yourself up, there is no way that's going to happen."

TWENTY-TWO

JONAH ROWE

JONAH DIDN'T KNOW what sucked more. The aftermath of what happened, or the fact that Eva was making sense.

Still didn't change much, though. This wasn't a television sitcom. This problem wouldn't be resolved in thirty minutes or less.

"Eva, hear this from my point of view," he relented. "As you know, before we had that mess in L.A., I went through a couple of things with Vera—"

"I know, Jonah," Eva said softly. "You needn't rehash it."

Jonah nodded. "Good, so we're on the same page. If you know those things, then you know that Mary Anna was a breath of fresh air. A rose amid chaos. Ironic, right? I fell for her so hard. I usually keep people at arm's length, a wise policy nowadays. But … I didn't do that with her. I didn't see the fact that it was a game. I feel like trash for not seeing it."

"Cut yourself some slack," Eva told him. "You *were* under the influence of poison."

Jonah shook his head. "It isn't much of an excuse. You know me well enough to know that I don't believe in one-eighties. The two of us had poison in us, sure. But the poison was so successful because it preyed on areas in which we already had issues."

"In your case, you've always feared a loss of control—with the Sibyl, the fame, the gods—the whole nine. The poison tore down your sense of control, which gave Albertson a much clearer path to possess you. In my case ...I 've always been leery of betrayal. Of duplicity, and all that. It's increased since Jessica, since Creyton, since losing Mr. Steverson—you get the point. The Venaré crushed the walls I'd built. Mary Anna ... *Persephone* had a clear path. Signs were staring me in the face, and I got played again. All I'm saying is that I can't blame it entirely on the poison."

Eva said nothing during Jonah's speech, so he figured that he'd gotten through. Not so.

"I figured out why you're beating yourself up so badly, Jonah," she said. "All the stuff you just said helped me figure it out. You wanted someone to rescue you."

Jonah frowned. "Excuse me?"

Eva nodded. "Yeah, that's it. Think about what you said. All the betrayals. All the crap going on in the ethereal world. You're the Blue Aura, so all roads lead to you. The savior, the main one. It does a mind job, Blueberry. You know that I can relate. You carry the weight well; you've had hero moments with the Elevenths, as well as with us. But that's got to take a toll ... got to be overwhelming. So, you wanted someone to save you for once. And the supposed answer to your prayers came in the form of the rose-wielding, pickup-truck-driving, family-values-having, but freak-in-the-bed cow-gal, Mary Anna Greene. Complete with a thick southern twang, no less! She was exactly what the doctor ordered, and then it turned out to be a lie. Your golden rescue got snatched away. And it's crushed the hell out of you."

Jonah looked at Eva in awe. He hadn't actually deciphered the true root of his hurt, and Eva had hit the nail on the head. Mary Anna *had* represented a rescue from all the bullshit he was dealing with. Just about everything about her was perfect, and then it was taken away. He hated Persephone for that. Of all the men she could have screwed with, she chose him. The so-called "perfect specimen of a man".

And it had all been one big lie.

"You deserve a whole hell of a lot better than an instant union, Jonah," Eva continued. "That was where Persephone got it wrong. She tried to cram the time-honored forging and bonding of a true connection into some—pardon my French—instant gratification clusterfuck. It's much like what WWE tried to do when they made Carlito the United States champion his first night on *Smackdown!* back in 2004."

Jonah slowly turned his head in Eva's direction. "So when—and how—did Terrence get you to play his WWE trivia game?"

Eva grinned. "Last night, when he came over and you refused to come downstairs. He brought it and he looked so crushed, I played it with him."

Jonah had to laugh. It was impossible not to. "The fact that you found a way to plug in a WWE statistic to get through to me shows that you really care."

"Of course, I do." She sat up and held onto the sides of the pool. "My point was the fact that you can do better. True relationships are built, not streamlined."

Jonah returned his gaze to the pool. "I hear you, Superstar. It's a good truth. But I'm still pissed. I'm not sure what to do about it."

"You'll be pissed for a while. Hell, you'll be hurt for a while. That's the nature of the beast, Jonah."

Jonah stared at the clear water before he looked over at Eva. "What'd ya say we get out of our heads? Terrence don't need an excuse for a barbecue. It'll be like old times. You refusing to eat more than two bites. Reena giving me hell because she cares."

Eva's grip tightened on the side of the pool. Now, she was the one watching the water. "I don't think that's a good idea, Jonah. I'm not up to a party considering the Networkers will be here at dawn. But that doesn't mean you can't go to the estate to see them. It's probably better if you aren't here when they show up. You've been through enough. I don't want to add this to your plate, too."

Jonah grabbed Eva's hand. "Fuck it, then."

"Jonah, don't put yourself on hold for me."

"Shut up, Eva." There was no hardness or venom in his tone.

Just fatigue. "If you won't do dinner, then I'll just stay here with you. I'll be damned if you await these motherfuckers alone."

Eva looked down at their hands before she pulled hers free.

"If you're going to stay here, I'll let you take control of the remote. Least I can do. *Big Bang Theory*? I bought the series on Prime for you not too long ago. I don't think you ever watched it."

"Only if you watch with me," Jonah said. "Non-negotiable."

"Yeah. I'll watch it with you."

"Seriously? You got the whole series for me?"

"Yes. And a supreme pizza is only a phone call away."

Jonah felt a small smile light his features. "I am there!"

He rose, and Eva didn't tug him back down this time.

"Ready to begin putting this behind you?"

Jonah pulled out his phone. "Almost."

He scrolled through his photo gallery until he reached a picture he'd taken of Mary Anna three days after they'd first met. He spent a couple of seconds looking over every line and curve of the quietly beautiful and serene face that, at the time, represented such possibility and promise for the future.

It had been a false future. Courtesy of a very troubled goddess.

Maybe he'd forgive her someday. Maybe.

But on this day, the only thing he had on tap was tons of Leonard, Sheldon, and Penny.

"Goodbye, Mary Anna," he said.

With that, he pressed *Delete* on the picture and followed Eva back into the house.

———

Jonah enjoyed binging with Eva. It was a huge blessing. A wonderful distraction.

The only problem was when she left, it came back. Full relief. Yeah. He'd been poisoned. Bewitched, if you will.

And he still felt like a heartbroken, violated piece of scum.

It took all the strength he had to go to Eva's door. This wasn't her problem. Given the things Jonah had said to her, he was surprised she had even let him back in the house, much less tried to make him feel better. He'd never forgive himself for what he'd said. Ever.

Jonah wanted her to know that. He needed her to know that. Especially since this was going to be his last chance to see her for a while. Last chance to speak to her.

He went to her door and knocked. After hearing movement, he braced himself.

Eva opened the door, looking surprised to see him. He was surprised, too. She looked like she'd just come from a photoshoot. Floor-length black gown. Diamonds. Every strand of blonde hair in place.

"Jonah, what's up? I'm ... kinda busy."

"Eva, I have no right to ask you this, but I need some help." Jonah came right out and said it. "I'm not okay. I thank you for helping me get out of my head all day, but I'm not okay. I need some company. Yours."

Eva looked puzzled. "You need me?"

Jonah nodded. "I do. I need to talk with you. I need to apologize for what I said."

Eva stared at him for a moment before she stepped aside.

Jonah came into the room to see a single wine glass on the desk next to her journal.

"Jonah, you don't have to apologize. You were being poisoned." She shut the door and rubbed her forehead with two fingers. "It's fine. I swear it."

"Eva, it's not fine!" Jonah said firmly. "I'm finally spiraling. Because I've had a ... fucked-up realization."

"Oh?"

"He was right, Eva."

"Who was right?"

"Cyrus." Jonah gritted his teeth. "Who'd have thought after all this time, Cyrus was actually *right* about me? They were all right. I'm a piece of shit, like he said. Like Priscilla said. Like *everyone* said. I *am* useless, Eva. I might as well be dead."

Eva stared at him.

He nodded. "It's all true. Every word."

"So, let me get this straight. You get poisoned, say some things to me that I forgive you for, and you equate yourself to Cyrus?"

"He was right—"

"He was *not* right, Jonah!" Eva's eyes flashed. "You are absolutely nothing like him!"

"But—"

"But nothing! I refuse to let anyone trash you. That extends to you, too! You are *not* useless. You are not a piece of shit; do you hear me? You are a hero, Jonah. You are a kind person who got twisted up under a fucked-up goddess. That does not discount all the good you have done now or in the future."

Eva was shaking so hard; Jonah could see her clench her hands into fists to try and control it. She gritted her teeth, then continued.

"Do you not realize how fucking dark this world would be without you in it? Do you not see the good you do for the people around you? Jonah, if you were to die, a lot of people would die with you. You wouldn't just be taking yourself out. You'd be taking out Reena, Terrence—every single one of the people who love you. And for what? Words you said under Persephone's poison? No. You can't let her keep twisting you, Jonah. You can't."

"Eva, I called you a mistake," Jonah said. "That's right out of Cyrus' playbook. I tore you down like he used to. I can't believe that came out of my mouth."

"You were poisoned, Jonah! You had no idea what you were doing!"

"Eva—"

"You used to tell me that I was wrong for believing the bad shit people said about me. But you're doing it now! Jonah, please. Your mind is cleared up now. I know it is. So, *think*. Please." Eva's tone became one of pleading. She hugged herself as she studied his face. "Don't say you'd be better off dead because of one fucked-up instant. Don't call yourself those horrible things because it's easier to listen to the past than it is to move forward. Please."

Jonah was silent. For a bit.

"Will you let me stay with you tonight?"

"Jonah, you've been here for three days. I kinda assumed you were going to stay."

"I mean, in here. In the same bedroom with you. I want every moment I can get with you before tomorrow."

Now, Eva was quiet. She looked away from him towards the desk then faced him again.

"Why?"

"I need you, Eva. I need you to be a presence right now."

Eva closed her eyes for a moment and Jonah steeled himself for her rejection. Instead, she nodded. "Alright."

"Really?"

"Yes. Really."

She released herself and went over to the desk. Jonah watched her close the journal and pick up the wine glass. She slipped into the bathroom to flush the wine down the toilet.

"You didn't have to do that," he told her.

"Yes, I did."

Eva went over to the bed and sat on the edge of it. She buried her face in her hands and Jonah had a feeling she was trying to square herself with something. He sat beside her but didn't touch her. After all the shit with Joey, the Curaie, and now, him? He didn't feel that he had the right.

"You have to swear something to me," Eva muttered through her fingers before she dropped her hands. "You have to swear that you will never say that again."

Jonah sighed. "Alright. I really am sorry. You aren't a sob story, Eva. You aren't a cloud of negativity, either."

Eva didn't respond. He didn't expect her to, though he knew those words were swirling around in her mind. He wished he could have taken them back. He wished he'd never said them in the first place. Jonah knew Eva well enough to know that she believed the worst about herself.

Jonah didn't say anything for a while. Eva didn't either. He finally broke down and wrapped his arms around her shoulders. She stiffened, but he held onto her for dear life until she relaxed. Even then, he clung to her.

"Why are you all dressed up?" He mumbled against her shoulder. "As late as it is."

"I ..." Eva sighed. "I just wanted to feel better about myself. That's all."

"That's all? Legit?"

"Yes."

Eva tapped his shoulder and he lifted off her. She got off the bed, then snagged something small from the desk. She closed her journal, then went into her closet. Jonah stayed still on the bed, his arm over his eyes as he tried to calm down.

"Hey." Eva leaned over to shake his arm when she returned. "Are you asleep?"

"No." Jonah removed his arm to see the gown was gone. Eva was dressed in a long-sleeve shirt and yoga pants. "You changed?"

""Yeah. No point in going to bed in my evening gown."

"Hey." He leaned up, on his side, and grabbed her wrist before she could walk away. "Are we ok?"

Eva's expression softened before she nodded. "We're fine."

"You don't want to cuss me out or anything?"

"No."

"Eva," Jonah sat up. "Talk to me. What's going through your head right now?"

"I told you, I forgave you. That's the last I am going to say on the matter."

Jonah studied her face now free of the makeup she had put on. She had helped him see the truth despite the hurt he had caused her. Eva loved him enough to see past the poisoned words. She loved him enough to save him; from the poison, from himself, from his enemies.

She had always been there to catch him when he fell. Jonah blinked as he realized the one thing he'd never considered. He'd been looking for a hero in a villain when the one person who had always saved him was there all along.

"Will Hestia reconsider allowing you to take her oath?"

The question came out of nowhere, but Jonah felt it was relevant. Eva's ability to love someone after they hurt her was one of her most redeeming qualities. He envied her for that.

"No," She pulled her arm away. "She won't reconsider."

"Seriously?"

"Seriously. The Oracles told her that she would cause a huge shift in two different realms if I was to take her oath. So, it's never going to happen."

Jonah watched as she moved around the bed to crawl in under the comforter. Eva turned her back to him when she commanded the lights to turn off. Jonah studied her form in the darkness. Had he ruined their connection? Was she still hurt despite her claims not to be?

"Good night, Superstar," he whispered as he stretched out beside her. "Good night."

TWENTY-THREE
JONAH ROWE

JONAH WOKE up from a dead sleep at four a.m. It took him a minute to realize that he wasn't at the estate or in his bed at the Sullivan House. Instead, he was in Eva's bed as she tried to remove his arm from around her waist.

"Eva? What-"

"Gods, did I wake you up?" She sat up and twisted around. "I'm sorry. I was trying to be careful with your arm."

"No," Jonah swallowed. "What time is it?"

"Just after four a.m. I wanted to grab a shower before they showed up."

They. The Networkers. Spectral law enforcement who had orders to take Eva away from her life for six months and throw her in a damn cell.

Jonah rubbed the sleep from his eyes as she turned on a lamp. He watched her go to the closet and wondered what was going through her head in that moment. Was she packing a bag? Could she pack a bag? Jonah had never known anyone who had actually been sentenced by the Curaie. Sure, he'd dealt with the assholes who were thrown on the Plane, but they deserved the horrors they faced.

They weren't Eva.

"Superstar," He tried. "Maybe we can fight it. Maybe-"

"There's nothing to fight, Jonah. I had my trial. I lost." She stopped by the bathroom door with her clothes folded over her arms. "When they get here, I'm not going to make a scene or anything. I don't want to give them a reason to extend this sentence."

"You never told me about what happened at the trial."

"There was nothing to tell."

Jonah made a wry face but kept himself in check. Eva was resigned to this. She'd made her peace with it. So, any protests would make it harder than it already was. So, he bit his tongue. He'd need all the balance he possessed if and when he saw Lawson again. He reached into her nightstand drawer and found what he was looking for.

"Superstar, I want you to have this."

He extended a deck of cards. Eva raised an eyebrow.

"You want me to play Solitaire for six months?"

"No, Eva. I want you to do the Gotch Bible."

Eva's eyes widened. "You want *me* to do that? Jonah, that's your thing. And you know beyond running, I don't really work out-"

"First of all, it's not *my* thing," Jonah said firmly. "Please don't throw shade on things just because it is not your cup of tea. I ask you to do it because you're like me. When you're down or alone, your mind goes to the darkest places. Given your past, your spots are darker than most. Nothing helps pivot your mind like exercise. Nothing. It's how I've dealt with anger. Do it for me. You can even give it up entirely and return to running after this is over. Please."

Eva turned the cards over in her hands then nodded. "Fair enough. But if I break my neck doing this, I'm going to kick your ass when I get out."

Jonah chuckled at her words. "I'd expect nothing less."

Eva gave him a small smile before she shut the bathroom door. Jonah listened until the water started then climbed out of bed. He was still wearing his clothes from the day before, but he didn't care. He wanted to do something. He needed to do something for her. A small token.

Jonah headed downstairs and went into the kitchen. He set to work making eggs and bacon. He wasn't a cook, but he could manage the basics. Toast and fruit came next. By the time he heard Eva come downstairs, he was pulling her coffee from the Keurig.

"What's all this?"

"I know you won't eat much, but I figured you could use a home cooked meal before you had to go."

"Thank you." She took the coffee with a small smile. "I hope you're hungry though because I won't be able to eat a third of this."

Jonah pushed a plate in her direction, and he sat across from her at the kitchen table. True to form, Eva nibbled at the food. She barely drank her coffee. Jonah knew that meant she was nervous and trying damn hard to hide it.

He reached out to catch her hand then squeezed her fingers. "It's going to be ok, Superstar. We'll get through this."

Before Eva could respond, the doorbell rang through the house. She wiped her mouth with a napkin and stood as Jonah's stomach sank.

"Looks like my ride's here."

Jonah walked behind her as she crossed the house to pull open the front door. Agent Marlon Dubois was standing on the other side. A woman was with him.

"Miss McRayne, meet Agent Harriet Newman. She will be searching your person for any contraband before and after you arrive at the prison."

"Come inside. I don't want the neighbors to realize you're putting cuffs on me.

Eva stepped back and the two agents entered. Dubois gave Jonah a quick nod of greeting. Jonah was barely able to contain his sneer.

"Turn around, Miss McRayne, and put your hands behind your back, thumbs up."

Eva turned to face Jonah. Her expression was so empty, so devoid of emotion, he wondered how she managed it. Jonah had to look away when he heard the click of those ethereal cuffs, but he turned his focus back on the scene at hand when the female agent spoke.

"What is this?"

She had been patting Eva down apparently, because the woman now had the deck of playing cards in her hand.

"You are not allowed to take any outside effects with you."

"Now, wait a damn minute!" Jonah took a step forward. "She can't even have cards?"

"No." The woman rose up and sat the deck of cards on a side table. "These must remain here."

"It's fine." Eva gave Jonah a sad smile. "It's better that way. Can't break my neck if I can't do your exercises."

Jonah was instantly enraged, but Eva gave him a smile that was both disarming and reassuring.

"Don't *worry*, Jonah," She said. "I'll honor your request. You do realize I've watched you do more workouts than I care to admit. I've memorized the bodyweight ones. I'll do them every day for you."

Jonah felt his eyes sting, but he bawled his fists. There was *no* way he'd shed a tear in front of these motherfuckers. And to think, he respected Networkers at one time. No more. Marlon observed Jonah's face and cleared his throat to get his attention.

"Son, these are just standard protocols. It's not meant to be malicious or-"

"Save it," Jonah snapped. "First of all, I ain't your son. My fucking father is dead. Second of all, I was taught from a young age that if you can't say anything nice, don't say anything at all. So, it's best for everyone involved if you just stop talking to me."

"It is time for us to depart, Miss McRayne." Marlon turned his attention back to Eva. "Say your goodbyes."

Jonah took another step forward, but the woman held her hand out.

"No, sir. Stay back. We can't risk you interfering."

"Interfering?!" Jonah snapped. "I can't even hug her goodbye?"

"Miss McRayne was sentenced five days ago. There was plenty of time for that."

"Jonah, it's ok," Eva spoke when the agent shut up. "I'll call you the second they let me out."

He stared at her as he tried to keep his emotions in check. He needed to be as strong as she was right now. As strong as she always was.

"See you on the flip side, Blueberry," Eva gave him another small smile. "It'll be over before we know it."

Jonah popped his neck muscles. If Joseph dared to show his face anywhere near him, he was going to die. Jonah made that mental promise to himself.

"Yeah, Eva," He said. "It will be. Blink of an eye, right?"

Marlon regarded Jonah. "I wish for you to tell Jonathan--"

"I believe I told you not to speak to me for any reason. You want to tell Jonathan something, talk to him your goddamn self."

Marlon's expression hardened instantly. As though Jonah had any fucks to give. "Harriet, Miss McRayne, it's time for us to go."

He met Eva's gaze and she mouthed a single phrase before the three of them vanished.

"It's going to be fine."

Jonah wanted to believe her. He needed to believe her. The empty feeling in his chest just didn't allow for that right now. He was still reeling from Persephone. He needed Eva to help him get through it. He needed her more than anything to be there. To make him laugh. To distract him from the world. To understand him like no one else ever could.

But Eva was gone. Just…. gone.

Jonah didn't know how long he stood in the foyer. He recognized the sun brightening. He felt hollow. Like a statue.

"Jonah?"

He didn't move as Reena approached him from behind. He didn't even hear her come in.

"Jonah, are we too late?"

"Yeah," He tore his eyes away from the spot where Eva had been. 'Yeah. She's gone."

"Jonah, sit down." Reena glanced over at Terrence and Spader who had come in behind her. "You look like you're about to pass out."

"No." Jonah grabbed a cold piece of bacon and bit into it. "I'm going for a drive. I need to get some air."

"Let one of us come with you." Reena studied him. "Or come home. We'll smoke weed for the rest of the day."

Jonah was well aware of what he was about to do, so he smiled.

"Cool. I'll get lit with you. Sounds fun."

Reena wrapped her hand around his arm. "The gazebo is waiting. Let's go."

"There's no chance Lawson will be there, right?" Jonah couldn't get his first name out. "He's being detained, too."

Reena and the other two shared a look. She cleared her throat.

"Um, no. Joey was cleared of all charges except conspiracy since he wasn't on that plane transporting the narcotics. He can't come to the estate. He's banned from ethereal lands, too."

Jonah stared at Reena. He was dead silent. It was as though a million words swirled about in his head, yet his mouth couldn't settle on any of them. His silence was long enough to make Reena look concerned.

"Jonah?"

"I'm fine." It was like a switch flipped. A notification that Jonah could speak. "Okay."

"Jonah," Reena looked genuinely unnerved, "Please be cognizant of the fact that *we* are pissed too. Seriously. Jonathan had to talk me down from leaking stuff to *TMZ* about him. Terrence and Malcolm suspect that since Joey is Clorox bleach white, he slipped between the cracks. If he shows his face anywhere around--"

"It's fine, Reena," Jonah said quietly. He didn't know how people achieved it, but he'd done it. He'd reached a level of anger so pronounced that he wasn't angry. "You don't have to explain anything. Isn't like *you* guys did anything wrong. Let's just go smoke. All good."

———

Jonah did something he'd never done in all the time he'd partake in cannabis. He focused on his own body and balanced away the effects.

He had never intended to be talked down. He humored his

family because they meant well. But his mind was on Eva in a damn ethereal detention center, all because she signed documentation that authorized bullshit Joseph and Pedro did. Pedro was in a place his actions couldn't hurt him.

That left Joseph.

Jonah seemed to be void of his emotions when Reena dropped the bombshell earlier. But now, all was back. In full effect.

It was one of the reasons Jonah needed to get out of Dodge.

Very quietly, he slipped out of the front door of the estate and went to his car, which he'd smartly parked facing the exit so he wouldn't make a ton of noise maneuvering. He fired up the engine and sailed down the drive. Worked like a charm.

Now for the next bit. He had to choose his words *very* carefully.

He stopped at the nearest gas station to fill up, but before he exited his car, he whipped out his phone and pressed a speed dial. It was picked up on the second ring.

"Jonah?"

"Hermes." Jonah sighed. "How are things now that you're no longer getting grilled by the Fates?"

"Peachy," Hermes murmured. "Though I'm still pissed off about Albertson escaping me. However, Olympus--those of us on the right side of history, anyway--have a lot of anger going around."

"Figured," Jonah said, his voice terse. "Same on my side of things. That's why I saw fit to contact you instead of Apollo."

"Oh?" Hermes was silent for a moment. "You've piqued my curiosity."

"Joseph Lawson." Jonah said the name with the purest, most undiluted hatred. "He got off scot free. Eva is in a detention center and can't even have playing cards because of those assholes in ethereal law while he got a sentence tantamount to a restraining order."

Hermes sighed. "That is most infuriating, Jonah. Is there a certain significance to the playing cards?"

"Yes," Jonah answered instantly. "I wanted Eva to keep her mind and body active to combat the depression she'd been feeling by doing the Gotch Bible."

"I'll get her a deck," Hermes said.

"They'll be dicks about it, Hermes."

"Laws written by men, even ethereal ones, are of no consequence to us, Jonah." Hermes' voice was intractable. "If Eva is dealing with depression, isolation without healthy stimuli can exacerbate it. That makes this a health issue. If ethereal law enforcement isn't seeing to the physical and mental well-being of the daughter of Apollo, it would be looked upon as an act of war. And Jonah, this is no disrespect to the Ghostly Ones, whose powers still largely remain mysteries to us. That said, your ethereal government has never seen Olympus at war, nor do they want to. Trust me, I'll handle it. I'll get her cards. And I'll tell her the gift was from you."

Jonah closed his eyes, so full of gratitude that he didn't know what to do. "Thank you. But...I called for another reason as well. Lawson got off with a slap on the wrist, Hermes. I... I can't have that. I can't tolerate that."

Silence. "Jonah, surely you aren't asking me to smite the boy."

"No," Jonah said. "I'd never ask that. At least I don't think. But...do *something* to him, Hermes. He can't be emboldened like that. Eva still has to work him once she's free, and if he's been in smug bliss all that time, he could prove to be detrimental to her again in the future."

"Fair point." Hermes' tone was pensive. "I'll think of something, son. I am, after all, the trickster."

"Indeed, you are, sir." Jonah smiled for the first time in hours. "Thank you again."

"Are you at the estate?"

"No," Jonah answered, breathing through his nostrils. "I'm gassing up to hit the road. I need to put distance between me and Lawson. It's necessary."

"No worries at all, son," Hermes answered. "Leave the cards and cameraman to me. But perhaps, I can make a suggestion."

"What sort of suggestion?"

"Wilderness training in the way of the ancients. The Nerds are allies of Olympus, and Thor has decided to spend his days training our soldiers in the way of the Vikings. Would you be interested?"

Jonah leaned his head against the window. "Could I stay six months?"

"I'm sure we could make the proper arrangements."

"Where do I need to go?"

"Moscow. Thor himself will contact you with the information to get you to the training grounds."

"I'll head that way tonight, sir. Thanks for everything."

"Go in peace, boy," Hermes said. "I have a feeling you are in desperate need of it."

*** END ***

Dear reader,

We hope you enjoyed reading *Gods & Reapers*. Please take a moment to leave a review, even if it's a short one. Your opinion is important to us.

Discover more books by Cynthia D. Witherspoon at https://www.nextchapter.pub/authors/cynthia-d-witherspoon

Want to know when one of our books is free or discounted? Join the newsletter at http://eepurl.com/bqqB3H

Best regards,

Cynthia D. Witherspoon and the Next Chapter Team

ABOUT THE AUTHORS

T.H. Morris has been writing in some some way, shape, or form ever since he was strong enough to hold a pen or pencil, and was born and raised in Colerain, North Carolina, then resided in Greensboro, North Carolina for twelve years. He is an avid reader, primarily ofin the genres of science fiction, paranormal, and fantasy because he enjoys immersing himself in the worlds that have been created. He published his first novel, *The 11th Percent* in 2014. He now resides in Colorado with his wife, Candace.

Cynthia D. Witherspoon is an award-winning writer of Southern Gothic, Paranormal Romance, and Urban Fantasy. She currently resides in South Carolina, but spent three years in Fayetteville, Arkansas. Always an avid reader, she began writing short stories in college. She graduated with a Bachelor's Degree in History from Converse College, and earned a Masters in Forensic Science at Oklahoma State University Center for Health Sciences.

Lightning Source UK Ltd.
Milton Keynes UK
UKHW041836020421
381458UK00006B/189/J